Moose, Bette Moose

This story is dedicated to my youngest sister Vicki Wilson Catoe. I took a lot of grief that she didn't make it into my first book, *You've Got a Wedgie, Cha Cha Cha* and she won't find herself in *Jaybird's Song* either, but if she had, I think I would want the world to know about the fun times Linda and I had hanging her upside down by the straps of her stirrup pants from the clothes hooks in the back seat of our family's station wagon. And her extraordinary ability to love out loud. Good times, Moose. I love you.

PROLOGUE

American astronauts landed on the moon the day I almost lost my virginity. It was July 20, 1969, a Sunday afternoon just a little more than a year after my Daddy died.

The world was focused on America and the first-ever mission that might really bring astronauts to the moon, beating the Russian cosmonauts to the feat. My sisters and I had been cutting newspaper articles from the *Atlanta Constitution* for weeks to put together a scrapbook Mother said we would want to show our children some day. Everyone I knew had plans to watch the televised moon landing later that afternoon.

But it was the middle of summer and my new best friend LaDarla and I had been invited to Lake Allatoona with the Carr family. We spent Saturday night at Karen Carr's house and on Sunday we drove to her family's lake house with plans for an entire day of boating and skiing.

The three of us had been spending a lot of time together that year. Karen was the last of the three of us to turn 16. I'd been 16 for two and a half months.

Karen's mother fried chicken and made a big Tupperware-full of macaroni salad Saturday night while Karen and LaDarla and I listened to my "Tommy" album by The Who and made up dance routines to "Pinball Wizard."

"Is everyone excited about the lake?" asked Mrs. Carr as she held out a plate of brownies. All three of us extended an arm, each wrapped in identical macramé bracelets, toward the plate at the same time.

"Don't stay up too late tonight girls. We'll leave early in the morning."

Mrs. Carr looked more like a typical mother than my mother did. She wore a pinafore-style apron over her shirtwaist dress, and her hair was cut short and curled around her face.

"We're really glad you can join us, girls," she added smiling, but she was looking directly at me.

That feeling again.

It had been 15 months since my father's death, but I still felt people lingering when they looked at me like they had more to say, but couldn't bring themselves to do it.

"Thanks for the brownies, Mom. We'll go to sleep soon," Karen shouted as she turned up the volume of the record player.

I sensed that Mrs. Carr might still be looking at me, but I pretended to look for something in my overnight bag and didn't look up. I saw LaDarla dancing in front of the mirror as I pulled out my shorty pajamas from the bag and Mrs. Carr shut the door with a melodic, "Well, good night, ladies."

The next morning we packed the car with the picnic lunch, beach towels, a change of clothes, extra life jackets and a cooler of Cokes and Sprites. The three of us rode in the backseat of the Carrs' mint green station wagon to the lake house.

Karen's brother Steve had just finished his freshman year at North Georgia College and was taking summer classes to get ahead. I had met him many times at the high school football games before he graduated from Northbridge and he'd never given us much attention, but I knew he had good manners. He'd won the citizenship award at our school's honors day.

He and four friends from college arrived in a yellow Volkswagen soon after we arrived at the lake house, and they all jumped out of the tiny car like clowns at the circus — if clowns were shirtless, tanned and good looking and had much nicer bodies than high school boys.

We packed the pontoon boat with the picnic supplies, extra gasoline and coolers while Steve and his friends loaded the skis and ski ropes into the Carrs' ski boat, which was already hitched to an old truck they kept parked on a gravel driveway next to their lake house. The plan was to drive both boats to the marina where we would put the boats in the water and then anchor the pontoon out in the water while the ski boat carried up to six skiers and spotters at a time. Those on the pontoon boat could swim aside the boat or sun on the deck.

LaDarla, Karen and I had all tried on our bathing suits the night before and fussed over how we were going to look in them in front of college boys. Karen ended up letting me borrow one of hers because she and LaDarla thought it was a lot cuter than mine.

"It makes you look rounder at the top, Josie," Karen said. "And that's a good thing."

But the boys were much better looking than we had anticipated, and I was really grateful for the cutoffs and t-shirt I'd worn over my suit as I tried out excuses in my mind of why I might not take them off all day.

"Mine's the one with the blond hair!" LaDarla teased when we were alone in the kitchen.

"They're all dolls!" said Karen in a half-squeal, half-whisper. "This might be weird because my brother thinks I'm a big dork. No telling what he's told these guys."

We were just preparing to leave when Mrs. Carr crawled over the trailer hitch between the station wagon and the pontoon and sliced her leg all the way from ankle to mid calf on a sharp piece of rusty metal on the side of the hitch.

"Jim! Oh my gosh! Jim!" she screamed. We all came running.

The bright red blood was running down her leg, becoming dark, grainy and coagulated as it mixed with the dusty gravel of the driveway below her.

She looked like she was going faint. Steve rushed to pull her arm around his shoulder as Mr. Carr took a closer look.

"Okay, this is going to require stitches and fast," said Jim Carr, an accountant who clearly knew how to stay calm in a crisis.

"Karen, get some towels and some rope or tape. Steve, there is duct tape in the ski boat console. Get that," he ordered. "Karen, get your mother a big cup of water, and the rest of you boys unhook the boat so we can get the station wagon clear. I'll get your mother to the car. We'll go to the emergency room in Cartersville."

Mr. Carr took over as the shoulder to lean on and led his wife to the back seat of the station wagon as his children darted into action.

"Josie, get a blanket off of one of the beds and bring it to her," he yelled as he helped her settle her into the car.

Mr. Carr wrapped her leg in a towel and taped it with the duct tape. He covered her with the blanket and handed her the water, checked the then-unhooked hitch and was ready to leave in just minutes.

"Should we go with you, Dad?" Karen asked.

"You all stay here," he said wiping sweat from under his chin with the back of his arm. "Steve, take the extra gas cans to the station on Highway 41. I forgot to stop on the way in. That way we won't have to pay the marina prices."

He pulled a twenty from his wallet and handed it to Steve.

"Hopefully, we will be back quickly and your mother will still be up for some boating this afternoon."

Karen peeked into the back seat of the car where her mother was looking pale. LaDarla and I stepped up behind her.

"Karen, go ahead and bring the food into the house because y'all will be getting hungry," she said. "We'll be back as soon as we can."

Dust kicked up from around the station wagon as they took off down the driveway and up the gravel road toward the main highway.

"I guess that means we can't take out the speed boat until they get back?" asked one of Steve's friends.

"No. I don't think so," Steve responded. "I think my dad would have said so if he thought that was okay."

"I've driven lots of boats," he tried again. "You don't have to worry about that."

"I'm sorry, Cary. I think we are stuck here at the house until they get back."

The one named Cary rolled his eyes and looked at the other guys.

"Well, at least we can go get the gas your dad wanted you to take care of," offered the tallest boy, Nate. "I'll ride with you. Anyone else want to go?"

"We'll stay here," said Karen looking at me for assurance.

"I'll stay too," said Cary looking at the remaining two guys and nodding. "The rest of us will stay here and hang out until you get back."

"All right," Steve shrugged as he threw two empty gas cans into the back seat of the VW and grabbed a shirt from the back seat and pulled it over his head. "We'll be back soon."

The rest of us entered the house and the girls went to the back porch while the guys went to the living room. The awkwardness was debilitating as LaDarla, Karen and I tried to find something to do that didn't involve peeking or obvious eavesdropping on these three college guys we found ourselves alone with. Starting a game didn't seem right. There wasn't a television there. It was too early to get out the lunch. And when we tried talking, we found ourselves whispering so the guys wouldn't hear us, and that felt weird too.

Finally, LaDarla picked up a *Tiger Beat* magazine she'd found in a rack by the sofa and headed out to the outdoor swing. Karen found a book on the shelf and curled up on the sofa. I walked out to the screened porch where I could sit and look at the tops of the trees that blocked the view of the lake beyond. Dark clouds were rolling in.

I could see LaDarla's back as she moved back and forth on the squeaky swing. It wasn't long before I saw the blonde boy, Jake, talking with her and then joining her on the swing. I looked again and he'd moved his arm around her shoulders.

I'd kissed my first boyfriend Tommy Wilson a lot of times. I'd tried kissing my neighbor Donnie Baker twice but both times were fails. Other than a spin-the-bottle game I played at a church youth group night and got stuck with two different guys I didn't know— one who pecked me on the lips, the other who just offered an awkward hug— my experience stopped there.

I was just wondering what my mother and Annie Jo would think about how this day was turning out when Cary walked onto the screened porch and plopped himself down beside me.

"Josie, right?" he said.

"Yeah," I managed. "Cary?"

"Yep. Steve was on my hall at school last year. He and Nate were roommates. My roommate was a dud so I hung out with Steve and Nate most of the time."

"At North Georgia College?"

"Yep. Dahlonega. Have you ever been there?" and before I could answer, "How old are you anyway?"

"No, I've never been there. And I'm 16."

"High school," he said. "I remember high school."

"Aren't you a freshman?" I knew my face was making the kind of snarl that my sister, Ansley, said made me look like a constipated ape.

"Sophomore as soon as I finish this summer quarter. I'll be doing ROTC starting in September."

We talked about the rain that was beginning to fall. He asked me about several people he thought I'd know from Atlanta, but I didn't. I warmed up to him a bit after he talked about his younger brother who had Downs Syndrome, and when he offered, "I'm just teasing you about high school. You actually seem older than you are."

Jake and LaDarla left the swing when the rain started and moved into the house. When Cary suggested we move inside too, I expected to find them in the living room but no one was there or in the kitchen.

"Come back here, I'll show you a picture of Joby," he said pointing to one of the back bedrooms in the Carr's lake house.

He picked up a duffel bag from the floor and pulled his wallet from the side pocket.

"This is my brother Joby," he said proudly. "He's 7."

The boy's ear-to-ear smile was bent about three quarters of the way through before it finished on the other side. His eyes were bright blue and his hair stood up with a partial crew cut, but the sides were a little longer, almost like Captain Kangaroo.

"He's so cute. And I like his name."

"It's really John Benjamin Grant, but we shortened it to Joby when he was a baby."

"Even cuter," I said. "Joby Grant. I'd like to meet him."

Cary tossed the duffel bag back to the corner of the room and walked toward the door and quietly closed it.

"Wait. So, you're Cary *Grant*?"

My mind was catapulting between the peculiar coincidence of his name and the fact that he'd just shut the bedroom door.

"Cary *R.* Grant. The 'R' is for Richard."

He sounded as if he'd explained this before.

"Besides," he added. "It's my *real* name. The actor Cary Grant is really named Archibald Leach or something stupid like that."

"No way."

"It's true, but who cares?" He sat on the bed and patted the spot beside him. "So Josie... I've only heard of one other Josie and she was in a comic book."

"It's short for Josephine. I was named after my grandmother."

"You have pretty eyes, Josephine-named-for-your-grandmother."

I swallowed hard and wondered what LaDarla and Karen were doing.

"Really, sit down. You are cute, and there's nothing to do until Steve's parents get back from the hospital anyway."

I sat down but pointed my knees toward him to keep a little distance.

It didn't work.

It wasn't long before we were sitting side-by-side kissing, and not long after that we were lying on the bed kissing and his hands were inching toward my breasts in nonchalant ingress and egress.

Ingress and egress.

We'd learned the terms in social studies when talking about cities. Reviewing the vocabulary words in my mind gave me something to think about other than that the hand of a college boy I'd just met was moving back and forth toward my right boob.

And then more ingress, and this time through the sleeve of my t-shirt and with a slip of several fingers right underneath the elastic of my bathing suit top.

"Um, maybe we'd better see what everyone else is doing." I tried sitting up but he put his face over mine and pushed forward with another deep French kiss.

"They're all doing the same thing we're doing, Josephine. Relax."

I wondered if that were true.

"Well, just kissing, okay?" I said, noting the teasing inflection as he said my formal name.

"Just kissing. I promise," he smiled. "Sorry about that little slip. It won't happen again."

He *was* cute. The dimple on his left cheek was as deep as Mother's when he smiled. His eyes were a greener-blue than his brother's but still had a lot of blue.

And he promised.

I relaxed while my mind whirled.

I'm kissing Cary Grant. I'm kissing a college guy. And he thinks I have pretty eyes. Are my friends kissing their college guys too? LaDarla and the blonde one? Karen and the one with the blue shirt?

I'd almost forgotten about Mrs. Carr's leg and the picnic and the lake plans as I got more and more comfortable making out with Cary R. Grant on a bed in a lake house more than an hour's drive from my sisters and mother and grandmother and my school and our house and our dog Cupie. It occurred to me that Cary didn't know anything about what happened to my father and to our family.

I don't want him to know, I thought as Cary stood up, pulled off his bathing suit and dropped it to the floor.

My heart was beating wildly as I pulled up to my elbows and leveled my eyes to his faded Rolling Stones t-shirt with the gnarled face of a cartoon Keith Richards before I got the courage to look further down.

Up to that point, I don't think I'd ever even said the word *penis.* My friends and I whispered about boys' *willies* or *things,* but this was no willie or thing. It was a fully engorged penis.

Engorged. I'd hated that word even when I saw it for the first time in the "Wonderfully Made" book Mother had given me after I started my period.

My eyes shot back to his eyes and he was smiling at me. But this time he didn't look cute at all.

I jumped off the bed and reached for the doorknob.

"Um, sorry. No," I stammered. "I've got to find Karen and LaDarla."

I was halfway down the hall before I finished my sentence, with my head reeling with whether I should have expected that or not.

I found the other four bringing the picnic in from the boat and setting up lunch on the kitchen counter.

"There you are. We've been wondering about you," LaDarla sang with a teasing smile.

"Where's Cary?" the third guy asked.

Fortunately Steve and Nate walked through the door before I was forced to answer.

"We've got the gas. Have y'all heard from Mom and Dad?" He looked at Karen.

"Well since we don't have a phone here, no," she said. "I guess you could go check for smoke signals."

I saw her glance at LaDarla to question the smart aleck tone, but

LaDarla dropped her face toward the ground, uncertain herself.

Steve ignored her. "Well I'm starved," he said, grabbing a paper plate and piling it with macaroni salad and three chicken drumsticks.

By the time we'd all made our plates and were heading for the porch picnic table, Cary emerged. He was still wearing the Keith Richards t-shirt but had changed from his bathing suit into a pair of blue jean cutoffs.

Steve brought a transistor radio from the car, and we all listened to the broadcast from NASA, where the Apollo 11 was approaching the first moon landing.

The rain had stopped, so Karen, LaDarla and I walked down to the lake after lunch.

"Well, how did it go with Jake and Cary?" Karen asked. "Are they nice? Do you like them?"

"Jake's really cute," said LaDarla.

"Did you kiss him?" Karen whispered urgently.

"No. We just talked." She seemed surprised by the question, and my heart fell. "But he asked me if I'd like to see a movie sometime," she added. "Why, did you kiss Rick?"

Rick. That's the one with the blue shirt.

"Yes. Three times," Karen boasted.

"What about you, Josie? Did you kiss Cary?"

"Once or twice," I lied. "But it was nothing."

"Well, it didn't seem like nothing. You were gone almost 30 minutes."

"No. Nothing," I said and headed back up to the house. I couldn't think of anything except wishing I were at home, wishing my Daddy were alive, wishing I could go back in time to before everything happened, and knowing full well that the protrusion I saw poking from under the Keith Richards cartoon was going to haunt me forever.

It was after 4 o'clock before the Carrs drove back down the gravel driveway and hobbled through the door together. Mrs. Carr had a crutch under one arm and the other around Mr. Carr. Her leg was bandaged and splinted from her ankle to above her knee.

"Thirty stitches," said Mr. Carr. "But we'll fill you in on all that in a few minutes. Apollo 11 is landing any minute."

"We've got the radio on in here," Steve yelled.

We all hurried to gather around the radio.

"Houston, Tranquility Base here," said the static-filled voice we'd come to recognize as Neil Armstrong's. "The Eagle has landed."

The lake echoed our cheers long after our group had quieted from the clapping and hugging.

I stole a look toward Cary, but he was keeping his distance from the group and fortunately, though I was afraid to look, I never felt his eyes on me.

".... about every variety of rock you could find," Armstrong's voice continued. "The colors—Well, it varies pretty much depending ... it looks as though they're going to have some interesting colors to them. Over."

In between checking in on the astronauts, Mrs. Carr described the day's ordeal at the emergency room, the stitches, the splint that she'd have to wear to keep the stitches from opening, and the nice woman they'd met in the waiting room who returned after her husband had been treated and released for shortness of breath with bologna sandwiches and a thermos of coffee for the Carrs' lunch.

"I'm so sorry to ruin the day on the lake, everyone," she said. "I do hope we can try this all again. I just feel terrible."

"It's fine, Mrs. Carr," offered LaDarla, as the boys' voices concurred. "We found plenty to do."

"Roger. Tranquility," came a voice from NASA's headquarters "Be advised there's lots of smiling faces in this room and all over the world. Over."

I wish mine was.

April 1, 2003, 8:45 a.m.

The fact that it was April Fools Day hadn't even crossed my mind as I poured myself a second cup of coffee. Uncharacteristically, given my aversion.

I'd already called work to say I'd be in mid-morning and was enjoying my quiet house when the phone rang. I saw the scroll come across my handset with the words "Charlotte, NC" and recognized my sister and brother-in-law's number.

"Daisyhead Maisy!"

My cheerfulness was always genuine for my youngest sister. "It's always a good day when I can talk with you! Hi Daisy, how are you?" I drawled the "are" just like I'd heard my daughter do with her friends.

"Josie, listen," her serious call to attention was sobering.

I set my coffee cup on the counter and my free hand on the cool granite.

"Annie Jo's had a stroke," she said.

The words pounded my forehead in cadence and faded the volume of her words as she continued.

"She's at Piedmont and it's pretty bad."

Please not Annie Jo.

"I'm leaving for Atlanta within the hour," Daisy said.

I bent in slow motion toward the kitchen chair.

Please no. Erase. Get back to the innocence of the morning. Please no.

I could hear my heart beating as I pushed my shoulders against the wooden slats at the back of the chair.

Images of my grandmother flashed before me as if I were looking through the View-Master slide projector I got for my eighth birthday.

Daisy's words grew fainter and harder to grasp as each new image of Annie Jo — the Flint family's rock — pulsed through my mind and the click of the imaginary View-Master grew louder in my head.

Click

Making homemade noodles with Annie Jo and adding pink food coloring for Ansley's birthday dinner. Chicken and pink noodles, her favorite.

Click

Annie Jo dressed as a clown and twirling a baton through the Inman Park July 4 parade while I rode my bike at her side dressed as a ballerina.

Click

"Who's with her?" I finally managed.

"Mother's there. I haven't called Ansley yet," she said.

As the oldest, I'd always been the organizer for the Flint sisters, but once Daisy married and had a son, she'd noticeably shed her baby-of-the-family role and proven herself masterful with all family matters.

"I'll call her as soon as I hang up with you," she said. "I'll leave for Atlanta as soon as I make arrangements for Charlie and the dogs. Doc's on his way to the hospital now."

Each step of her pre-crafted organization swatted at the nerves behind my eyes as I tried to think through logistics in my head.

What day was it? Oh right. Tuesday. Work is fairly clear. Dentist appointment. Bridge club Wednesday night. Client meeting on Friday, but Bud can handle that.

"Why didn't Mother call me?"

"She was driving to the hospital, Josie! She probably came to my name first on her phone, I don't know," Daisy said impatiently. "She asked me to call you and Ansley right away."

"All this is just so scary, Daisy."

"I'm sorry, Sissy," her voice steadied. "I know you're upset. I'm really anxious to see you, though. Can you go meet Mother there now? I should be there by 3."

"Yes. Of course, I'll leave as soon as I get dressed," I said, trying to ignore the role reversal. "Do you want me to call Ansley?"

"No, you're the closest to the hospital. Just get there for Mother. I'll call Ansley."

"Daisy?"

"Yes."

"Where was she? When she had the stroke?"

"Oh, that's the lucky part. She was outside getting her newspaper and collapsed on the steps near the mailbox. Mr. Faulkner saw her when he was walking the dog and called an ambulance. Otherwise, who knows how long it would have been before we would have even known? Mrs. Faulkner called Mother before the ambulance even got there."

The View-Master's click.

The Faulkner family. The brick steps we sat on when we ate homemade Popsicles at Annie Jo's duplex. 42 Mathis Street. I could almost hear sounds of the Northbridge High marching band practicing behind the dirt hill a few blocks away.

Annie Jo's yellow sun hat.

Annie Jo: Our rock.

"Okay. I'll see you there. I love you. And I'm anxious to see you too, Daisy. What are you going to do about Charlie?"

"I'll worry about that. You just get moving! And I'll see you this afternoon."

"Okay. Thanks Dais. Love you and be careful driving."

I gulped the rest of my lukewarm coffee and grabbed my calendar.

April 1. April Fools Day.

Of course.

June 1966

Laura Liz and I played Dot-to-Dot on a yellow steno pad as we bounced awkwardly on the back seat of the black '59 Rambler on the way to the fruit stand, the drugstore, and probably the Dairy Queen if we were good and didn't nag.

We were inseparable that summer just like we had been for five years back. Laura Liz would be 14 in October. I'd just turned 13 in May, but my boobs were already bigger than hers. You could see air bubbles in her A-cup, but I was definitely filling a B. At least the right one was. The left one was a little smaller, and I blamed Ansley for the time she kicked me in the chest when I was in the bathtub and had just started to bud.

The Rambler's seats were deep. Laura Liz and I had to stand or stretch if we wanted to see out the window. Mother was listening to WQXI-FM. She called it "her station" ever since Daddy had installed an FM converter in the car. Everyone in Atlanta listened to "Quicksy."

I grew bored with the Dot-to-Dot as Laura Liz filled the boxes with her LL initials, so I started thinking about what I would get at the Dairy Queen. Probably a Mister Misty Float. Cherry, for sure. But maybe lemon-lime.

The Rambler didn't have air conditioning, so we usually rode with the windows all the way down from March to October. The dank, muggy air wafted through the back seat as we waved away the smoke stream from Mother's cigarette and passed the steno pad back and forth.

I had just blocked a string of 11 boxes and was filling in my fancy JGF initial signature when we heard a loud scraping sound from the back of the car followed by *Klaaa Bamm!* and a string of pops and long, dragging and scraping sounds.

Laura Liz jabbed me in the thigh with her pencil as we both jumped. We turned backward and vaulted to our knees so that we could crane our necks over the rear seat and see through the thick back window as our car continued past the Hallmark store and the Ben Franklin Five and Dime. The only other cars on the street were at least half a block away.

Another metal screech pierced through the sounds of the car radio and a pipe fell from the car, scraped across Johnson Road and sparked against the pavement before skidding to a stop on the shoulder.

Mother was smoking a Virginia Slims and singing along to Elvis. I guess she didn't even notice the noise. I whipped my head and stared at her, but she just continued the long drag.

"Momma!" I shouted. "Something big just fell off of the car! Momma!"

"What's that, *sug-ahhh*?" she drawled as she turned down the radio. She smiled at both of us from the reflection in the rear view mirror then cut her eyes to Laura Liz and winked. Her lipstick was bright red and perfect.

"Look out the window! A piece of the car fell off!"

Mother squinted her eyes as she studied the reflection in the mirror, and then gracefully stretched her long, thin neck to look back over her shoulder and out the rear view window. Just as quickly, she turned her head back toward the road.

"Oh that." She put on her blinker to make a left on Piedmont. "Yes. Well, we didn't need that part anyway."

Mother just kept on driving. She took another drag on her cigarette and then dropped it into an almost-empty Coke bottle that was sitting in a plastic cup holder hanging from the dash. Nancy Sinatra came on the radio. Mother had some white crushed leather boots just like Nancy's. She turned the volume back up.

I rubbed the spot on my leg where the pencil had dragged across my thigh. There was a scratch, but nothing more. Laura Liz and I cut our eyes toward one another, shrugged and went back to the Dot-to-Dot.

Before Nancy Sinatra had finished her last note, Mother took a sudden swerve into the parking lane where two meter spots were open in a row. She smiled into the rear view mirror and said, "Well, look who we've run into, girls!"

A city bus spit out black exhaust as it pulled away, but as it cleared Annie Jo's bright yellow sun hat came into view like a single sunflower growing in a field of concrete. She'd probably taken the bus to visit her friend Anabelle because she didn't have any groceries in her hand. Just her blue handbag on one arm and a tiny flowerpot she held gently with both hands.

"It's Annie Jo!" Laura Liz screamed.

"Can we get out and go catch her, Momma? She's walking pretty fast. We could miss her," I pleaded.

"Get out on Laura Liz's side," Momma said. We'd slammed the door and were running down Piedmont Road before she had drawled out *s-i-i-ide's* second syllable.

Annie Jo heard us calling the full distance of the Woolworth's. She turned around with a smile and held one arm out as she balanced her handbag and flowerpot in the other. We ran to her partially opened arms as she kissed our heads and hugged us tightly. Each of us spilled words over one other as we heard about her visit with Anabelle and she showed us the violet her friend had sent home with her. We told her about the possible trip to Dairy Queen and Mother in the Rambler just down the street and the whereabouts of Ansley and Daisy. And, of course, Annie Jo asked about Laura Liz's family and added like she always did, "Please give my love to your mother, Rita. I've known that girl since she was..."

"Knee-high to a grasshopper," we finished her sentence in trio.

We paraded arm in arm back to the Rambler where Mother had lit another cigarette as she watched us approach. The three of us quickly spilled our just-hatched plan to share a banana split at Woolworth's and then walk back to Annie Jo's where she'd show us her latest craft project and the new puppy that lived next door.

"I've got one of Cooper's lasagnas thawing for supper," Annie Jo said to Mother. "The girls can have dinner with me and walk home afterward."

"Well, that sounds nice then," Mother said. "But Laura Liz, you call your momma and let her know. And Josie, you be careful and be sure you are home before dark."

Mother opened her handbag and pulled out a lace handkerchief to blot her lips as she stretched to look in the mirror.

"You look pretty in *thaaat collaahhh*, Annie Jo," she added as she folded it back into a neat square. "It suits you."

"Y'all have fun now," she added.

The three of us sang, "We will," as we turned and hurried toward Woolworth's.

We were the three Musketeers, loud and confident with the affirmation that fun was ahead. It just always was when Annie Jo was involved.

April 1, 2003, 10:30 a.m.

"Thank you, Bud. I knew I could count on you," I said to my assistant on the phone. I'd already showered and phoned the kids and Joe with the news.

"No problem. I hope your grandmother pulls out of this all right. How old is she?"

I stared at the tiny blocks of glass tile behind my kitchen sink as I did the calculations.

"Annie Jo was born in 1916," the numbers came quickly using the 'subtract from 100; add 3 for 2003' method I'd learned when Joey and Grace were in elementary school. "Wow. That makes her 87 next month."

"Well, I know it's going to be okay. Don't worry about anything here, Josie. I've got it covered."

Images, lists and random facts ran through my mind as I drove. *We were both born in May. She'll be 87 on May 9. I'll be 50. 50! 50 on May 3. Northside to Collier Road. Park in the newest lot; the turns aren't so tight. Piedmont is where our children were born. Where Joe was born, too. Where Ansley had her twins. Where Mother had gallbladder surgery in '75. Where Laura Liz's mother passed. When was that? 10? 15 years ago now? Was it pancreatic cancer or thyroid cancer? You'd think I'd remember that.*

I parked my car and paused as I listened to my heart beating and tried a few deep breaths. *Should I go to the emergency room desk? Where do they have an information desk here?* I couldn't remember. After a quick "Our Father" prayer I headed toward a sign marked "Hospital."

"Josie!"

Did someone call my name?

"Josie! Over here!"

I whirled around and saw Doc hobbling toward me with a big smile, a cane in one hand and a vase of pink tulips in the other. Annie Jo's favorite.

"Oh, Doc. You're such a sweetheart."

"They don't make many women like Annie Jo Flint," he laughed as he peered at me sweetly over his wire-framed glasses. "She's a special one. Your mother, you and your sisters are included in that category, too, of course."

I hugged him tightly.

"Have you heard from Mother?" I asked.

"Yes. Annie Jo's stable and in a private room. She hasn't spoken yet, but her vital signs are good."

Doc's aftershave always made me smile. It was just a little too much of a good thing, but so perfectly Doc. He was the last of a generation of true dapper men. And he was never without his spit-polished shoes, pressed pants and shirt, and his signature aftershave. The day he and Mother married, he'd worn a blue seersucker suit with black and white saddle oxfords. And a smile as big as the Mississippi.

As we exited the elevator and rounded the corner, we spotted Mother at the nurses' station asking for an extra blanket.

"Momma!"

I was much louder than I meant to be and several people turned to look at me as I ran to my wafer-thin and ever-beautiful mother. Her dimples, even deeper with age, were a familiar comfort, and my embarrassment for the outburst faded.

"Jaybird! Thank you for coming so quickly, sweetheart." Her strong arms wrapped around me as if she were twice her size.

Jaybird.

Mother very seldom called me by my nickname. Without warning, tears welled in my eyes.

"Don't you worry, sweetheart," she said drawling the '*sweet heaaart*' with a familiar flow that felt like a warm cloak across my shoulders.

The cheekiness that had once defined my mother had faded years before. "Annie Jo is stable and sleeping soundly. I just wanted to get another blanket for her. The room is kind of drafty." Her *'dra-ahf-ty,'* had three syllables, and it made me smile.

Mother nodded toward the second room, and I swallowed hard as I read the placard next to the partially closed door: Room 433. Josephine Louise Flint. Dr. Paul Raymond.

Mother opened the door with a sweet but quiet-voiced, "Annie Jo, you'll be happy to see these visitors." She walked in, and Doc held out his arm and nodded for me to follow.

The tubes and equipment that surrounded her hospital bed were alarming. The room was patched with stark white and light blue décor, its only accents machinery with blinking lights and faint humming sounds. Annie Jo was sound asleep with tubes and clips attached to her shoulders and hands. She showed no sign of hearing Mother's introduction.

Doc placed the tulips on the table next to her bed as the three of us studied her face. Her curls had gotten much thinner over the years, but they still kinked like corkscrews when her hair wasn't set and styled. Her lips were dry and chapped, and she was breathing heavily through her mouth, but her face was peaceful. She didn't look like she was cold, but I felt a cool draft, too, and helped Mother cover her and tuck in the sides.

"How long was she outside before Mr. Faulkner found her?"

"Just minutes," Mother said. "Melanie said that her husband waved to her when he saw her coming out the door to get the paper. He went back in to grab the leash and fill his coffee cup and when he came back out he saw her lying across the stoop. She cut her leg and scraped up her elbow. But they've been bandaged and will be fine."

"So is she going to be okay?"

"Say your prayers, Josie. So far, the vital signs are good, but she's had a stroke. All we can do is send up our prayers. It's all we know until she wakes up."

Mrs. Faulkner popped in the door and was almost immediately followed by Dr. Raymond and then someone from the church.

The crowded room felt wrong and frustrated me as I glanced across the chatter of concern-mixed-with-small-talk to watch Annie Jo sleep. Her closed eyes and mostly steady sleeping sent no message at all.

"How are the twins, Mrs. Faulkner?"

"Doing well, Josie," she said. "Both boys are in Florida now. One in Tampa, the other near Pensacola. I'm sure they'd love to catch up with you and your sisters when they're in town."

I forced a smile.

"Please let Mr. Faulkner know how grateful we are that he found Annie Jo so quickly."

Just as the doctor and two visitors left, Ansley walked in looking like she was headed for a tennis match at the yacht club where she would be accepting a crown or a diamond-studded bag tag or something. She had on a pink and green toile tennis skirt with a white sleeveless top, pearls and white tennis shoes that looked like they'd never seen a court. The only blonde in our family, her enhanced-with-highlights hair was pulled back into a sleek ponytail that only served to emphasize her perfect cheekbones and size 6 Barbie doll figure. At 47, Ansley was gorgeous in all the ways Mother was.

We filled her in on what we knew and then looked around helplessly.

Ansley broke the ice, "Well, this place brings back memories."

"I had four grandchildren born here," said Mother brightly.

"I don't think I've been here since my twins were born," Ansley added. "Unless it was your surgery, Mother. I can't remember which came first."

I could see Mother thinking.

"I was here with Rita before she died," I added. "What was her cancer?"

"Pancreatic," Doc confirmed.

Then, just as quickly, Ansley transitioned.

"Oh wait, I forgot! Josie, do you still drive that black Avalon with the 'Bush/Cheney' sticker on the back?"

"Yes. Why?"

"I saw it being towed from the parking lot when I came in."

"What!"

My eyes flew to Annie Jo's bed, but nothing had changed. I darted around looking for where I'd put my bag, stood up and grabbed it with a painful, "be right back."

"April Fools!" I heard after I rounded the corner of the door. Ansley's voice grated across my nerves as I heard her add an exaggerated giggle.

April Fools! April Fools! April Fools! A reverberating cadence pounded my head opening the gates of a painful past.

August 1964

*D*addy called me "Jaybird."

I was named after his mother, Josephine, but hardly anyone knew that was her real name because she'd been called Annie Jo long before I was born. In fact, she wasn't even an Ann or an Annie. Her nephew Dexter started the name when he was a toddler: Aunt Josephine became Aunt Jo, which sweetened into Auntie Jo, and then later just slurred into Annie Jo. Pretty soon, everyone was calling her that. Even my grandfather, Papa Ray, who died when I was 6.

Josephine Grace Flint: Born May 3, 1953. 5-3-53. The oldest of the three girls born to Cooper and Beverly Flint of Atlanta, Georgia. Green eyes. Brown hair. 'A' student, mostly.

Daisy called me Sissy a lot. Mother called me Josephine Grace when she introduced me to someone at church. Daddy called me Jaybird. But thanks to Laura Liz, most people just called me Josie.

Thw ee eeeet. "Jaybird?"

Daddy would whistle between his teeth before he whispered my name with a plan he knew I'd love. "There's a scary movie on tonight. Up for it with me?"

Daddy and I shared popcorn and milkshakes late at night after everyone was asleep. We'd watch Johnny Carson long after my bedtime and scary movies in the middle of the night. We'd share a blanket and hide under the covers during the scary parts, but we were both peeking, of course. During commercials we'd talk about school or fishing or the Georgia Bulldogs. I was the only one in the family who shared his love for the Georgia Bulldogs, so when he won free tickets in a drawing at the Piggly Wiggly, he took me to see the Dawgs play Georgia Tech at Grant Field.

Daddy grew up near Athens, Georgia, and cheered mightily for the Georgia Bulldog football team. All through high school, he and his friends would hang out near campus. He loved to brag that he saw every home football game from a bridge near Sanford Stadium for 16 years straight. He also took a job right out of high school with the university's facilities department and made friends with all the coaches and players.

"Man's best friends are always Dawgs," he'd say.

One of Daddy's best friends was George Elliott, an offensive coach for the Georgia Bulldogs. He and Mr. Elliott would talk every week on the phone about the Bulldog team or fishing or the Atlanta Braves. He had a boat on Lake Lanier and would often invite Daddy to go fishing with him. Sometimes they'd fish all night long and come home with a cooler full of fish that he'd clean and grill for our Sunday morning breakfast. And every summer, Mr. Elliott and his wife would take our whole family out on the lake for a day of boating, skiing and fishing.

One year he promised to teach us all to water ski, and naturally Ansley got up on her very first try.

"Lean back and let the boat pull you, Josie," Mr. Elliott said as I held on to the boat's ladder. I was embarrassed after five failed attempts and could feel my chest and neck burning bright red and moving toward my face. The six boat passengers looked at me with pity, but didn't want to give up. I really wanted to water ski.

"Do you want me to get in and show her how, Mr. Elliott?" the skiing expert of the universe asked.

Daddy gently pushed Ansley into the seat and kissed her head.

"That won't be necessary, Ansley. I think Josie's got it this time."

He winked at me and I let go of the ladder as Mr. Elliott restarted the boat's engine.

The ski rope straightened and I unfolded my legs as the movement of the boat pulled me right out of the water. Mother, Daddy, Mrs. Elliott and Daisy were cheering and waving their arms. I saw Ansley move to the front of the boat and pull a Fanta Orange out of the cooler as I took three loop turns around the big cove behind the red and white boat, "Salty Dawg."

When Daddy was skiing, Ansley asked Mr. Elliott if she could help drive the boat. He gave us both a short turn, but Ansley went first.

Daddy's closest friend, though, was his cousin Dexter. Dexter was six months younger and was the only child of Annie Jo's brother, Uncle Lee, and his wife Lola. Daddy was an only child too, so the two grew up just like brothers and went to the same grammar school and high school.

Dexter and his wife Shalene moved to Atlanta in 1964 about the same time we moved to our house on Duberry Street.

Our house was just a few blocks from Annie Jo's duplex, and it put me at the same school as Laura Liz who'd been my best friend since we met in Sunday school a few years before. We moved in on a Saturday. I started the sixth grade at Seaton Ferry Junior High two weeks later, while Ansley started fourth grade and Daisy started first at Seaton Ferry Elementary.

On the day we moved in, Daddy carried Momma over the threshold of the front door. Ansley took pictures while Daisy and I sang, "Home, Sweet Home" to the tune of "Home on the Range." Afterward, we toasted with grape Kool-Aid from the bathroom Dixie cups because we hadn't unpacked any glasses yet. Momma said we were "high cotton."

That night we spread all of our mattresses on the floor of our new living room and jumped up and down laughing and screaming together. Momma unpacked a box of towels and we made pillows with some and used others for covers. It was a happy night for the Flints.

Our two-story house had four bedrooms, but Ansley and I shared one. Daisy had the smallest room, and we kept the downstairs bedroom for sewing and guests. The house had a brick front, a large picture window on the top left and a driveway that wound around the right side of the house to a garage. Daddy loved to tinker with things in the garage, so there was rarely room for our car.

Ansley and I had twin beds in our room. We arranged them in an "L" shape with a card table covered with a yellow tablecloth at the foot of each bed. We could easily look at each other if we wanted to talk, but geometrically, our heads were about as far apart from one another as they could be if we didn't. We had a narrow desk with two chairs. Above it, Daddy hung a large framed corkboard. He covered the left half with red burlap and the right side with yellow burlap to make a bulletin board. Annie Jo brought over her pincushion and we put yellow pins on my side and red pins on Ansley's side. The very first day I hung a picture of the Mouseketeers that came inside our Mickey Mouse Club album and the Georgia Bulldog football schedule on my side. Ansley hung a photo from her first dance recital and a list of rules for our room.

Most all of our neighbors came by the week we moved in with a casserole or a pound cake. There was a family next door — the Bakers — who had a boy and a girl both in my grade.

"Irish twins," their mother explained. "Donnie will be 12 next month and Dena is 11, but because of how their birthdays fall, they will both be starting sixth grade."

"The same as our Josie!" my mother said with a higher, more enthusiastic pitch than was typical. She wrapped her arms around my neck and pulled me in front of her as if she were presenting me as a trophy.

"The kiddos are in Kentucky for two weeks with their grandparents," said Mrs. Baker. "But they'll be back before school starts. I'll send them over to meet you, Josie, so they can show you around Seaton Ferry and introduce you to the kids in the neighborhood."

Across the street was Mrs. Dean. She had recently lost her husband to complications from a blood clot, she said. She wore thick glasses and explained that she mostly just warmed TV dinners, so she brought over a plastic pitcher filled with sweet tea.

The telephone company hooked up our phone about a week after we moved in, and our phone number had the same digits as my birthday: Amhurst Seven-5-3-5-3. To dial it, the number was 267-5353. Daddy said the Amherst Seven was made up to make the numbers easier to remember. It made me feel like we'd moved to the right place.

We shared a party line with Mr. Grogan, the butcher at the Piggly Wiggly, and his wife Mabel who lived on the street behind us. Their children lived out of state, so they rarely used the phone except for Sunday afternoons when their kids called. Mrs. Grogan walked through the neighbor's gate in the backyard to bring us a pound cake.

Momma and Daddy fussed with our hand-me-down furniture and moved it around five or six times before they settled on the right spots for our sofa, love seat and two matching chairs. Most of our stuff came from Annie Jo's next-door neighbor who moved to Savannah to live with her sister. We even got her gold velvet draperies with tie-backs. Daddy hung them and they fit perfectly in our big living room window. That's where all our important photos were taken — framed by the tie-back velvet drapes — for everything from the first day of school each year, to pictures of Momma and Daddy every time they got dressed up, and me on my first date with Tommy Wilson.

We were allowed to walk to Annie Jo's duplex any time we wanted. She lived on the right side and rented the left side, and she always found interesting people to be her tenants. One summer, a fortune-teller lived there and she told us all about her tarot cards and read our palms. She said Ansley would be a dancer and I would be a poet.

"Grab a salt shaker on your way out," Annie Jo would say every time we visited and we'd follow her out the back door to her garden.

Every spring, Annie Jo planted a garden with flowers, cucumbers, bell peppers and tomatoes in the back yard that was surrounded by a white picket fence. The fence surrounded both units of the duplex, and every year she made her garden a little bit bigger. We helped her plant and pull weeds and can tomatoes at the end of the season.

She kept a basket by the door filled with Tupperware salt shakers that had a snap-down lid. We'd pick a red juicy tomato, wipe off the dirt on our shorts or shirt, salt it and eat it as we chatted and strolled through the rows.

Everything was fun at Annie Jo's house. I was interested in everything Annie Jo talked about. And she was interested in everything she heard and everybody she met.

"Stand next to me because I'm a lucky charm," she would say. "I don't even know what I did to deserve the greatest son in the world, but I got him. Then I got luckier still to get the greatest daughter-in-law and then the greatest granddaughters, too."

"We're the lucky ones, Mom," Daddy said.

Every year Daddy took Annie Jo to the Waffle House for breakfast on her birthday. And he ordered a corsage for her to wear to church every year on Mother's Day.

Daddy drove a red truck. He installed a speaker and tape player in the dash to play the Georgia Bulldogs' fight song. Sometimes when he came home from work, he'd play the song as he drove into the neighborhood. All the kids knew that when they heard the familiar, "Glory, glory to old Georgia..." it was a signal to run to Mr. Flint's truck. He'd let us all pile in the back where he would drive us to the Dairy Queen and get us all an ice cream cone — plain or dipped — and we'd drive back home singing the fight song and licking our cones.

Daddy loved to cook.

"Daisy, Ansley, Jaybird," Daddy would call. "Y'all wash up for supper. Spare ribs on the grill."

Lots of times he'd just skewer everything from the refrigerator on a stretched out clothes hanger and we'd have shish kebabs.

Every night that he'd cook supper he'd make an extra plate or two and cover it with foil for Mrs. Dean across the street. She was crabby most of the time, but always friendly when she saw Daddy. She had bursitis and often couldn't find her glasses, so she'd ask our names every time she saw one of us girls. She always recognized Daddy, though. Daddy charmed everyone he met.

"Cooper, you are too kind to an old lady!" she'd always say when he brought her a plate across the street with a grand description of its contents and warming instructions. And then no matter how many times we would tell her, she would look at whichever daughter he'd brought along with him and ask, "Now which Flint girl are you?"

The kitchen table at our house on Duberry Street sat against the window. Mother and Ansley sat on the left side, Daisy and me on the right, and Daddy on the end facing the window.

"How are the ribs tonight, Jaybird?"

"The best you've ever made, Daddy."

"Heh, heh!" he laughed. "What do you say we go fishing this weekend? I made a grill basket I want to try out. Maybe some barbecued catfish," he said as he playfully poked me in the ribs. "How's that sound?"

Daddy had spent the afternoon tinkering in the garage where he'd soldered some mesh wire to a handle from Annie Jo's old frying pan to make the grill basket. He had been working on it earlier in the day when Laura Liz and I were looking for skates.

"Can I go, Daddy?" pleaded Ansley.

"Me too!" screamed Daisy.

"Yes, yes, yes, Lady Bug Flint Muffins. We can all go. I'll wake you all up real early on Saturday morning. We'll stop at the Waffle House for breakfast on our way home."

Daddy could fix anything, but he never wanted to fix it back like it was supposed to be. He thought it was more fun to make it into something new.

For Ansley's seventh birthday, he rewired our old toaster that would no longer heat with an old alarm clock. Then he cut out seven blocks of wood in the size and shape of a piece of toast. On each one he painted, "Good Morning, Ansley, it's Monday" or "Good Morning, Buttercup, it's Tuesday" with cartoon pictures of Ansley on each one. On the back of each one he wrote a Georgia football statistic that he thought she ought to memorize.

When he tucked her in at night, he would change the inserts so that when her alarm clock went off in the morning, the "toast" would pop up at the same time with her morning message. The alarm clock sat on the table at the foot of our beds, with the sides with the football statistics facing my side, but I pretty much had all that memorized before the toast clock anyway.

Another time he made a bird feeder for Momma to look like our house on Duberry Street. He put a latch on the base of a box that held a tape player. Then he recorded a 90-minute cassette with bird sounds, mostly from just sitting outdoors recording the morning birds, but he added some duck calls and a few minutes of Ansley, Daisy and me making our own bird sounds. He made a remote control that would activate the recorder from inside the house.

The birds soon figured out how to open the door, and we found the tape recorder pecked apart the very first week, but the birdhouse hung in our backyard until the day we moved.

When I was in first grade, Daddy made reading benches for my class. Mrs. Jacobs requested that they be simple semi-circle wooden bleachers to fit up to eight kids each, but Daddy had a better idea.

We had dozens of University of Georgia seat pads stacked in our garage given to Daddy by Mr. Elliott. Daddy glued eight of the cushions to the benches and added book holders made from old steering wheels he found in a junk yard.

The kids loved the benches, but by the time Ansley got into first grade, she said Mrs. Jacobs had taken off the steering wheels and re-covered the seat pads with a yellow chintz print.

For every ounce of Daddy's charm, Mother had two. But hers was combined with a pound of guts and a sharp tongue that many didn't understand. Lots of women didn't care for her, but men were always drawn to Beverly Flint. Her hair was thick and brown, and she had a dimple so deep on her right cheek that she could hold a dime in it when she smiled.

Her sister, my Aunt Pauline, told me once that she was so jealous of my momma's dimple when she was a little girl that she actually pressed dimes into both cheeks, squeezed her cheeks around them and then taped them shut with duct tape one night before she went to bed. When she got up the next morning, her face was sore and bruised, and by noon that day she had giant blisters on both of her cheeks.

"Now, Josie, don't go tellin' her I told you that story," Aunt Pauline said. "I never admitted that I knew how I got the blisters to your mother. Just keep that between us, you hear?"

Momma used her dimples, her perfectly painted lips and her thick southern drawl when she spoke. She was sweet as sugar until she had a reason not to be, and she held the attention of those around her as if they were expecting a lashing from her sharp tongue, which reared itself when you might expect it and sometimes when you didn't. When she spoke to men, she'd add in the eyes. She'd look right into their eyes and linger there just a fraction longer than seemed necessary, pop the hint of a smile and then throw in the dimples, lips and drawl.

If Ansley and I were fussing, she'd drop her chin and stare right between us with a little purse of her lips. We knew that meant we'd better shape up or we'd be doubling our chores. If Daisy was whining, she'd cock her head to the left, raise her eyebrows and look right at her. She didn't speak, but you could hear her eyes counting "one... two... three." Daisy learned early on to pipe down before the end of the "three" and Momma would snap back to whatever she was doing.

Those who knew her well, knew that when her eyelids grew heavy, something unpleasant was coming. They'd stay closed just long enough for her to gather some steam, then she'd start spouting her sharp-tongued, not-to-be-argued-with precepts with a slow, deliberate drawl in a cadence that seemed to go on forever and could stop your heart. Then, she'd smile and cock her head just like it was a punctuation mark and walk away. Then, as if it had never happened, she'd offer you some iced tea and tell you how pretty you looked in *thaaat collaahhh*.

She worked at the Frito Lay plant in the payroll department during the day, but many weekends and nights she volunteered answering phones at the church for a suicide hotline that it sponsored. She always came home happy, which was kind of funny considering the sad state of the people she talked to, but I guess that's why she was so good at the job. Some people probably questioned whether Beverly Flint would be the right person to help someone who was contemplating suicide, but we Flints understood the boundaries of her edginess. Need her and she was gentle and comforting; cross her and that was a different story.

Mother went to Agnes Scott College for one year before she met Daddy and quit, but she dated a boy from Georgia Tech during that year, and his fraternity made her a little sister. They entered her into the Miss Greek Week pageant and she won first place.

She wore her Alpha Tau Omega jersey, with "Beverly – Lil Sis" stitched across the back, almost every Saturday that I can remember. She'd pull her hair into a ponytail and wear her jersey with short cut-off jeans and high heels. Aunt Lola told her once that it might be time to dress and act her age. Momma spat back, "Lola, honey, my age and my clothes are none of your business."

Then she drooped her eyes to Lola's floral printed house dress and let them linger a few seconds before snapping back to her eyes and giving Lola a dimpled smile.

Momma was only 120 pounds but Daddy always told her 115 pounds were pure guts. She'd say, "Really, Cooper? What about the other 5?"

He'd just smile.

She was gentler with Daddy. They always seemed to be secretly smiling through their disagreements. She couldn't resist Daddy's Rhett Butler smirk, and he couldn't resist her Scarlet O'Hara-style charms. Their fusses always turned into flirting and Momma would tease his Bulldog sensibilities with stories of Georgia Tech and the ATOs.

"Maybe those wussy frat boys can try their secret handshake on the 1966 SEC Champions," he laughed. "Face it, Bev. Tech oughta just hang it up."

"Cooper Leon Flint! You're just jealous that the ATOs won first place in Greek Week thanks to me," Mother drawled.

"Yes, Baby Doll, you're right. I'm jealous all right," Daddy laughed as he headed out to the garage.

September 1964

The first year at Seaton Ferry Junior High, I got Mrs. Sanders for homeroom, math and P.E. Sandra Sanders was tall and skinny. She had a scarf for every outfit. If she didn't have a scarf around her neck, there was one around her waist or fashioned into a headband or tied to her handbag. She would have been pretty, except that her mouth turned down at both ends making a permanent scowl on her face.

If it wasn't for P.E., I would have liked Seaton Ferry right away. Sixth graders had to dress out for P.E., and the girls' locker room was just one giant room with mirrors on each wall. There was a backorder for the girls' uniforms — an awful, striped one-piece short jumpsuit that snapped at the shoulders — so Mrs. Sanders assigned me a faded used uniform that was too tight. The very first day we played a horrible game called Bombardment with teams hurling kickballs at one another. The girls were mean and strong and I hated the game. When I finally got the courage to reach for a ball, my uniform's shoulder snapped completely apart and my bra flashed for all to see.

I grabbed my shoulder and instinctively crouched down and ran to the bleachers just a few steps away.

Mrs. Sanders walked over and put her hand on my arm. "New schools can be scary, Josie," she said. "But you're going to like it here, I promise."

A new order of uniforms came in after two weeks, and we started badminton, which I was pretty good at.

In math though, Mrs. Sanders started in the very first week with factorization and GCFs — greatest common factor, and I got lost right off the bat.

Daddy spent hours with me at the dining room table going through everything we'd covered. I made an 80 on the first test, and once we started covering LCMs —least common multiples —Daddy helped me again and I made a 99. I would have made a 100, but Mrs. Sanders marked off because I dotted the "i" in Josie with a heart instead of a "proper pencil mark made directly over the letter."

Lots of things bugged Mrs. Sanders. Like girls who put their eyeliner on the top of their lower lashes.

I was rushing to put my school clothes back on one day and had only my skirt and my bra on when she came into the locker room and stood behind Belinda Roach who was in front of the mirror putting on makeup.

"You girls need to learn the importance of hygiene," she said. "And stop putting that eyeliner on the inside of your lower lashes. That's just chemicals, ladies. You could go blind using all that makeup."

I confided to Annie Jo that I wasn't sure I was going to like Seaton Ferry Junior. "It will get better, sweetheart," she said. "Just you wait and see."

April 1, 2003, 2 p.m.

*B*y 2 p.m., we had visits from two more women from the church and a physical therapist who did nothing more than to tell us that he'd be checking in on Josephine and would begin therapy with her as soon as she was awake. It felt so impersonal. *"Her name is Annie Jo,"* I stopped myself from saying out loud.

Daisy arrived just before 3 o'clock bearing a bouquet of balloons and a poster Charlie made for Annie Jo's room. He'd carefully printed his name and a neatly penned 'Age 9' at the bottom of the poster.

Mother, Ansley and Doc had taken a break to the cafeteria and were gone when she arrived.

Daisy's face had rounded since I last saw her, but her hair cut was an adorable bob and her dimples were all Mother— more fabulous than ever as she bopped into the stark room with the world's greatest smile, a bear hug and the most comforting levity I'd felt all day.

"I've missed you, Sissy!" She smiled brightly and wrapped her arms around my head as she kissed my forehead.

"Missed you, too, Dais!"

She carefully carried her eyes to Annie Jo's bed and let them linger before she pulled back her head and closed her eyes and smiled.

"Do you remember the Dip and Drape dolls she taught us to make?"

Wow. Dip and Drape dolls. I'd forgotten those.

Annie Jo showed us how to make dolls she'd found in a craft magazine. We started with a Coke bottle and put a Styrofoam ball on the top for the head. We shaped it into a face with other pieces of Styrofoam and covered it in gauze dipped in glue. After it dried we made clothes by dipping fabric in glue and shaping it around the bottle so that it would be stiff when it dried.

Wow. I hadn't thought about those in years.

"Oh my gosh, I do!" I said. "I don't think I'd ever have remembered those if you hadn't said that."

I stood and wrapped my arm around Daisy's waist as we studied Annie Jo together.

"Anything new?"

"No. Just say your prayers, Daisy. It's all we can do. Where's Charlie, by the way?"

"Sweet Vivian," she said smiling. "She drove from Spartanburg and picked him up from school at 2:15. She'll stay with him tonight at our house until Allen gets back from D.C. tomorrow afternoon. She's the greatest friend ever."

Mother and Doc returned with a half piece of chocolate cake in a Styrofoam box and warm greetings for Daisy.

"Momma, do you remember those Dip and Drape dolls?"

"Oh, of course, I do," Mother said. "Do you remember the popcorn balls?"

"And the marzipan!" Daisy and I said in unison.

Between the three of us, memories of fun times with Annie Jo tumbled over one another faster in our heads than we could account for in the three-way conversation.

"Do you remember the time Daisy had strep throat on Halloween and Annie Jo dressed as a hobo and trick-or-treated for her?"

"Oh my gosh!" Daisy answered. "She brought home more candy for me than you and Ansley had put together!"

Daisy closed her eyes. I could see her reliving another memory before she snapped back to reality and asked, "Where is Ansley? When I phoned, I thought you said she was here."

"She's making a quick phone call. She'll be right back."

I looked at the clock. It was almost 4:15 and Joe and the kids should be getting here soon. Joe would be coming from downtown; Joey and

Grace were meeting at our house and driving together.

Daisy stepped out of the room and returned just minutes later entwined arm-in-arm with Ansley, and the room filled again with chatter. The seriousness of the day couldn't flatten the joy I felt to be with my family.

My little sisters. I was Jaybird again.

From the corner of my eye, I saw Annie Jo's head turn toward the conversation.

1962

Laura Liz Roberts and I were sort of related. Her mother, Rita Roberts, was the second cousin of my Aunt Lola, who was married to Annie Jo's brother, Uncle Lee.

Mother said she thought the connection made us fifth cousins or maybe third cousins twice removed, but that we could pretend to be actual cousins if we wanted to.

We liked to pretend that we were cousins from different countries and make up accents like Patty Lane and Cathy Lane on the "Patty Duke Show." Laura Liz and I watched the show every week.

It was third grade, though, that Laura Liz and I became best friends.

She sat next to me in Sunday school. I liked how her too-long bangs separated around her eyes that were the exact color of a sea-foam-colored Crayon, one of my favorites.

"Josie?" She swiped her bangs to the side and unsuccessfully wrapped them around her ear. "Do you know how to tie a bowline knot?"

Of course I knew because Daddy had taught all of us Flint girls about knots every time we went fishing.

"My brother Butch found an old canoe back in the woods and he wants to take it down the Chattahoochee River this afternoon," she said. "He says he won't take me because I don't know how to make a bowline knot and I'll just get in the way."

She reached in a purse that she carried with Indian-style fringe and beads and pulled out a small piece of rope. I showed her a bowline knot and we stayed in the Sunday school room after class and I showed her a cleat hitch too.

It turned out that Butch still wouldn't take her on his river trip, but I spent a lot of time thinking about our conversation that week, and on the next Sunday I brought two ropes and showed her another one I knew that Daddy called the sheetbend knot. Laura Liz and I were pretty much inseparable after that.

We went to different schools for 3rd through 5th grade, but we could walk a few short blocks and meet in front of Harmon's Pharmacy on the way home from school. She came home with me a couple of days a week. Then she would have dinner with us and Daddy would drive her home afterward. We never seemed to waste time talking about what we should do. We just found something to do until it faded into the next fun thing. Once in a while, I would walk home with her to her house and we would hang out climbing trees, walking along the creek by her house or poking around in her attic.

At our house, we would play board games or gather some of the other kids nearby and play kickball or monkey-in-the-middle. Other days we'd pretend we were crime solvers like Nancy Drew. She loved that I had younger sisters and always said she wished she'd had one. Ansley and Daisy liked her too, and I suppose I was nicer to them when Laura Liz was around.

The Roberts lived outside the neighborhood just a few blocks away, but Laura Liz was embarrassed about their house because their furniture was old and the kitchen was pretty dirty most of the time. The house sat deep in the woods. The driveway was gravel, but needed more rocks because there were a lot of potholes on the long drive to their house. Except for when her brother Butch was around, I kind of liked hanging out at Laura Liz's house because there was a swinging vine in the backyard and a creek that ran along the side of the house and usually some stray puppies or kittens to play with.

By the time we moved to Duberry Street and I started sixth grade at Seaton Ferry Junior, Laura Liz and I had been best friends for two years.

In our neighborhood the kids would come out just before dark to play a game we called "Bloody Tiger." One person would be the Bloody Tiger and would hide in the woods while the rest of the players would put one hand on a tree that would be "base," hide their eyes and count to 50 before scattering in search of the Bloody Tiger. As soon as someone got close, the Bloody Tiger would jump out screaming "Bloody Tiger" and try to tag someone before they made it back to base. Whoever was tagged would be the Bloody Tiger for the next round.

Laura Liz joined the game whenever she was at our house. Her mother, Rita Roberts, worked at the telephone company and her father, Hank, drove the school bus until he ran a red light just outside the school and was pulled over. His alcohol level was .09 and he'd only been awake an hour or so that morning. He spent 30 days in jail and lost his job.

By the time we were in sixth grade, he mostly just drank Pabst Blue Ribbon all day long. He was mean and sloppy. His sleeveless t-shirts were always stained and needed bleach. Even their dog, Amos, hid when Hank was around. Her mother had the night shift so she slept all morning and afternoon, so we had to be quiet when we were there. It was no wonder that Laura Liz spent most of her time at our house.

Hank Roberts had a beautiful singing voice, though. Aunt Lola liked to tell the story of him singing *Love Divine, All Loves Excelling* when their son Dexter got married. She said she had never heard the hymn sung more beautifully. Aunt Lola had a photo of Hank, Dexter and my daddy, all wearing white suits that I loved to look at when I was at their house. Hank had a beautiful voice and played a mean guitar when he was sober, but by the time Laura Liz and I became friends, those days were mostly over.

After the school bus incident, Rita started taking Hank's beaten up truck to and from work at night, so it was pretty much up to us Flints to get Laura Liz to and from after-school programs.

At the school Honor's Day, the principal asked the parents of the kids who won an award to stand when their child was recognized. Laura Liz won an award for three years of perfect attendance and it was Mother and Daddy who stood up and cheered for her.

I saw the relief on her face when she saw them stand up. Everyone knew that it was the Flints, not the Roberts, but I think the audience was as relieved as Laura Liz was. I noticed she was looking at the ground when the principal called her name, but she glanced up just for a second and saw Momma and Daddy cheering and waving. A big smile spread across her face and she timidly waved back with her hand at her waist.

When Laura Liz got an A+ on her book report on *Moby Dick*, it was Momma who made her a pan of brownies and decorated it with her name and a big smiley face.

Mother and Daddy insisted that we Flint girls call our neighbors by Mr. and Mrs., and always speak using, "Yes, Ma'am" and "No, Sir." For whatever reason—maybe because we were almost related—we all just called Laura Liz's parents Hank and Rita.

1965

Two very bad things happened at the Roberts' house that I never told Mother or Daddy about.

The first was in seventh grade when Laura Liz and I were working on a skit for social studies class about the Bill of Rights and we wanted to dress up like two of the Founding Fathers.

"Let's look in the attic," Laura Liz said. "I know how to get up there if we bring the ladder from the shed. I saw a wig up there one time when I went up with Momma once."

We dragged the dusty ladder from the dilapidated wooden shed that sat in the Roberts' back yard to the hallway in their home. No one took notice or seemed to care.

We only had one flashlight so we moved her bedroom lamp to the attic's entry for more light. It was musty and dirty and filled with boxes, plastic bags, old shoes and books. The ceiling was too low for us to stand so we scooted around on our knees or butts looking through the mostly unmarked boxes. We found some old jackets to wear and a blonde wig we figured we could pull into a ponytail like Thomas Jefferson.

"Hey, here's a picture of your brother," I said, pulling a black and white photo from the box.

Laura Liz scurried over right away to see what I had found. She was always complaining that she never had any pictures from when she was little. Since Annie Jo took lots of pictures of Ansley, Daisy and me and always gave them in nice frames to my parents for their birthdays and Christmas gifts, there were lots of photographs at my house.

It was a tattered baby picture taken when Butch was about a year old wearing a rounded collar shirt and white suspenders. On the back someone had written "Butch, 1950." That made sense because he was three years older than Laura Liz and three and half years older than me.

"That's Butch?" she cried. "Ughh! Just goes to show you're not home free just because you're cute as a baby."

We tossed the picture aside, knowing that Butch wouldn't care about such a wonderful treasure. He'd just shrug and mumble something ugly and tell us we were stupid idiots. We ratted through the box looking for photos of Laura Liz, but only found pictures of people we didn't recognize or had never met. There were a few of her Nana and Pa Roberts so she put them in a stack of things she'd found to keep in the seashell box under her bed in her room.

Underneath the photos we found an old Bible. Across the inside cover was written, "Roberts Family Bible" in fancy script. Page 3 had a chart with names that dated back to a person who was born in 1845 and died in 1879.

I held the flashlight as Laura Liz read the names as best she could. We laughed at some of the names, but none of them meant anything until she got to her grandparents, Zachary Beauregard Roberts and Patricia Jane Holden Roberts. Underneath were entries for their children Henry Beauregard Roberts (her dad Hank) and Jacob Collier Roberts (Laura Liz's Uncle Jake, who lived in North Carolina.) Next to Hank's name was Laura Liz's mother, Rita Sue Reynolds and next to Jake's was his ex-wife Doris Wannamaker. Underneath Hank and Rita was a different handwriting with the name Dalton Beauregard Roberts and "Butch" in parenthesis next to it.

There was no entry for Laura Elizabeth Roberts.

We turned another page and pulled out an index card-sized paper that had an elaborate crest at the top. A stain under the crest made some of the writing illegible. It was a membership card. Blank lines had been filled in with broken type from a typewriter. Laura Liz read out loud:

"...this 17 January 1928 date certifies that Zachary Beauregard Roberts is an initiated member of the Toccoa, Georgia chapter of the ..."

Both sets of our eyes had already dropped to see the words, "Ku Klux Klan" before she got to that part out loud. She stopped mid sentence and we both just looked at each other.

Her seafoam-colored eyes were glassy and dark in the dim light.

Underneath the Bible was a folded white garment of stained and dusty cotton. Laura Liz tugged on it and the pieces separated. She held up a cone-shaped piece and we both inhaled and held our breaths before she wordlessly refolded it and tucked it back under the stack.

My mouth filled with sour saliva as I took the card from her hand and tucked it at the back of the Bible and thumbed through the other documents stuffed inside. There was a newspaper clipping with a picture of a burning cross. Someone had written "Booger Creek" in a blue fountain pen in perfect penmanship at the top of the clipping. I'll never forget how those words looked with such perfect penmanship.

There was another membership card with a name we didn't recognize, plus a black and white photograph of a bunch of Klan members in white robes and pointed hats standing in front of a grove of trees.

I whispered, "Is your granddaddy in this picture?"

"How would I know? All their faces are covered."

Laura Liz had a point.

Clipped behind the card was a grainy black and white photograph, but you could tell it was a Negro man wearing nothing but his underwear. He had a sack over his head and was hanging from a tree with a rope around his neck. The man was barefoot and his feet were kind of hugging each other with his toes pointing down.

"Put it away, Laura Liz!" I whispered hoarsely. "Let's get out of here!"

I think we were both screaming, but I'm not sure if it was out loud or in our heads. We tossed the Bible and the photos and robe to the corner of the attic. I was first and rushed down the ladder and Laura Liz slammed the door shut.

We heard Rita hollering from the bedroom about the ruckus, but we knew it was almost time for her shift so I doubt we woke her up. We carried the ladder back to the shed and I went home soon after. We met before school the next morning to finalize plans for our Founding Fathers skit, but we'd both lost our enthusiasm for it.

I never told Mother and Daddy about what we found. I guess I figured it could get Laura Liz in trouble. Or maybe I was afraid they wouldn't want me to go to her house anymore. I knew I'd never forget that photograph or the shape of the tree or the smell of the attic.

The second terrible thing happened a few months later.

Laura Liz had invited me to spend the night at her house and after I'd already packed my overnight bag, we found out that her cousin Ginny would be there that night too.

Ginny was our same age, but we really didn't like her. She was kind of fat and she talked like a hillbilly and lived in the north Georgia mountains with her mother, Doris, who had divorced Hank's brother Jake when Ginny was a baby. She had long, dark hair, but it was always greasy and her bangs hung in her face. She didn't know anything about music or any of the things that Laura Liz and I tried to talk to her about. She couldn't name any of the Beatles or any of the girls on "Petticoat Junction." She didn't like to dance or play any of our favorite games.

When it was time for bed, we agreed that Laura Liz and I would sleep in her double bed and Ginny would sleep on the sofa in the living room right outside Laura Liz's room. Rita gathered blankets and a pillow for Ginny and made her bed.

Sometime in the middle of the night, I woke up with the distinct feeling of someone's hand tugging at my panties. I opened my eyes and silently tried to get my bearings. As I stared at the ceiling, someone pushed their fingers under the elastic of my panties and was reaching inside right over my barely sprouting pubic hair.

The room was dark with only a little moonlight shining through the gap in the curtains. The hand moved closer and I shot up straight in the bed.

The hand retreated.

I looked over at Laura Liz who was sleeping on her stomach. I could tell that her face was pointing toward the other side of the bed and one hand was hanging off the side. I could hear her breathing deeply.

As my eyes adjusted to the darkness, I saw movement as a figure slowly crept along my side of the bed, around the bottom and out the bedroom door.

I was stunned with silence. I stayed upright in bed waiting for something else to happen, but nothing did. My head was racing. It was so dark I couldn't get any clue as to who it was as the figure crawled right out the door.

After a long time, I lay back down trying to listen for a sign of who had been at my bedside. *Could it have been Butch? Was it Ginny? Hank?* I waited and listened to nothing for what felt like hours just listening to my heart beating. I wanted to wake Laura Liz, but I couldn't imagine what I would say. I couldn't scream or jump up and turn on the light. I was so scared, but I couldn't bring myself to identify and blame.

I left early the next morning, before I saw anyone but Rita and Laura Liz. I never told anyone what happened, not even Laura Liz.

I only spent the night there one other night though, and it was years later. I never saw Ginny again either. She and Doris moved to Kentucky and I think the Roberts lost touch with them completely.

April 1, 2003, 6:15 p.m.

*J*oe brought a sack of barbecue sandwiches and a gallon of tea to the waiting room lobby just a few doors from Annie Jo's room. It made me proud as I watched him hug and comfort my mother and sisters and shake hands with Doc before they both moved forward for a hearty hug. Joe was an Annie Jo fan too. Had been since the day he met her, a month or two after we started dating more than 25 years before.

We'd moved down to the waiting room when our group grew too big and loud and the nursing staff asked us twice to keep quiet so that Annie Jo could rest.

Daisy corralled a stack of Styrofoam cups from the nurse, and we were all enjoying barbecue and lukewarm tea when my children, Joey and Grace, arrived.

Ansley filled them in on the latest news about their cousins, who were freshmen at Auburn University. Chip and Carly were twins, though you'd never guess it. Chip was tall and blond and sleekly chiseled like Ansley. Carly had dark hair, olive complexion and bright brown eyes and a big smile like Ansley's ex-husband Trey. They would be driving back to Atlanta together on Friday to see Annie Jo.

"Can we see Annie Jo?" asked Grace.

Now 21, my daughter was a nice mix of the Flints— Ansley's beautifully chiseled nose and chin, Daisy's big eyes, Mother's dimples and my long lashes — and Joe's side, the Kings — who had taller, leaner physiques than most of my family.

Joey was two years older. He had his dad's wavy hair and thin nose and had surpassed Joe's 6'1" by at least an inch since before high school.

The King family: Josie, Joe, Joey and Grace. To say it, sounded a bit like talking with a mouthful of peanut butter, but we were a solid family and I was proud of my husband and my kids, both of whom were working steady jobs. Grace had two years of college under her belt. Joey was a full-time student at Georgia State and would graduate with a degree in accounting in two more semesters.

Mother hugged them both and signaled for them to follow her down the hall. I smiled as I saw Joey and Grace move to each side of her and hold her arms as they entered the room, and I followed them in.

Annie Jo had not spoken all day, though her vital signs remained strong. We knew she could hear us because she would occasionally move her head toward the conversation, but there was little expression in her face. During her few conscious moments, she'd managed to sip a few teaspoons of beef broth at dinner thanks to the help of a nurse and Mother's patient prodding.

"Hi Annie Jo!" Joey whispered.

"It's Grace and Joey," Mother offered. "They came to check on you. Are you feeling better?"

Joe and Daisy moved in behind me, and soon the whole family was back in the room peeking at Annie Jo with quiet hope.

Her eyes were open but cloudy as she studied our faces with feint awareness. She looked at each of us in the face, but her lips had a sad quiver, accented by raw cracks and dry flaps of skin. They searched the room as my insides teetered between the extremes of hope and dread.

"You're at Piedmont Hospital, Mrs. Flint," said Doc, who had always held Annie Jo in the highest esteem and often called her Mrs. Flint instead of Annie Jo to show his respect. "Do you remember walking outside this morning?"

She answered with a single blink and returned stare, but somehow we all knew that meant, "no." She had not remembered the morning, but was just trying to understand.

"You fell, Annie Jo," I said with surprising control. I glanced at Doc who offered an encouraging nod before I continued. "Mr. Faulkner found you on the stoop. An ambulance brought you here."

I felt Doc place his hand on my shoulder. He held both of mother's hands with the other.

"You're going to be just fine, Annie Jo," Ansley added.

She blinked again and turned her head back as she looked at the ceiling, working to internalize the words.

We each held our breath, and I prayed that no one would mention the stroke. We had not discussed whether we should tell her or not, and I was not certain that we should.

The new shift nurse arrived, and we took the timing as a grateful interruption to delay more conversation. We turned our attention toward the nurse and the cup of ice chips she held in her hand when we heard a skeleton version of Annie Jo's voice and our hearts fell with a collaborative thud.

"Cooper?" she asked.

March 1966

"I couldn't find the scissors, so I brought this to cut the string," said Dena as she slipped into the girls-only fort we'd made in the woods behind our house on Duberry Street.

She pulled an orange paring knife out of a kitchen towel and cut several pieces of string. Laura Liz held the miniature American flag so that Dena could tie it to the dogwood tree in the middle of our fort and let it reign over the list of fort rules that Ansley had penned on a page of Mother's best stationery. Underneath was our cigar box filled with pencils, notepads and Bazooka gum. Six Bulldog cushions — one for each of us and two for potential guests — surrounded the tree.

To make the fort, we tied rope about four feet from the bottom of four pine trees and clothes-pinned beach towels to the rope, then leaned long sticks around the towels as camouflage. We made a roof with an old shower curtain that Dena brought from her house.

Our meetings mostly consisted of listing boys we thought were cute, making plans for future meetings and reviewing rules regarding who was allowed to use the fort and how it should be kept clean and organized. One night Dena's mom packed us dinner to eat out there.

As we chatted about our fort business, Laura Liz fiddled with the knife and purposely slid the blade across the bark of the tree. The bark sliced off easily with the pass of the sharp blade. Underneath the wood was dewy and bright white.

"Let me try that," said Ansley.

Ansley was on the other side of the tree. She pushed the knife down the side of the bark and took a long scalp. The bark easily fell away. We all took turns with the knife until the bottom section of the tree's trunk was bare and the wood underneath was fresh and white and smooth.

"This makes our fort look like a real girls' fort," Dena announced.

We all agreed and complimented ourselves on the special touch, but it wasn't long before we had abandoned the fort and moved on to a rope swing, skateboarding or something else. Just a few weeks had passed before Daddy spotted the dogwood tree, now dead from our scalping of its bark, with the paring knife still secured to its trunk with string.

It was the maddest I'd ever seen him.

He found Ansley first who ratted out the rest of us, and we all had to gather that afternoon for a funeral of sorts around the tree. The tree was no longer white and moist, but gray and dry. It looked about half the size we remembered. Daddy talked to Hank and to Mr. and Mrs. Baker and they all agreed that we would work in each family's yard over the weekend to earn $15 each. With the money we earned, we would buy and plant a new dogwood tree for each of our houses.

We never worked at the Roberts' house because Hank said that he had Butch to handle all the work that he needed and he didn't need any new trees, but I never saw Butch work in the yard in all the years I knew them. For that matter, I never saw anything growing in their yard but a few weeds and lots of pine trees either, but Hank did think it was a good idea for Laura Liz to participate in the punishment at the other homes.

We worked a whole weekend while Dena's brother, Donnie, just watched. Donnie sat behind me in Mrs. Pate's Science class, and he was always poking pencils and flicking wads of paper at my back. And when I'd see him at the bus stop or in the halls at school, he'd hum the words "Naked as a Jaybird" to the tune of "Na, na, na, na boo, boo." He didn't even say the words, but I knew what he was singing. He'd just hum the tune as he bobbed his head stupidly staring at me. Daddy suggested that teasing was how a boy flirted with a girl, but I did my best to ignore him at school, even though I had to see him on the bus everyday and when we played Bloody Tiger.

We hauled sticks and raked leaves to make a big bonfire in the Bakers' yard. Then we worked in our yard cutting grass and mulching Momma's flowerbeds. Then Daddy helped us dig a hole to plant a dogwood right next to the garage. In the afternoon we planted a dogwood between the Bakers' driveway and walkway.

For the first part of the day Donnie stood around calling us "tree killers" and dumb head girls until that grew old and he started in on some slightly more obvious flirting. It was clear that Ansley thought he was cute because she started calling me "Jaybird" and turning cartwheels around the tree.

"Her name is Josephine," said Daisy.

I felt Daisy's shoulder leaning against the back of my hip.

"Right, Sissy?" she added with clear-to-me snubs to Ansley and Donnie.

"I know Josie the Jaybird," Donnie answered, "and I know you too, Miss Daisy May Clampett."

Daisy cut her big eyes at me, and I could see the lump in her throat. She moved sideways to cower behind me.

Ansley broke into another cartwheel and once upright quickly glanced to see if Donnie had seen it. It wasn't clear whether he had seen it or not, so she launched into the chorus of a Tommy Roe song as she turned another cartwheel, singing the chorus as she completed the landing. Her blonde ponytail snapped to her neck at the final beat of her song.

But Donnie was focused on Laura Liz and missed Ansley's bonus cartwheel completely.

"L-squared, I wouldn't have taken you for a dogwood murderer," said Donnie. "Didn't your momma teach you any better than that?"

"Well, we didn't know it would kill..." Laura Liz stumbled. I knew she was hoping he couldn't see that she was staring at him as she dropped her chin and looked at him curiously from the tops of her eyes.

His stick-straight platinum blonde hair was cut a lot like Paul McCartney's, and it swished against his head like the long mop-like brushes at the car wash when he talked. "I'm just thinking you should be spending your time cutting up with me instead of cutting up a tree."

"Oh, Lord," Dena and I groaned simultaneously.

"You're pathetic," Dena added.

"You must think we're idiots, Donnie Baker," I said. "Good grief! Do you think anyone would fall for that lame line?"

"It's really Laura Elizabeth," Laura Liz said with a syrupy drawl I'd never heard her use. "Everyone just calls me Laura Liz."

Even Ansley's jaw dropped. None of us could believe that this absurd version of amateur flirting was happening — and actually working — right in front of our eyes. And between my best friend and Donnie Baker of all people.

"Would have never guessed that one, L-squared," Donnie answered.

We all knew Donnie knew Laura Liz's name. She'd played Bloody Tiger with us many times. Their act was miserable.

"By the way, have you ever seen the dirt hill in this neighborhood?" he asked.

The dirt hill was huge and covered with fallen pine trees. The trees had dried out over the years and were patterned almost like an obstacle course, so we'd been crawling around and hiding among them, building forts and playing games there since we'd moved to Duberry Street. Laura Liz had been there with me hundreds of times, and Donnie knew it.

"I don't think so," she said. Her seafoam-green eyes batted twice.

My jaw dropped and my eyes shut, I suspect in perfect cadence with Dena's, because our heads turned toward each other at the exact same moment and her face was as shocked as mine. Neither of us could muster anything to add to the shocking conversation.

Donnie spent the rest of the afternoon helping Laura Liz with her part of the yard cleanup and then stood right next to her when Mrs. Baker took our photograph with the new dogwood tree.

Afterward, Laura Liz asked if I'd mind if she walked over to the dirt hill with Donnie and took a rain check on our plans to bake sugar cookies.

"Sure, L-squared. Do what you want."

"You're not mad are you, Josie?"

"Just make sure this new boyfriend of yours doesn't call me 'Jaybird' again."

She and Donnie walked off, and I was in the bathroom when she came back into the house. I purposely stayed there when I heard her say her mother was there to pick her up.

"Josie, I'm leaving..." she sounded concerned.

"Okay, Laura Liz. I'll see you around. Bye," I called through the bathroom door.

I came out of the bathroom and watched Laura Liz and Rita get into their truck from Daisy's window. But Laura Liz turned around and looked across the upstairs windows and I quickly jumped back, pretty sure she didn't see me.

The next week, we had a science test at school. Mrs. Pate handed out answer sheets that had to be bubbled in with a No. 2 pencil. Only a few teachers used the automated scoring forms for chapter tests, but Mrs. Pate liked them because her tests were long, multiple choice tests and she could get the grades back to us quickly.

I took a sheet and passed the rest back to Donnie. He rolled his upper lip under to expose his teeth and made a stupid smile at me while wiggling one of his eyebrows. I snapped back to face the front.

"Students, have two No. 2 pencils on your desk ready for the test. If you need to use the pencil sharpener, do so quickly."

I reached inside my desk and pulled out my Jetsons pencil bag, quickly selected two sharpened pencils and placed them at the ridge at the top of my desk.

"Write your name, last name first, first name and date across the top, one letter per box as you have done many times," said Mrs. Pate.

I carefully filled in the boxes for my name with capital block letters.

"And then bubble in the corresponding letters underneath, being careful to fill in completely and not let your pencil marks go outside."

As I prepared to start filling in the bubbles, I noticed an ink mark on the corner of my sheet and turned over my right hand to find ballpoint pen ink all over my palm and baby finger. It was still wet and oozing.

"Mrs. Pate?" I said and raised my other hand.

"Josie? You've filled in these sheets many times."

"I know Mrs. Pate, but the ink pen in my pencil bag exploded." I showed her my hand.

I heard a couple of kids chuckle. Mrs. Pate said, "Okay, give your sheet to Donnie to bubble in the top part for you as we continue. Go quickly to the lavatory and wash up. We'll wait until you're back to start the test."

I couldn't get rid of the ink completely, but I found enough of the pink powdered soap between three of the soap dispensers to scrub it until it was nothing more than a blue stain and quickly dried my hands. Donnie handed me my sheet, and I sat down as Mrs. Pate handed out the science test questions and took the test.

The next day we started a new science chapter, and Mrs. Pate told us that she would be passing out our grades at the end of the period. Just a few minutes before the bell was to ring, she called out each student and handed back their test and grade, but when she got the last two in her hand she said, "Donnie Baker and Josie Flint, I would like to see you two in the hallway."

I panicked. I knew I hadn't cheated. Maybe she thought Donnie had cheated off my paper and he was in trouble. *Maybe he did cheat off my test. Maybe...* I could hear my own heart beating as I walked in front of the class toward the door.

"I think you know what this is about, don't you, Donnie Baker?"

Mrs. Pate said as she closed the classroom door.

I saw a smirk move across his face as he dropped his head, "Yes, ma'am."

"I have already spoken to Principal Britt," she said. "And he is expecting you in his office. Go directly there, and I will meet you there after the bell rings where we will discuss your apology to Miss Flint, among other things."

His smirk had disappeared. He looked at me sheepishly and turned toward the principal's office.

"Directly, Mr. Baker," Mrs. Pate said sternly.

She turned to me and handed me the computerized calculation sheet. My grade was written in red ink with a circle around it at the top of the page. I had made a 91.

"Nice work, Josie," she said. "It seems, though, that Mr. Baker thought he would be funny when he bubbled in your name for you."

She pointed to the corner of the printed page.

In tiny block-typed letters across the side of the printout where I would expect to see "Flint, Josie," it said instead, "Jaybird, Naked As."

April 1, 2003, 11:35 p.m.

$\mathcal{M}$other, Doc, Ansley, Daisy and I were at her bedside when the machines just stopped pulsing and the green line across the screen took its last leap. The doctors said the stroke was massive and damaged her heart and likely other organs.

The collective drain of hope among the circle of my family was almost visible as we hovered over our family's matriarch with our minds and hearts pulsing to the fatiguing beep of her heartbeat amplified by the cloying pitch of the cold machine.

Mother must have sensed death first, because she bent to kiss Annie Jo's sweet head and walked silently into the hallway. I peeked at my sisters and Doc and one by one we were all looking at one another when Doc gave an almost indiscernible nod of confirmation.

Annie Jo died. Just a few minutes before midnight on April Fools Day. Thirty-five years to the day after Daddy died. And 35 years from the day that my life story split in half.

A cold chill moved through my arms and chest.

My beloved grandmother, my Annie Jo, never spoke another word after calling for Cooper. *My father. Her son.*

She just left the earth quickly and without sound. Annie Jo left our lives with none of the color and vibrancy that she'd put in to them, but rather just faded away.

I remember it as though she was walking through a fog in her yellow sun hat. She walked past us and became fainter in the fog with each step. And then in a moment, she was gone.

I had never pictured this day. Annie Jo had never given us reason to. Other than a bad bout with shingles once, she rarely even had a cold. I don't think I had ever even imagined a time when she wouldn't be the center of my history and the constant that was my being.

We lingered at the hospital until nearly 2 a.m. We moved to the third floor lobby where a nurse came and went at a desk and a man we didn't know slept in a chair under a nappy green blanket.

"Remember how proud she was when she won the blue ribbon for her tomatoes at the fair?" asked Daisy.

"I loved her blackberry pie," said Doc.

"Remember her clown costume?" I asked.

The click of the imaginary View-Master continued as a collective murmur of our voices, our smiles, our nods affirmed each story. For hours as we sat, then paced the floor, then held one another, and cried, all the while finding a surprising but healthy dose of laughter between the tears.

The next morning we met at Mother and Doc's to talk about the arrangements.

We held the funeral on April 4, the same date that we'd buried my Daddy. It was a fitting service that filled the church. The preacher knew enough stories to share about Annie Jo himself that though we kept the service to his sermon and tribute, it still lasted more than two hours. The organist helped us select Annie Jo's favorite music, and we sang *Love Divine, All Loves Excelling* and six more at the top of our lungs, just like Annie Jo would do every Sunday.

Mother selected the dress that Annie Jo had worn to Daisy's wedding for the burial. It was robin's egg blue with a lace bodice. She chose the tiny diamond necklace that Joe had given Annie Jo for her birthday just before we married to sit where the lace bodice opened at her throat.

We buried her right next to Papa Ray, her husband of 26 years until he died in 1959.

Afterward, we came back to the fellowship hall where her long-time friend Anabelle Levy had prepared a gigantic bowl of chicken salad, fresh-cut fruit, homemade biscuits and ten gallons of sweet tea.

Friends from Atlanta and around Athens and as far away as Kentucky were there. Several people brought photos of Annie Jo we'd never seen. Everyone who came had nice things to say about Annie Jo Flint.

We arranged almost 70 chairs in a circle to share chicken salad, sweet tea and another round of stories about the woman we would never forget.

September 1966

*I*n eighth grade, Seaton Ferry Junior High desegregated.

Laura Liz and I walked to school together that day, and the difference in the first day of school from the years before was clear before we ever walked through the front door.

"Are you scared, Josie?" she whispered as we walked past the school's marquee sign with "Welcome All Students" messaged across three lines in block letters. I noticed the "e" in students was really a backward "3."

"A little," I lied.

Negro students — 25 in all — entered the school with their heads low and eyes looking at the floor. It was understandable that they would be afraid since they were starting at a brand new school, but Seaton Ferry felt unfamiliar to me too. Instead of excitement and chatter on the first day, there were groups of kids whispering and looking around through the crowds of students, parents and teachers. Our principal, Mr. Britt, stood by the flagpole and helped students off every bus that pulled to the front of the school. Lots of parents were there on the first day, too, just standing around in packs.

Six Negro girls and four Negro boys joined my grade. One in my homeroom was Bailey Jackson, who I'd met a couple of times before. In the bathroom some girls wouldn't go into the stall after one of the Negro girls had been there. It was obvious to everyone what they were doing, and I know that the new girls noticed too, but mostly the students just whispered.

The Negro students stuck together too. They always sat together in the lunchroom and moved to the corner of the dressing room when it was time to dress out for P.E.

Some of the parents were organizing meetings away from school. Hank even asked Daddy if they could hold one of the meetings at our house, but I heard Daddy suggest that maybe the Elk's lodge or the community room at the library might be a better idea. Daddy didn't attend the meetings, but I know Belinda Roach's dad did. Probably Hank Roberts too.

Right after school started that year, a terrible race riot broke out not far from our house, close to the Atlanta Zoo. A policeman shot a Negro man because he thought he was stealing a car and a riot started that lasted four days. The news showed crowds of people throwing bottles and rocks at Atlanta's Mayor Ivan Allen as he tried to calm the crowd in Summerhill.

Annie Jo came to stay with us for a while because she didn't want to be alone, and Daddy drove us to and from school for most of September because he didn't want us riding the bus. A lot of kids didn't come to school at all while the riot was going on. Two of the Negro kids never came back after it was over.

Mrs. Sanders switched from teaching sixth grade to eighth that year, so I had her for social studies. She showed us newspaper photos of two young people who had been hospitalized after the riot in Summerhill. She also talked about the Ku Klux Klan and a man named Stokely Carmichael, but somehow I felt it was really a subject that she wasn't supposed to teach us. I often overheard other teachers talking and whispering about Mrs. Sanders and her "ideas."

At night, Mrs. Sanders volunteered with the Bo Callaway campaign. Callaway was running for governor against Lester Maddox and Mrs. Sanders placed signs around her room to support him. One day she pitched a fit in the principal's office because someone added the words "to Hell" with black Magic Marker on the "Go Bo" bumper sticker on her car. I happened to be in the front office that day delivering a note about Ansley having pink eye to the school secretary and I overheard the whole commotion.

Lester Maddox, a "bigoted racist," according to Mrs. Sanders, won the election. The adults around me talked in whispers about him and Martin Luther King and Negros and the Ku Klux Klan. There was always something on the news about fighting and preaching, fairness and civil rights, but my family just carried on as if it didn't concern us. Mother and Daddy would watch the news, but I never heard them discuss it.

Mrs. Sanders, however, wanted the eighth-grade students to discuss current events every day and we barely used our book the whole year. She reminded us every day that no one should ever use the word "nigger" in her classroom. The truth was we heard it all the time, either whispered, or in an ugly, hateful way like the way Hank would say it. Mrs. Sanders suggested we say "Negro" or "black people" and "white people" and to remember that God created all people equally and no one was better than another. I think the discussions had to be most awkward for Bailey and the other Negro kids, and I was glad none of them were in my social studies class.

In science class, Mrs. Huffstachler assigned Bailey to be lab partners with LaDarla Dalrymple. They had known each other for years because Bailey's mother, Rubelle, was the Dalrymples' maid. LaDarla was sweet to introduce Bailey to her friends and try to make him feel comfortable. Mrs. Huffstachler assigned me to partner with a Negro girl named Verna.

One day, Verna and I both came to school wearing the same dress. It was a red gingham top with a blue bodice and skirt dress that I picked out when shopping with Mother at the Lemon Frog shop at Sears. I was embarrassed when I saw her walk in to school that day, but when she looked at me, I realized that she was even more embarrassed than me. When we passed in the hall, both of us dropped our eyes to the ground, but I regretted it immediately and turned around and pushed my arm through hers and locked arms with her as we strolled down the hallway.

"Didn't y'all hear it's 'lab partner dress alike day?'" I said loud enough to get attention from the other kids in the class.

Verna looked embarrassed, but I saw a little smile move across her face.

I stood taller and she followed by doing the same as we strolled arm in arm.

"I've got art," she said as we reached Miss Grove's art room.

"Well, I'll see you in science, lab partner!"

We became pretty good friends. She invited me to her birthday party at the skating rink and we ate lunch together a few times the weather was nice and the eighth graders were allowed to take their lunches outside.

She introduced me to her brother Jimmy who was a really good artist. He could draw a great portrait in just a few minutes and would use the side of his pencil to create shadows and his eraser to make highlights in the eyes. They really looked professional and the kids started asking him to draw them and then hung the pictures on their lockers. Jimmy became popular for his portraits, and the drama teacher asked him to head up the set design for the play that year.

But I only wore that dress a few more times that year, and I noticed Verna rarely wore hers either.

About a month after the Summerhill riot quieted down, twin boys Mason and Dixon Faulkner moved from Shreveport and registered at school. They were identical twins and really cute, but looked a lot like trouble. They were tall and had Cajun accents, with dirty blond hair down to their shoulders. I had Dixon in English and math, Mason in social studies and both of them in P.E. and science.

Over the intercom that morning, Principal Britt introduced the Faulkner twins and asked all students to welcome the new eighth graders, Mason and Dixon, to Seaton Ferry Junior High. He mentioned that the Faulkners had been transferred to Atlanta, where Mr. Faulkner would be working with General Motors.

Later in social studies, Mrs. Sanders asked Mason to tell us about his previous school and about his twin brother. He stood up and said that his brother, Dixon, preferred to be called Dick and that his father worked on a shrimp boat when they lived in Shreveport. I knew he was lying and I think Mrs. Sanders did too, but she just welcomed Mason and asked him to take the seat near the window.

Turns out, they moved into a duplex across the street from Annie Jo. She called right after school that day to tell me she had met a new family and that they had twin boys in my grade.

"I saw them today, Annie Jo," I said quickly. "They are in some of my classes."

"Maybe I can have them over after school one day this week for some pie and you can invite Laura Liz and some other friends from your grade."

"Maybe, Annie Jo."

I quickly changed the subject to find out if the dog next door had had her puppies yet and pushed the Faulkner twins out of my mind.

April 4, 2003

J poured a glass of wine and headed to the back deck. Ignoring the yellow pine pollen that covered the lounge chair cushions, I stretched out on it, kicked off my shoes, pulled up my swollen feet and looked at the dark sky.

My dress was ready for the dry cleaner anyway, and I was exhausted.

There were few tears at the funeral. My mother and sisters and our families maintained ourselves as we greeted long-time friends and family and nodded when we were reminded over and over again about what a lovely, full life Annie Jo had led.

It's what she would have wanted. No tears. No sadness. Just friends, loving friends and chitchatting about the weather and how much the children had grown.

I heard the back door open and watched Grace's slim shape drag a lounge chair across the deck and position it next to mine.

"You doin' okay, Mom?"

"Better now that you're here," I said. "I miss having you around. But, yes, I'm just fine."

A bright light, maybe a plane, moved toward the top of the sky, and I pictured Annie Jo riding atop it as Grace settled into the chair.

"I was really proud of you this week, Grace. Annie Jo would have been, too."

"We were lucky to have her," Grace said. "We're all going to miss her. I know you especially."

"Yep," I managed. "It's going to be different, for sure."

She reached for my hand and we watched the stars twinkle and listened to the evening sounds of birds and early season cicadas.

"I guess it's too early for lightning bugs?" Grace asked.

I smiled.

When I was a kid, Daddy would tell me that you should always wink at the first lightning bug of the night, because it was really a fairy signaling the lightning bugs that it was time to come out.

I'm sure he'd heard that story from his mother because Annie Jo had passed it on to my kids and to my niece and nephews, too.

"Probably not until next month, as I recall," I said, knowing exactly what she was thinking about. "Annie Jo had some good stories."

"My friends love Annie Jo's crazy bridge idea," said Grace.

"Hold your nose!" we both said together.

"Hold your nose when you drive under a bridge!" Grace exclaimed. That way, if the bridge collapses and falls on you, your nose won't get broken."

We both laughed, and I sighed as I watched a star twinkle three times from black to bright.

Annie Jo was everything to me. And my whole life I wanted to be a part of whatever she was doing, every conversation she had, and play along with every crazy idea. She was the first person I wanted to talk to when I got my acceptance to Georgia State. She was the first call I made when Joe proposed. She was the one I most wanted to meet my baby when Joey was born.

Accepting life without her was difficult. The lump in my throat was already there every time I thought about her.

October 1966

Seaton Ferry Junior High hosted a Halloween carnival, but Daddy had an extra ticket to see Georgia play the Tar Heels in Athens on the same day. It was a tough decision, but I decided on the carnival and Daddy took Daisy to her first Bulldog game.

I came with Dena Baker, Laura Liz and Candy Saylor, and we all wore matching outfits — red shirts and white shorts. We'd planned to all wear white Keds, but Candy showed up in her new Go Go boots. I decided right then that our friendship would not likely go very far.

Mason and Dixon Faulkner had already made a lot of friends and showed up at the carnival with a crowd of boys that I didn't know very well. Verna was there with a Negro girl I didn't know and Bailey Jackson.

The Boy Scout troop smoked barbecue and sold plates with chips and coleslaw as a fund-raiser and the school brought in snow cone and cotton candy machines and tubs of bottled Cokes on ice.

There was a fortune teller (the principal's wife, Mrs. Britt), games with prizes of candy, stuffed animals or goldfish in plastic bags, a haunted house set up in the classroom hallway and a stage where the school chorus sang and Ansley's dance group performed.

We waited in line for the fortune teller for a while, but it wasn't long before word got out that every single fortune was either "mind your parents," "study extra hard this week," "go to church on Sunday" or a combination, so we left the line and headed for the Go Fish booth that Mrs. Sanders had organized.

It took two tickets to play. The fishing poles were baited with a magnet. I dangled it over the pool filled with water and plastic fish.

For prizes, all the parents were asked to donate a white elephant gift—it could be something new, but was more likely something used, but is still in usable condition. It didn't have to be anything valuable, but it should be something that someone could enjoy. Mother had rolled up an old set of six placemats and tied them with a ribbon for her donation. One of them (the one from Daisy's place) had a bad stain, but Mother put that one on the bottom. She said that many families would just need four or five of them anyway.

Other people donated things like picture frames, jars of home-made jelly, coasters, maybe a pot of flowers. Then each gift was as-signed a number. Plastic fish with magnets on their backs were float-ing in the "fish pond"—a plastic blow-up pool that belonged to Mrs. Sanders' three kids—and each were assigned the same set of numbers.

I caught number 82 in a matter of seconds, probably much more related to the fact that these were strong magnets than to my 13 years of fishing experience.

Mrs. Sanders wore a pink and white flowered scarf with her navy SFJH t-shirt. She unhooked my fish and walked to a table at the back of the booth piled with miscellaneous boxes, bags, flowerpots and gifts. She picked up a beautiful large white box with a huge gold ribbon tied vertically and horizontally around the box. On top was a great big gold bow with smaller glittery ribbon intertwined in it and a tag with a large "82" on top. She placed it in my open arms.

"Looks like you're the lucky one, Josie," said Mrs. Sanders. "We've all been eager to see what's inside this box. Mrs. Dalrymple donated this gift, so it's likely a great one! Be sure and let me see what you've won once you've got it open."

CeCe Dalrymple was the richest—and the prettiest—woman in town. She was married to Winston Dalrymple II, a periodontist whose office was on Maple Drive. They lived off Clifton Road and they were loaded. They were the family with the maid, Rubelle. Their daughter LaDarla Dalrymple was in my grade. They also had two sons: Winston Dalrymple, III, was already in college, a freshman at Duke in North

Carolina; and Kenneth was in Ansley's grade.

I opened the box to find a fluffy white, brand new bathrobe. It had a gold crest from The Plaza, a hotel in New York City. Mrs. Sanders walked over to join the crowd that gathered around me as I opened the box. Candy Saylor whistled through her fingers when I pulled out the robe and held it high. Dena and Candy helped me put it on over my shorts and Keds. It hung all the way to the ground. I felt like a princess as I tied the belt that hung from terrycloth loops on either side. A receipt for the bathrobe—$55.00— from the previous October with Dr. Dalrymple's name on it was tucked under the tissue paper. It was Mrs. Sanders who knew that The Plaza was a fancy hotel.

It was like she'd never even opened it. I couldn't image why, but lucky for me, she sent it to school for the Halloween carnival Go Fish booth. I couldn't have been more thrilled. I wore it for the rest of the day until I noticed it getting some grass stains around the bottom. Luckily, Annie Jo had a solution that took them out in the wash.

That bathrobe was my pride and joy and the envy of Ansley and most of my friends. I hung the '82' tag from the box on my side of the bulletin board. Daddy fashioned a hook from an old water nozzle and attached it to the back of our bedroom door so I could hang the bathrobe from a loop inside the collar. I was ceremonious as I put it on every evening before bed and every weekend morning before breakfast, especially when I knew Ansley was looking.

The next few months, though, were all about Donnie and Laura Liz. His apology for the "Jaybird, Naked as" incident sounded sincere in front of Principal Britt and Mrs. Pate, but starting the very next day on the bus, he hummed the "Nana nana boo boo" tune every time he saw me and I knew he was putting "Naked as a Jaybird" into the tune in his mind.

But as bored as I was with Donnie Baker, I couldn't help but admit that he and Laura Liz were good for each other. She gained a lot of confidence and he grew a lot less dorky during their time together.

He asked her to the Junior High winter dance and we went shopping together for dresses. Rita came through with $50 from her pay-check for a dress and shoes, and I had never seen Laura Liz so excited. Annie Jo picked us up and took us downtown for lunch at Rich's and shopping in the afternoon. Annie Jo paid for my dress and for our lunches.

We found dresses on sale, some great shoes with a medium heel that we bought in different colors, and had enough money left to buy earrings for me and a necklace for Laura Liz. My dress was powder blue with straps that crossed at the back. Laura Liz's was a pale yellow with a tiny Swiss dot pattern on the top and capped sleeves. She bought the shoes in white and I bought mine in navy.

We twirled in front of the three-sided mirror in the dressing room as Annie Jo clapped with approval. Then we each stood side-by-side looking at our fancy images in the mirror and talked about how we would look to our dates.

After we shopped, we went to the Magnolia Room restaurant for chicken salad, frozen fruit salad and iced tea. I'd been there before, but it was Laura Liz's first time. She was positive she wouldn't like the chicken salad, but as we left she proclaimed it her "favorite food above pizza and pancakes and strawberry shortcake!"

I went to the dance with Tommy Wilson and we doubled with Donnie and Laura Liz. Daddy drove us and Mr. Baker picked us up after the dance. Tommy and Donnie had biology and shop classes together so they got along great. Tommy and I started going steady after that so the four of us hung out the rest of the year.

Tommy's older brother Glenn even drove us all to Athens for a Georgia game the Saturday after homecoming. Glenn taught us the Junior Bird Man song and we sang that, the University of Georgia fight song, camp songs and the theme songs from Gilligan's Island and the Beverly Hillbillies all the way to Athens. Tommy's brother sang along too.

April 12, 2003

"Ansley wants us all to come to her place for Easter dinner," Mother said as we spoke on the phone.

"At her condo? Really? That sounds crowded."

Most of our family get-togethers were held at my house. Joe and I had bought the two-story Tudor home near Emory University with entertaining in mind. It had a finished basement that the kids had enjoyed with their friends during their high school years and where the cousins hung out for family parties. We had all traveled to Charlotte to spend Memorial or Labor Day weekends with Daisy and her family many times. Often we would meet at Mother and Doc's Buckhead home, or at the country club where they were members, but we rarely gathered at Ansley's, even when she and Trey were still married and they lived in a big, beautiful home in Brookwood Hills.

"She's hoping we can make the meal very casual and take our plates outside onto the common area lawn. She says we can have an egg toss and play croquet. Everyone can bring lawn chairs and we'll just enjoy the outdoors if it's a pretty day."

"Well if we are going to tackle Annie Jo's place on Saturday, the casual meal part sounds good," I admitted opening my refrigerator for a quick inventory.

"Let's just put the men in charge of that," she offered. "I'll ask Doc to pick up a ham. Joe can rally the kids to put together some salads and deviled eggs while we're working at Annie Jo's. They'll have fun being all together. The twins will be home on break and they can help too."

"Allen and Charlie will be here in time to help too. They arrive from Charlotte on Friday and they'll join Daisy at our house," I added, pulling a bottle of orange juice from the refrigerator. "We'll make a bed for Charlie on the sofa and put Daisy and Allen in the guest room. Joe will love having Allen around and he'll be a big help on Saturday."

Daisy was single until she was 34. She met Allen Tucker through mutual friends when they were all gathered watching a house fire near where Daisy was living at the time. They married six months later and had their only child, Charlie, when Daisy was 37. It turns out that Allen and Joe had both played rugby years before and had a lot of mutual friends from the league, so he was a natural addition to our family and he fit in right away. I often wished we lived closer because Joe and Allen got along so well. Joe rarely had time to spend with friends and I thought it would be good for him.

"LaDarla's coming too, right, Mother?" I was counting the crowd in my head.

"Yes. LaDarla's bringing a pound cake. Almond, I think," she added. "There will be three from her family, plus Kenneth and his new girlfriend. That's five."

"So the 13 of us, plus five more. Eighteen," I said confidently.

Our extended family get-togethers included LaDarla, her husband and son. Since we'd been best friends in high school, it was another natural addition. Lately, her brother Kenneth had been included as well. My mind skipped to Laura Liz, who had been an extended part of our family for such a long time when we were young, when mother's voice — and math — threw me back to attention.

"Seventeen, Josie. I think you're counting Annie Jo."

Ughhh. Twelve of us Flints now. I'd grown accustomed to the heavy lumps that would fill my throat without warning and the thick tears that would burn the backs of my eyes.

"I miss her so much, Momma."

"We all do, sweetheart," Mother said. "I've picked up the phone every single day to give her a call. It's so hard to believe she's really gone."

I poured a glass of juice as I looked out the window of my kitchen and noted the crepe myrtle tree just beginning to bud for spring. Annie Jo would decorate the tree outside her duplex every year for Easter. She taught us to blow the yolks and whites out of raw eggs by punching a needle hole in both sides. Then she'd dye them in pastel colors then hang the empty shells from ribbons on the tree's branches.

This Easter would be different. This *everything* would be different.

"What time should we get started on Saturday?"

"Let's start at 9. We'll just sort one room at a time," Mother said. "Annie Jo's will was very simple: All assets and personal belongings should be divided among the family. No suggestions beyond that, so we have our work cut out for us."

I hung up the phone and thought about the deviled eggs. Joe was very handy in the kitchen. He would be thrilled to be assigned such an important role, and he and Allen and the kids could have a lot of fun putting some food together for a casual Easter get-together.

But it was Annie Jo who always made the deviled eggs before. She never lost her love for crafting and making things special and fun. One year she turned the eggs into little chicks with tiny peppercorns for eyes and a wedge of carrot for a beak. Another time she just made a big bowl of egg salad and served it in a basket she'd made by weaving long rolls of bread dough and baking it around a bowl.

And marzipan, of course. It was just last Easter that she'd made each of us a basket and eggs out of marzipan.

There wouldn't be any marzipan this year.

I tossed the untouched juice into the sink.

March 1967

That spring Seaton Ferry Junior High had an open house night where parents could see the student's art projects and visit classrooms. Rita had the night shift and Hank was drinking again, so Mother walked around with Laura Liz to her classes, while I took Daddy to mine.

I couldn't wait to introduce Daddy to Miss Paulk and for him to see the essays we had written and that she had hung on the wall. Miss Paulk had told me several times that she thought I had a real talent for writing. The notes she wrote on my papers were always sweet and encouraging and it was clear she really liked me. One day when she thought she'd left the lights on in her car, she gave me the keys to her Mustang and asked me to go out to the parking lot and check. All the kids knew she drove a yellow Mustang with a Tri Delt decal and an Ole Miss sticker on the back. She didn't realize that I didn't even know where lights were on a car, but I stood in front of them and could tell they weren't on anyway, so I strolled ceremoniously along the outside windows of the classrooms swinging her keys and then down the long hall back into class to announce that all was fine.

I worked hard in her class and was really excited when she told us about an advertising campaign assignment that we would be starting the next month. She said that we'd be writing radio and television spots and designing bumper stickers and writing newspaper releases and such. I told Daddy and Mother and Laura Liz all about it on the way to the school for the open house.

Mrs. Sanders was standing at the school entrance when we arrived.

"Good evening Flint family, so nice to see you," she said. Daddy shook her hand and offered a dimpled smile.

"And you too, of course, Laura Liz," she added as we entered the school's atrium.

We visited my homeroom where I showed Daddy my desk and he met my homeroom teacher, Mrs. Mathison. He looked at all the campaign posters that were on the wall that year and asked why I wasn't running for student council, but I said I was helping Tommy with his campaign for treasurer and was concentrating on that.

Coach Layson talked to all the parents about the year's P.E. curriculum and noted that we would continue with Bombardment on rainy days. I moaned out loud and Daddy put his hand on my shoulder. He knew I hated that game.

I rushed him through Mrs. Peters' music room, and I got a break on science because Mrs. Huffstachler had a death in the family and wasn't there that night.

Exactly as I'd hoped, Miss Paulk was wearing her white shirtwaist dress with the cherries pattern and red patent leather pumps. She had a matching purse that went with that dress, but it was probably in her desk drawer. She usually wore a red headband with that outfit, but today she wore her hair pulled into a low ponytail with a red ribbon around it.

She was busy talking with CeCe Dalrymple when we walked in so I took Daddy to the wall of essays. Mine was on the top row with "Excellent ideas! Very well crafted," written in red next to my name.

Daddy smiled and looked at some of the other essays until I got the chance to introduce him to Miss Paulk.

To me, Miss Paulk was perfect.

She was about 30 and exactly the kind of person I wanted to be when I got older. On most days she teased her hair so it would be poofy on the top and then flipped up a bit on the ends. Once in a while she would wear a long fall in her hair and another day her hair might be about 10 inches shorter than it had been the day before. She had a headband or ribbon to match every outfit and she probably had 15 different pairs of shoes.

She had been engaged to marry a man named Tripp Stand, whom she told us about when we had studied oxymorons, but they broke it off soon after she had started teaching at Seaton Ferry. She lived in an apartment near Oglethorpe University with her roommate, Cheryl, whom we had all met at a school car wash at the beginning of the year.

"Well, you must be Mr. Flint," she said as she walked toward the circle of parents and students and extended her hand.

Yep. I wanted to be just like her.

"Please call me Cooper," said my Daddy offering his best Clark Gable grin. Then for good measure, he actually kissed her hand.

Miss Paulk giggled, then quickly recovered.

"Why, you're so kind. I want you to know that Josie is one of my best students this year," said Miss Paulk. "She's a natural writer and I've been very impressed with her work."

I beamed inside and out. Daddy offered to be of help in case she needed anything constructed or repaired in her classroom. I told Miss Paulk about the reading benches with steering wheels and she laughed. That gave her an idea and she told Daddy about the upcoming advertising campaign assignment and how she'd love to have a theater backdrop with a cutout like a puppet show where the students could present their television commercials.

"Jaybird's told me all about that project. I'd be glad to help you with that, Miss Paulk."

I beamed again. Except for calling me *Jaybird* in front of Miss Paulk, I was so proud of my Daddy that night, and of the essay that was hanging on the wall for all to see, and of my favorite teacher in her red patent leather pumps.

"It was a pleasure to meet you, Mr. Flint."

"Please, call me Cooper."

He smiled at Miss Paulk as Dr. Dalrymple walked over and extended his hand to introduce himself to her. He put his arm around LaDarla and she stepped into our circle.

"Good to see you too, Cooper Flint," he said turning to Daddy. "How are your Bulldogs looking for next season?"

They quieted their conversation when Miss Paulk turned to address all the students and parents. She pointed out the wall of essays and introduced the upcoming advertising project.

Daddy took my picture with our Polaroid camera in front of the display of essays before we moved on to the next classroom. Then before we left for the night, he took a photo of Laura Liz and me standing along side the life-sized paper maché Seaton Ferry Rifleman mascot that art students had made for the school lobby.

The following weekend was Easter. Daddy's cousin Dexter invited us to Lake Sinclair, to stay with him and his family in their trailer on the lake.

His wife Shalene had inherited a pop-up camper from a relative, so they offered to park it outside their larger trailer to give plenty of room for our family, but Daddy thought it would be fun if we took a tent and pitched it somewhere nearby. Mother, Ansley and Annie Jo opted to sleep in the pop-up and Daisy stayed in the trailer with Dexter, Shalene and their kids, Vivian and Luke. I joined Daddy on a hike to find a spot for our tent.

We built a fire and popped Jiffypop, eating it while we talked about the television commercial I had been thinking about for my English project.

The assignment called for us each to pick a product or concept to sell, and I'd decided on season passes to Six Flags over Georgia, a new theme park that had just opened that year. Miss Paulk explained that we could choose students from the class to actually help deliver the message for our commercials, but if our idea was more conceptual and involved different kinds of visuals than what would be available in the classroom, we could present our ideas in the form of a storyboard. She described a series of drawings depicting what a viewer might see during each second of the 30-second spot.

Tommy Wilson's older brother Glenn agreed to drive us to Six

Flags so we could ride the rides all day and then get some photos of the rides for my project. I had also spoken to someone in Six Flags' management office on the telephone about getting some copies of their brochures so that I could cut them up and use them on my storyboards.

Daddy suggested that I take the tape recorder too and record the sounds of people screaming on the roller coaster to use in the commercial.

We also talked about the theater design. Daddy got the idea of hanging window shades sideways behind the theater opening. That way anyone using the storyboard idea could tape their pages in order onto the blinds and then roll right through each segment of the commercial. I told him that the idea sounded perfect and I started to imagine how I would create the storyboard for my Six Flags project.

He suggested that we start the project next weekend, but I'd made plans with Tommy for Six Flags. Daddy spent the whole Sunday working on that storyboard screen.

Daddy rigged an old paint roller to the window blind so the presenter could stand behind the theater and crank the blind smoothly through. He wired the whole thing for electricity too, then added a spotlight at the top and mounted a tape recorder to the inside. He painted the whole front to look like a console television. Instead of Zenith or GE, he put "Paulk Electrics" as if it were the brand name.

He made the theater with three hinged panels so that it would stand up and the student could be inside without being seen from the sides of the "television."

Daisy helped by donating a spring toy they reconfigured into an antenna for the top.

Meanwhile, Tommy and I spent the whole day kissing at Six Flags. We'd kissed several times before that day beginning with the homecoming dance, but they were always lip pecks. They'd grown from quick to a little more lingering over the past weeks, but neither of us had ever gotten the nerve to poke out our tongues.

That day at Six Flags, the two of us were sitting in a little boat for the Okefenokee Swamp ride. We were straddling a bench with me in the front as we entered a misty cave where mechanical beavers, opossums and bears wearing overalls and straw hats or dresses with aprons and bonnets were dancing and singing.

A cheery theme song about the Okefenokee looped over and over as we watched juggling rabbits and rows of carrots and vegetables with faces that moved up and down as if they were singing to the ragtime song. The faint squeaks of metal and jolted mechanical movements of the stiff-smiled menagerie didn't take anything away from the wonder.

I watched the show and was oblivious to what Tommy had in mind because when he said my name I just kept looking at the dancing animals assuming he wanted to make sure I saw something in particular. When he didn't say more, I turned my head to look at him and his head bobbed right into mine. My neck was craned around to the right in an awkward position, so when he grabbed hold of my shoulders, I tried to break free, but before I had the chance, he'd moved his hand to the back of my head and smashed his lips against mine. Then without warning, I felt his tongue shoot straight into my mouth.

I choked, pulled back and screamed.

We both looked around to see if people in any other boats were close enough to have seen us, but we were clear. When I saw the look on Tommy's face, I felt bad. I could tell he was blushing even in the dimly lit Okefenokee cave.

The truth is, I'd wanted to see what French kissing was like but I couldn't imagine actually doing it. There was no place for either of us to run and pretend like it had never happened, and I really did like Tommy. As pathetic as it was, I didn't want him to regret that awkward try. I turned around and looked him at about nose level.

"How about a Mulligan?"

"What do you mean, a Mulligan?"

"A do-over. Like in golf," I said, getting the nerve to raise my eyes to his. I think I must have been channeling Momma for ideas. "A pretend-it-didn't-happen, try-it-again kiss."

Tommy swallowed and looked only slightly hopeful.

"Hold on," I said, and took his hand.

I wasn't known for my grace, so I gingerly stood up while he helped me balance. The boat rocked to one side and my heart jumped as I imagined tipping us over into the exaggerated blue water. Tommy held my hands as I switched my right foot to the other side of the bench, then moved my left foot to the other side. I sat down facing him knee-to-knee.

He took a moment to take in the situation, and then said, "Try it again?"

I nodded.

He leaned in and cocked his head to the left. I answered by leaning in and cocking my head the opposite way. We moved a little closer together and kissed that same familiar kiss, then we both opened our mouths a little bit. It took a few seconds before Tommy got the nerve to move his tongue toward me and just about the time he did I realized that my eyes were wide open. His were closed, but I saw his lashes start to flutter open, so I quickly slammed mine shut.

I couldn't stand not knowing how he felt about what we were doing, so I peeked to see if he was looking at me. His eyes were closed and I think I saw his eyeball gently rolling back and forth under the lid.

I relaxed and moved my tongue around a little bit and moved it toward his lips and then just barely into his mouth.

I was just getting comfortable when a light fell across our eyes and I opened them to see a boy a few years older than us wearing a blue and white striped shirt and pants with a hat similar to Donald Duck's. He had big, oozing red zits on his face and was holding a long pole.

We snapped apart and sat straight with guilty faces.

"Thank you for visiting the Okefenokee," he said through his nose as if he had a bad cold. He reached in to help me out of the boat.

I was embarrassed about being backwards in my seat, but Donald Duck didn't seem to care, and there was a family of four anxious for us to get out so that they could load in. We stumbled out as quickly as we could and didn't get the nerve to look at each other until we'd long cleared the exit stanchions.

"I'm glad you told me about Mulligans," said Tommy.

"Me too."

I rushed to walk a few steps in front of him so he wouldn't see me smiling.

Next, we rode the Hanson old-fashioned cars. Tommy drove and he waited until he was far ahead of the car behind us and stopped. I was anticipating just this move, so I settled in for another French kiss. This one was even better, but we had just started when we heard another Model-T coming from behind. Tommy took off and we laughed as we raced back to the end of the ride.

We bumped noses when we tried another kiss on the roller coaster and Tommy's nose bled off and on for about three hours, but we found plenty of time when it wasn't bleeding to continue practicing.

After a jarring ride on the Runaway Dahlonega Mine Train, a stream of red was inching slowly from his nose. I pointed nonchalantly to my own nose and Tommy took the hint. He spent a while in the bathroom and came out with a fresh face and a wad of toilet tissue in the pocket of his shorts.

At the end of the day, we took the sky lift across the park to put us close to the exit, where we were to meet Glenn. I agreed that it was a good idea, but we both knew that there was an even better reason for riding that sky lift: Practice!

We waited in line counting the people in front of us and watching the cars as they slid slowly toward the sky lift station. I tried to imagine what Tommy was thinking and if he liked the way I was kissing back or if I was doing it all wrong. I had the distinct feeling that he liked it as much as I did, but it made me nervous to wonder.

The sky lift cars were coming in a pattern of yellow, green, blue, red. I made up a little game in my head that if we ended up on a yellow car it meant he liked me as a friend; a green meant he would break up with me tonight; a blue meant that we would fall in love and go together through high school; and red meant that we would both go to the University of Georgia, marry as soon as we graduated and live happily ever after.

I matched the groups in front of us with the cars as they approached one-by-one over the Six Flags skyline and Tommy and I perfected our French kiss as we rode across the sky in that red car. And it felt just right as we rode the second half with Tommy's arm around my shoulder looking out over the treetops. His pinky and ring fingers moved nonchalantly to the very top of my breast and I didn't argue a bit. Instead, I thanked God that it was the right breast that was a little bigger, and just smiled, thinking about our destiny now that it was set.

We spent the last few minutes of our time taking the pictures I needed for my English project, but I'd forgotten to record the sounds until we were outside the gate, so the tape was mixed with a lot of street noise and Tommy's brother's voice yelling at us to get in the car.

When I got home, I took a long bubble bath and put on my fluffy Plaza bathrobe before Daddy took me out to the garage to show me the theater he'd been working on all day.

April 19, 2003

"Oh my gosh," cried Carly. "It's petrified marzipan! How old is this?"

Grace leaned over her cousin's shoulder and peered into the Tupperware lined with waxed paper. On top of each carefully placed layer were tiny little pieces of candy formed from almond paste and shaped to resemble apples, peaches, grapes and bananas.

"I loved making those!" exclaimed Grace. "Let me see!"

"Let me see, too," said Charlie.

I realized just how long it had been since I'd taken a break as I sat in a kitchen chair and took in the chatter of voices that filled Annie Jo's house. The cousins were enjoying one another, and we'd found a rhythm to the work when it wasn't interrupted by another memory of craft projects, adventures and rituals with Annie Jo. I stared at the sheer curtains that covered the window and thought of the red gingham ones that hung there all through my childhood.

"I think I made this bunch of grapes," said Charlie, as he pulled out a disfigured piece of marzipan candy that was well more than twice the size of the rest of the fruit bowl pieces.

Marzipan making had not missed anyone in the Flint family. It was a favorite pastime of Annie Jo, and she never missed a holiday season for mixing up the almond-flavored dough with food coloring and sitting around the kitchen table with all her children, grandchildren and great-grandchildren working to fill her candy dish with the tiny almond treats. Some years she made little pumpkins to put on top of cupcakes at Halloween.

I loved the flavor, but the candies became less and less appetizing through the years as the thought of germs from all the hands rolling the dough into different shapes became more obvious.

"Can we eat it?" asked Charlie.

"Better not, Charlie," said Carly. "It looks like it's several years old."

Mother, Ansley and I took turns trying to organize the clearing and sorting efforts. It seems just as one of us would get on a roll, we'd find ourselves lost in memories from another closet or drawer.

All the kids opted to help with the sorting at Annie Jo's instead of the Easter cooking preparation, so we settled on leaving the husbands with picking up a pre-cooked ham and prepared salads. The sorting was more difficult than we expected so we were grateful for their help as we pored through Annie Jo's closets and kitchen.

Charlie, Joey and Chip served as runners back and forth from the house to the front porch as we assigned items into "giveaway," "sort among the family" and "trash" piles.

Every drawer and every cabinet unveiled another memory of the adventures and fun she had shared with each of us.

Daisy found Annie Jo's stack of albums and pulled out her turntable record player. Annie Jo had the entire collection of the Ray Conniff Singers albums and Daisy stacked three of them on the magnetic arm. With flashlights and a hair brush as microphones, Ansley, Daisy and I sang along to "We've Only Just Begun," songs from "Mary Poppins" and the chorus' rendition of "These Boots are Made for Walking" with the living room window as our stage backdrop.

Grace found her old guitar behind the coats in the hall closet and sat down to try out some of the chords she remembered and she was pretty good.

"Imagine what you could have done if you'd practiced and not given it up," I said, knowing she'd probably take offense as I sat down to listen and take a break.

Grace shrugged and continued with the tune as Joey entered the room.

"What? With the perv!" he exclaimed.

Grace shot him a look and went back to the guitar.

"What are you talking about?" I asked. "What do you mean 'perv'?"

"Nothing. It was nothing," Grace whined in her "you're-nagging-again-Mother" singsong voice as she stopped playing and steadied the guitar against the edge of the coffee table.

"Grace's guitar teacher was a pervert," Joey yelled from the next room.

"A pervert! Mr. Crews? What are you talking about? That was a legitimate music school. Grace? What is he talking about?"

"Well, he was kind of a pervert. He made me uncomfortable," said Grace.

She shifted to the back of the sofa and pulled a throw pillow to her lap.

I worked to formulate my next question carefully, but she answered before I asked.

"He always placed his hand on my leg while I was playing for him."

"Where on your leg? What do you mean? Is there more?" I panicked.

Ansley came around the corner and stopped next to me to be a part of the conversation.

"On the middle of my leg. And no, not really."

"Well, why didn't you ever mention it? And what do you mean, 'no, not really?'"

"How old were you?" interrupted Ansley.

"Probably 12," said Grace to Ansley, and then to me, "Just once he did this creepy thing."

Clearly Daisy was catching our conversation from the bedroom. "Charlie, I need you in here right away," she called.

Ansley stepped to the kitchen door and called for Charlie, who was looking through a photo album at the kitchen table.

"Charlie, your mom needs you in the bedroom. Come right now," she said.

We halted the conversation until Charlie was safe in the bedroom with Daisy.

I picked back up, but with more calm and less decibel, determined to get the full story: "What creepy thing, Grace?"

"Once he was looking at me really weird, then he leaned back and looked down at his crotch. I looked too and his pants were stretched across his crotch, which was bulging. I looked back at his face and he was smiling this creepy smile."

"Oh my God, Grace! Why didn't you tell me this? What did you do?"

"That's when I told you that I needed to quit guitar so that I could concentrate on my grades and that I wanted to try cheerleading in the fall instead."

"But why didn't you tell me how you felt about Mr. Crews? Why didn't you tell me what he did?"

"I don't know, Mom. I just didn't."

I looked at Ansley. Her face read of surface sympathy, but I didn't trust the deeper thoughts I couldn't read.

Grace picked the guitar back up and announced that she thought she and Carly should start sorting things in the hall closet. I made a mental note to talk with Joe about what I'd learned, but as I moved back to the kitchen to empty Annie Jo's pantry, my head filled with thoughts of the night I'd spent with Laura Liz and her cousin Ginny.

I found myself with a less sentimental attitude than I'd had before the conversation as I pitched pantry items into the trash bag with little consideration. Before I knew it, I'd filled two bags and knotted the drawstring ties and dropped them at the back steps for the boys to carry to the trash bin.

Was it Ginny? Butch? Was it Hank who touched me? Why didn't I tell anyone? Why didn't I get up and turn on the light and catch whoever it was when I had the chance?

Was it the same reason Grace kept quiet? And Joey was older. Why didn't he protect her by telling us what had happened.

I thought about Cary Grant. Cary *R*. Grant. Now *he* was a perv.

It was getting late in the afternoon so I pulled three medium-sized boxes out of the top of Annie Jo's closet to take home and sort there.

April 1967

$\mathcal{J}$ got an A-plus on my Six Flags project.

Daddy's theater set was a big hit, and Miss Paulk made sure all the students knew that my father had built it. There were some really great projects, but Miss Paulk only gave two A-pluses — one to me and one to LaDarla Dalrymple.

To present the project, I used the brochures that I got from Six Flags and Momma took me to her office at the Frito Lay plant because they had a blueprint machine that would allow us to make line drawing copies. I cut out pieces from them and used them on the storyboards representing what the viewer would see and how the screen would change every few seconds on the screen. The copies were light blue and white, of course, so Ansley helped me color them back in with colored pencil. Then I added my photographs and drawings of the other images.

I also designed a bumper sticker and a postcard mailer and wrote a radio spot and a press release about the benefits of season passes at the theme park.

Tommy was in two of the photographs on the storyboard, but I'd carefully taped information cards over his face to avoid kids in the class teasing us. I was grateful he wasn't in my English class because Miss Paulk asked me to describe the Okefenokee Swamp ride to everyone.

LaDarla's project was on Maybelline mascara. I thought it was good, but I didn't think it was any better than Dena's project on Tide laundry detergent, and Dena got an A-minus.

Miss Paulk was so impressed with our work that she selected six of us to make our presentations to the school before the chorus performed at an assembly that year. Ansley said that I talked too fast, but a lot of people said that they liked it that afternoon on the bus. They all agreed that it made them want to go to the new theme park.

I saw Laura Liz rolling her eyes at another girl when I finished my presentation. When I asked her about it, she denied it and we ended up having a big fight about how much time I was spending with Tommy.

"Don't you remember how you and Donnie were when you were going steady? We barely spent any time together then," I said. They broke up when Donnie got interested in an eighth-grader that Ansley had been in dance class with a few years before. Laura Liz cried for days and stayed at our house for almost two weeks without going home at all.

"I know, I just miss you, Josie. And I miss your family. I hardly ever see you any more."

We made plans to spend that Saturday with Annie Jo, and we ended up helping her bake six pies for a reception at the church.

We talked more than we had in a long time while we rolled out dough and filled the pies with apples and peaches. She asked me if I had talked to the new Faulkner twins much at school.

"No, not really. They seem a little wild."

"They are really sweet. You should try and get to know them."

"You know I saw them smoking cigarettes at the dirt hill one day."

"Oh, Josie, who doesn't smoke cigarettes? Your momma does, my momma does, Butch does, my daddy does... Besides, don't you think those boys are cute?"

"Yeah, they are cute, I guess. They are both in some of my classes but I can't tell which is which."

"I can only tell them apart because Dixon has one crooked tooth on the side and Mason has a mole on his neck. Also Dixon had stitches on his right knee and you can still see the scar."

"Their momma and daddy are real nice folks," offered Annie Jo from the kitchen sink. I hadn't even noticed she was listening.

"Will there be any extra pies that we can sample, Annie Jo?" I asked, changing the subject.

"Of course," Annie Jo replied.

Ansley was working on a science project that weekend. She and her friend Mary Ellen, Candy's brother, Roger Saylor, and two other boys constructed a beaver's dam with mud and sticks and somehow cut it apart so that they could label it showing the cross section. Then they wrote a paper about beavers and how their behavior affects the environment.

Just a day before the project was due, Mary Ellen and Ansley decided they should construct a beaver out of paper maché to add to the project. The boys felt that the project was perfect and didn't want to help, so Ansley recruited Annie Jo and we all helped after we'd finished the pies. We shaped the beaver out of coat hangers and masking tape. Then we dipped strips of newspaper in the glue and draped it over the figure. Once they painted it and glued on some old black buttons for eyes, it looked pretty good.

We brought it home that night and Daddy had an idea to cut off the tail and reattach it with a hinge and motor so that it would flap up and down. I thought it was a great idea, but Ansley just felt they'd run out of time.

Mrs. Saylor drove Ansley, Roger and Mary Ellen to school that Monday so that they wouldn't have to carry the beaver and the dam on the bus. Roger wore a tie and sports jacket, and Ansley wore a pair of Mother's heels and her Easter dress for the presentation. They got an A on the project, and by that afternoon, Ansley and Roger were going steady.

Roger bought two initial rings at the Ben Franklin store next to the Winn Dixie and gave them to Ansley after school that first week. One "A" and one "F." She couldn't decide if she should wear them on two different fingers of one hand or one on each ring finger, but it turned out they caused a rash on her fingers, so she just wore them on special occasions — the "A" on the left and the "F" on the right most of the time.

When our neighbors, the Richards, had a garage sale, Ansley bought a pair of cufflinks with an "R" on them for Roger. He didn't have a shirt that had French cuffs, so he poked them through the top two buttons of his shirt on Sundays for church.

Later that week I was waiting by the light pole for Laura Liz and saw her coming up the walk with just one of the twins. They were holding hands.

They were deep in conversation and as she walked toward me, she lifted a few fingers from her other hand that was wrapped around her science book and said brightly, "Hi, Josie."

Then she and whichever-one-he-was just kept on walking. She stopped once and called over her shoulder, "I guess I'll see you at lunch, okay?"

She didn't wait for my response. They just walked right into the building.

I didn't see a mole on his neck, so I guessed it was Dixon.

I saw Ansley in the hall after class, and she asked me if I could meet her in her science class after school so that I could help her carry the dam and the beaver home on the bus. I told her that she should get one of her partners to bring it home, but she knew I'd be there after the sixth period bell.

Ansley carried the dam because it was heavier and it was her project, so I carried the beaver. As we pulled out of Seaton Ferry Junior High, our bus drove right by Laura Liz and Dixon Faulkner walking down the road holding hands and looking very much in crush with one another. I peeked over the top of the paper maché beaver to take another look at him as we sped by.

That afternoon, Tommy's dad dropped him off at my house for the afternoon and we walked to the dirt hill.

"Do you know the new twins, Mason and Dixon, very well?"

"We played basketball one day in the gym. They were pretty cool."

About that time, four kids on bikes came flying toward the dirt hill. They couldn't see us, but we could see that it was two older boys that I recognized from the bus, and the twins, Mason and Dixon Faulkner.

One of the twins pulled out a pack of cigarettes and handed one to each of the other boys. Then they passed around a lighter and all lit cigarettes as they walked to the other side of the dirt hill.

Tommy and I stood up, and when we knew they couldn't see us, we walked home.

Daddy was cooking shish kebabs on the grill and Tommy called his parents to see if he could stay for dinner. We kissed once in the hallway after dinner, but Daisy came running from the kitchen and cut us off.

"Momma! Josie and Tommy are kissing!"

"Hush, Daisy!" I whispered sternly.

Momma had changed clothes into a short orange dress with a diamond pattern, her black boots, bright yellow beads and bright red lipstick. She smiled at us as she walked toward the front door.

"How's your Momma, Tommy? Please tell her I said 'Hi.' You kids have fun. I've got a hotline shift at the church tonight," she drawled as she sauntered down the hall and out the door without even waiting to hear Tommy's response. I looked at Daddy and he just smiled.

The next week Miss Paulk rearranged the desks into a completely different configuration in her classroom. I got there early and chose my desk. It wasn't long before LaDarla Dalrymple came in and plopped right next to me. We'd barely ever shared two words between us, but she turned right to me and asked about my favorite music.

We talked about Tommy Roe and the Monkees, but then I changed the subject to compliment her on her mascara project.

"Thanks. I loved yours too. Are you still going steady with Tommy Wilson?"

"Yes, but our parents won't let us go on a date until we're juniors. Once in a while his brother takes us places, but mostly I just see him at school and at parties and stuff."

"My brother knows Glenn Wilson."

"Your brother?"

"Yes, Winston. He goes to Duke," she said. "He knows Glenn from Boy Scouts."

A few days later LaDarla slipped a piece of paper on my desk. I opened it before Miss Paulk started class and saw that it was an invitation to her spend-the-night birthday party. I looked at her, and she smiled the sweetest smile I'd ever seen on her. I smiled back and tried to give the signal that I was excited and we'd talk about it after class.

She invited six girls for that Saturday night to swim in their pool, have pizza and watch Hollywood Palace, then spend the night in their basement. We were all to bring sleeping bags, pillows, toothbrushes, pajamas and a gift for LaDarla's birthday. The next morning, our parents should pick us up by 9 o'clock in time for families to go to church if they usually did.

The invitation was very thorough, with the exception of why she was inviting me.

"I really hope you can come," she said and she seemed very sincere.

"I'll check with Mother and Daddy and let you know tomorrow."

"Thanks for inviting me," I added.

"I've invited you, Lisa Crane, Karen Carr, Cheri Johns, Dena Baker and Belinda Roach."

I knew all of those girls, but the only one I'd ever really been a friend with was Dena. They were all real popular. I wasn't sure if I was happy to be invited or if I'd be happier if Mother and Daddy had a conflict to remind me of.

As the party got closer Laura Liz and I stopped meeting every morning to walk to school together. After the second time she walked past me holding hands with Dixon Faulkner, I quit coming to the light pole. One morning she held the front door for me as she saw me coming up the front steps of the school.

"Bye, Dixon. Bye, Mason," she drawled as she watched them walk toward the lockers.

"You guys are spending a lot of time together," I said.

"Well, they walk right by my house on the way to school, so they wait for me so we can walk together. Besides, it seems like you and LaDarla are best friends now anyway."

"Laura Liz, don't forget we poked our fingers that day and mixed our blood. We'll always be best friends, right?"

She shrugged her shoulder and looked past me.

When the bell rang we rushed to our classes leaving the question unanswered.

That weekend, Mother pulled lipstick and cologne from her gift basket she kept in the hall closet for me to take to the birthday party.

I thought a long time about bringing my bathrobe to LaDarla's house, but in the end I decided not to. It felt weird that it had been Mrs. Dalrymple's cast-off before it was my own prized possession. I brought my best shorty pajamas and one of Momma's short, light-weight robes that matched almost exactly.

Their house was really pretty. We put our overnight bags in her room that had a full-sized canopy bed and a whole wall of shelves filled with pretty figurines, books, games and her candle collection. She said we'd be sleeping in the basement, though, so we brought our sleeping bags downstairs.

I was picturing Annie Jo's cellar that had cinder block walls and pipes running across the ceiling and a creepy smell, but it was nothing like that in the Dalrymple's basement. There was a pool table, a long wooden bar with neon lights behind it, a three-sided sofa and a color TV, plus two bedrooms.

By their backyard pool, Mrs. Dalrymple set out a tray with cold Cokes in bottles, a bowl of M&Ms and a basket of popcorn balls wrapped in waxed paper that the Dalrymples' maid Rubelle had made for the party.

After we swam, LaDarla opened her gifts and everyone tried on the lipstick and the Love's Baby Soft I gave her. I thought the lipstick was way too red, but LaDarla said she liked it and sprayed the Love's

Baby Soft on all the girls' wrists and I think she liked that too. I saw everyone sniffing their own arms most of the night.

Karen and Belinda got out their makeup kits and hair rollers and brushes and "beauty shopped" us all.

Belinda put my hair in a high bun and then took Dippity Do and some pink sponge rollers and made curly sideburns on the side. She put light green eye shadow and thick eyeliner on my eyes with a sickly yellow color for highlight under my eyebrows. I liked everything but the yellow highlight. But I loved the sideburns and how she did my bangs. She parted them in the middle and smoothed in some Dippity Do to hold them in place.

Karen gave LaDarla a Mystery Date game. I noticed that she'd already had one when we were in her room, but she acted very sweet and excited anyway, and we played that for about an hour pretending each of the dates in the games were boys we knew at school.

We talked about the Faulkner twins and the consensus was that they were cute but trouble. Everyone wanted to know who I liked, but I lied about how much I liked Tommy Wilson, and instead said that I'd been writing a boy from Huntsville, Alabama, that I'd met the summer before at the pool. I really did meet a boy at the pool and we'd exchanged addresses, but I'd never written him and he'd never written me. He wasn't really that cute either, but I described him as better looking and without acne and braces.

"I thought you were going steady with Tommy Wilson?" asked Belinda.

"Oh, we're good friends. That's all." I'm not sure why I lied.

Belinda fully admitted she was madly in love with LaDarla's brother Winston, but we all just told her to set her sights on someone her own age. Plus, LaDarla said he was bringing home a girl that he'd been dating from Duke later that month for a weekend visit. He's sent a picture of them from the Delta Zeta formal dance and she was really pretty. Belinda didn't seem swayed, but she did suggest that we all have a dance party so LaDarla ran up to her room and brought down a huge stack full of albums.

After we danced, Mrs. Dalrymple brought down an ice cream cake and Dr. Dalrymple gave LaDarla a pretend spanking — one lick for each year plus one to grow on. Her brother Kenneth was there with his girlfriend, Wanda Jean Smith, but they left right after the song because Mrs. Smith was driving them to the movies.

We had a séance and tried to conjure up LaDarla's great aunt Boopie, but we got distracted with a knock on the basement window before she ever had the chance to send a message. Actually, I thought it was a message from Boopie when we heard three knocks on the window, but I think the other girls were already expecting a visit from some of the boys in our class. They all screamed and ran to the window and opened it. I was shocked to see that Tommy was there with three other boys I never saw him hang out with before. One was smoking a cigarette and I saw him drop it onto the dirt and squish the butt with his shoe.

I was grateful when Mrs. Dalrymple came downstairs with a bowl of marshmallows and chocolate sauce and we shut the window and waved the boys to go on home. Karen broke her fingernail on the window though and whined about it until we all faded off to sleep.

The next morning Kenneth served as our waiter at the breakfast table as Dr. Dalrymple cooked bacon and pancakes and Daddy picked me up right on schedule in time for church.

Momma wanted to know everything about the Dalrymple's house and everything about the party.

"Do they have a color TV?" she asked. "Was their house really fancy?"

I told her about the big porch in the front and LaDarla's full-sized canopy bed and their pool and their monogrammed bathroom towels.

Once she was satisfied, she said, "Now Josie, you call the Dalrymples right after church and thank them for their kind hospitality."

"Yes, ma'am," I said.

Annie Jo suggested that we all come to her house to make sugar cookies that afternoon and said I could invite LaDarla. Mrs. Dalrymple answered the phone when I called and she said that LaDarla's dad could drop her off. Ansley came with Roger and Daisy invited Vivian, and we baked and decorated six dozen cookies with everyone having plenty to take home to their own families.

When school ended after Memorial Day, the Dalrymples invited Belinda and me to spend a week with them at their beach house on Jekyll Island. Kenneth brought a friend and Winston was there for the first part of the week with his girlfriend from Duke, Lorna. She had a different bathing suit for every day — each in pink or green Delta Zeta colors. And every t-shirt, beach towel, even earrings had her sorority letters or a turtle on it.

Winston and Lorna rarely participated in any of the cooking or family games and always positioned their towels separate from the rest of us while we were on the beach. I don't even think Dr. and Mrs. Dalrymple were sorry to see them leave on Wednesday so that Lorna could get back to Charleston for a baby shower for her cousin whose wedding was just the month before.

Kenneth and his friend met some kids with surfboards, but they left and took the surfboards with them that day too. We walked toward the pier and found the beach covered with hundreds of starfish.

"Doesn't this look like the Big Dipper?" said LaDarla pointing to a group of starfish.

We spent the afternoon making up constellations from the arrangement of starfish spread across the beach and drawing shapes around them with sticks or our fingers in the sand.

"I think this one's called 'Pisces with Go Go Boots,'" said Belinda, drawing a shape of a fish that appeared to be walking with tall boots.

"Here's Lorna's bikini top," said LaDarla, circling two starfish. "Oops, looks like she lost her bottoms!"

We laughed as we walked the expanse of the beach identifying more made-up constellations.

It was a great week, but by the fifth day, Belinda and I were so badly sunburned that we had fevers and chills. I heard Dr. and Mrs. Dal-rymple talking about cutting short the vacation to get us home, but after dinner Dr. Dalrymple announced that he'd just learned that he needed to get back to the office for an important meeting and though he really apologized to everyone, it was necessary to all go home a day early.

We packed up and left for home the next morning. My back and nose and shoulders were sunburned so badly I was really just glad to get back to my own home. Annie Jo made a paste out of oatmeal and lotion and put it on all my worst spots. I was so miserable I even lay on my bed and let Ansley and Daisy pull the burnt skin off my back in a contest to see who could pull off the largest piece.

April 20, 2003

*I*t poured rain all morning on Easter Sunday so instead of going to Ansley's condo, we met for brunch at Druid Hills Country Club where Doc and Mother were members.

Allen brought Charlie in from Charlotte late the night before, and they joined Daisy in our guest room. Joey and Grace both stayed home for the weekend, so we all went to church services together before meeting the rest of the family at noon at the club.

Kenneth canceled at the last minute, which disappointed Ansley, but LaDarla was there with her husband Greg and their youngest son, Matt. There was a big holiday crowd so we had to split up into two groups: The cousins: Joey, Grace, Chip, Carly, Charlie and LaDarla's son Matt sat at one table. The older generation — Doc, Mother, Ansley, Daisy, Allen, LaDarla, Greg, Joe and me — at the other.

"Do you realize that except for the year we were in Italy, this is the first time I've ever celebrated without Annie Jo?" I said to Joe on the way to the club.

We compared notes with the others, and none of the others had missed spending more than a handful of holidays with Annie Jo.

Even at 86, she had remained the maypole that all the rest of us revolved around. She brought the laughter, the antics and the creativity to everyday things, evident to anyone outside looking in, but she also formed the deepest and most meaningful roots of our family tree.

After we'd eaten, Doc led the men on a tour of the newly remodeled pro shop, and the women took off for the pool cabana where we lined pool chairs under an awning to chat and watch the rain.

"What was Papa Ray like?" asked Carly.

Carly and her twin brother, Chip, had always been sentimental children and had enjoyed listening to Annie Jo and the other adults tell stories all their lives.

My memories of my grandfather were limited, and Ansley and Daisy were just 4 and 1 when he died.

"Annie Jo said he was the handsomest boy in three states," I said. "They met when they were both just 10 and married at 17."

I told her about the silver canister-shaped lunchbox that he carried to work each day. He'd plop it on the sideboard in their kitchen when he'd come home and scoop us up and tickle and tease us while Annie Jo would unpack the lunchbox and wipe it clean for the next day's lunch.

"Did Annie Jo ever work?" asked Grace.

"Not since I was born," I said, "but I remember my father telling me that she delivered the mail when he was young. She had a walking route to deliver to the businesses in the town so she did it while he was in school. In the summers he often made the deliveries with her."

"She was closer to me than my own mother," said Mother. "And a Godsend for me through everything — especially raising you girls after your father died."

I studied her face and feared she was going to cry until she added, "And she was my maid of honor when I married Doc!"

I thought of that day and the powder blue dress Annie Jo wore, very similar in shade to the dress we buried her in. It had an empire waist and lace bodice with long sleeves and a rounded neck. We picked flowers from her yard and she made flower chain headbands for herself and for my sisters and me to wear.

"I loved making pies and homemade noodles with her," said Ansley. "Do you remember when she dyed the noodles pink for my birthday dinner?"

"I do," shouted Daisy. "I loved those. And I loved the puppies and kittens that always seemed to be around to play with at her house."

Doc returned with Joe and the rest of the men and I noticed Joey's shoulders were now stretching broader than Joe's 6'1" frame. Joey and Chip were melding back into their best friend days, growing up as the closest of cousins, inseparable in the summers.

"By the way, LaDarla," Ansley clumsily segued. "How long has Kenneth been dating his girlfriend?"

Daisy shot me a look.

"I'm guessing they will be engaged by the end of the summer," LaDarla answered. "They met about a year ago at a Braves game. She's really great and they're good together. I'm looking forward to having a sister-in-law."

I could see Ansley's gears spinning and anticipated her next question before she even asked it. Her divorce had been final for nearly two years and despite her best efforts, she had not landed a new man yet. Now that the twins were away at college I knew she was lonely.

"A Braves game?"

"Yes, he was there with some co-workers and she was with a group of friends in the row in front of them."

"Well, tell him Miss Vernal Equinox Runner Up said hello," Ansley laughed.

"Miss Who, Mom?" asked Carly.

"Oh, something from school when I was in sixth grade. I'll tell you about it later. I'll try to find my school yearbook from that year."

The sky had cleared as we hugged the kids goodbye. Grace, Joey, Carly and Chip hopped in Chip's car with plans to spend the afternoon with a Frisbee in Piedmont Park.

We said our goodbyes to Daisy and Allen and Charlie as they loaded the car for the trip back to Charlotte. They made plans to come back in two weeks for what we hoped would be the final weekend of sorting and cleaning Annie Jo's duplex.

Allen started the car as we talked. Rod Stewart's version of "People Get Ready" was playing on the radio.

Rod Stewart was a favorite, but it was Curtis Mayfield's original version that filled my mind as I thought about the April my family and

I had shared 35 years before. Images of my father, television newscasts, the Roberts' attic... *that musty smell*, a flash image of the photograph Laura Liz and I had found and the newspaper article marked "Booger Creek" all shook the levity I'd enjoyed all afternoon.

I saw Joe looking at me in curiosity and I shook my head, smiled and pushed the melancholy thoughts back into hiding.

Mother opened the back seat and slid inside for another hug with Charlie before they left, then made the rounds to each of the rest of us. The wrinkles around her eyes were deeper than I'd ever noticed before, but they seemed to be pointing at her beautiful brown eyes, just calling more attention.

"Happy Easter, everyone," yelled Daisy.

"Drive carefully," said Ansley, as she blew two-handed kisses to their car. "Maybe we can all go to a Braves game when you're back in town next month."

Joe shot me a look and added a one-eye-squint and question, "Is she...?"

"Yes, darling. Looks that way," I knew what he was thinking because I was thinking it too. "Ansley's somehow set her sights on Kenneth after all these years. You heard LaDarla say he was dating someone, but I think you're right. Either that or she just thinks Turner Field is the place to meet her next man."

"Or she's just hoping to catch a fly ball," said Joe.

"Lame, but cute," I said as we got into our own car to head home. "There is something else I wanted to talk to you about though."

I told him about Grace and her story of Mr. Crews, the guitar teacher.

"I can't understand her not telling us that," he said. "What an ass, this guy. Do you think he's still teaching there?"

"It's probably been ten years. I doubt it."

I tried to imagine if I would have told Mother and Daddy if it had happened to me. I didn't tell them about what happened at Laura Liz's house. Was I afraid of getting someone in trouble? Did I feel I was somehow to blame? Grace had begged for guitar lessons and then just as quickly lost interest in it. She was no more to blame for Crews' actions than I was when I was asleep in Laura Liz's bed.

"If nothing more, I'm going to speak to Joey. He should have told us even if Grace couldn't," Joe said.

My mind filled with more thoughts as I tried to imagine why Joey wouldn't have told us. I thought we'd set up a very open communication with our children as they were going through adolescence. Did we do enough? Was there more we didn't know?

As Joe pulled into the driveway and hit the garage door remote, my mind readjusted to thoughts of the next week at work. I had a new client meeting first thing the next day.

September 1967

Ninth grade at Northbridge High School was a big change from junior high. In some ways I felt as if I'd walked to the end of my block and with a single step, found myself in a completely different place. Or like the lighting changed in my life, kind of like when Dorothy's black and white world in "The Wizard of Oz" turned to color once she landed in Munchkinland.

High school football was fun. I went to most games with Belinda and Karen and Karen's family because LaDarla and Dena were junior varsity cheerleaders and they had to be at the games early to sell programs.

Tommy was playing football so I went to the homecoming game with Donnie and Belinda, who had started dating. LaDarla was up for homecoming court and we wanted to be there to cheer her on. We met Tommy in the gym for the dance after he'd showered. I wore the chrysanthemum corsage he had ordered for me from the Beta Club's sale.

Annie Jo had made my dress – a red sizzler with white rickrack around the sleeves and neckline. It was called a sizzler because it was so short you had to wear bloomers underneath. She made them out of the same red polyester fabric. LaDarla was named to the freshman homecoming court and we all posed for pictures wearing her crown.

Meanwhile that fall, Ansley made cheerleader for the junior high basketball team. She had bloomed with a dancer's grace, aided by contact lenses and a newfound pretty-girl style just as my acne started flaring. She was named "Student of the Month" and came home with a construction paper sign, a rose and a $20 gift certificate to Sears on the same day I got my first period.

There was standing room only on the bus that day, and I was wearing a pale yellow skirt with my arm looped through a frayed strap from the ceiling of the bus when I noticed two boys whispering and laughing.

I heard the word "blood" just as the bus stopped. My stop was five stops away and on the other side of the river, but I pushed toward the door, jumped off and hurried behind a tree.

I turned my skirt around, held my notebook in front of the bright red spot as big as a tomato and propelled my legs and shame-filled self toward Annie Jo's house.

She opened the door just as I was running up her stoop. A new tenant on the other side of her duplex, a Fulton County policeman named Barry Hazelip, was sitting in her kitchen where they had been talking over a cup of coffee.

The sun was blazing through the red gingham curtains in her kitchen as I entered, so all I could see was his silhouette until he stood up and said hello. He was every bit of 6'3" and had a tan-colored mustache that looked like a caterpillar across his lip.

"Barry, let's talk again later this week if you don't mind," Annie Jo said as she put her arm around my shoulders and introduced us. He made a quick exit and I told her all about what had happened on the bus.

She made me a cup of tea and gave me a pair of stretch pants to wear and a pad she'd fashioned from a rag and a new kitchen sponge. We ended up dancing to the radio and singing at the top of our lungs together when they played "Up, Up and Away." We played two games of rummy before I headed home and Mother took me to the Piggly Wiggly for my first purchase of Kotex and Midol pills. Hiding the boxes under my arm, I took my place in the longest line at the store because it was the only female cashier working at the time. Mother didn't comment, but I think she understood.

April 2003

I joined Mays, Hayes & Greystone Public Relations — MHG, as it was referred to in the industry — when Grace was two.

I'd quit my job with the *Atlanta Business Chronicle* when I was eight months pregnant with Joey, so I was pleased to accept a copywriter position four years later even though the salary was well below where I'd been before the children were born. I moved up quickly the first five years and was named a vice-president when Mr. Hayes retired in 2001.

The Midtown Atlanta office building where we occupied the twenty-first floor had been dwarfed by sleek taller buildings built during the '80s and early '90s, but MHG was committed to staying at the mixed-use center that had started Midtown's development. As late as the early '70s, the area was overrun with shops selling drug paraphernalia and hippies sleeping on the streets, but today it was one of Atlanta's most important business districts.

"Josie, I'm sorry about the late notice," said Grant Greystone, the agency's only remaining original partner, as he held on to the door frame of my office on Tuesday morning, "but we are going to need you to travel to Houston this weekend to oversee the Banks Museum ground breaking."

He gripped the door frame as if he feared that if he let go, he might fly right on by to his next task without delivering his news to me.

"Our contact there has had a medical emergency and will be out of pocket until at least June 1," he said.

Daisy and Allen were due back in town on Friday afternoon, and we'd made plans to work at Annie Jo's all day Saturday. And we had tickets to a Braves game on Friday night.

"Bud can join you because we are expecting all the media big wigs in Houston, and there's a decent chance that 'Good Morning, America' will be there."

I saw Bud peer over his computer screen to see how I would react. The Atlanta skyline glistened from the full-width window behind his head. He shot me a sympathetic look.

Damn it.

"No problem," I lied. "Can we pow-wow on the details during team meeting in the morning?"

I saw Bud's head drop behind the screen, and I remembered that he had been making plans to propose to his girlfriend over the weekend. We'd discussed restaurant ideas last week.

"Oh, Bud, your big night..." I said as Greystone left the room.

"It's fine," he said. "I couldn't get a reservation at Atmosphere anyway, and French food is Jill's favorite. I'll reschedule our date and hopefully can get a reservation there. She's not expecting this, so she won't even know to be disappointed."

"I'd better call Joe and my sisters and let them know," I said. "Are you making our flight reservations?"

"On it," he said. "We can leave Thursday at 3:30 p.m. and catch a flight back on Sunday at 10:20 or 12:45."

"10:20," I said as my phone rang and I saw my mother's number show up on the screen.

And tell Mother, of course, too.

I picked up the phone.

December 1967

*J*ust before Christmas I stopped by Annie Jo's duplex and found her sitting in the kitchen with Barry Hazelip and Butch Roberts having coffee. A plate of her sugar cookies sat between them.

"Hi ya', Jaybird!" Butch said with a sick, sarcastic tone and then smiled at me. His teeth looked like they had each been outlined with a black Magic Marker.

"Butch?"

I looked to Annie Jo for help.

"Butch and Barry are friends," she said. "And as it turns out, Butch is going to take the second bedroom in Barry's apartment to help him out with the rent."

My heart sank at the thought.

Butch didn't graduate the year before like he was supposed to. He had failed a couple of classes and was supposed to make it up the summer before his senior year, but failed those too. He went to classes only about two weeks of his senior year before he took a full-time job at the bowling alley and started working days.

Rita and Hank didn't seem too surprised or even too disappointed.

Rita had lost her job at the telephone company and was working at the elementary school in the cafeteria. I knew that because a couple of mornings I saw her in her uniform on the back of Butch's motorcycle as he dropped her off as our school bus went by.

"So... Jaybird?" asked Barry.

"It's just a dumb nickname. You can call me Josie, please," I said with my eyes toward Butch.

"I've known Jaybird — ugh, Josie — since she was a little kid," offered Butch. "She and my little sister are good friends." His outlined teeth flashed again, and I made up an excuse about some homework I needed to get to and left.

By Christmas that year, Laura Liz and I were barely looking at each other. In fact, I guess we never looked at each other if we thought the other was watching. Her face was hollow and her eyes were thickly lined in black. She'd bleached her hair too, and I remember noticing that it exactly matched my yellow notebook pad when she sat a few seats in front of me at an assembly one day.

But without mentioning it to me first, Momma invited Laura Liz's family to our house for Christmas dinner that year. Rita, Hank and Butch all came, along with Annie Jo, Dexter and Shalene, Vivian and baby Luke. Mother did all the cooking and decorating. She was dressed in her white boots and a short green velvet skirt with a matching vest and a jingle bell bracelet that tingled all day long. She did a great job on the food, but the mix of company was completely wrong.

The Roberts couldn't stop arguing with one another. Butch left right after dinner, saying he had a "meeting." No one bothered questioning a meeting on Christmas Day because we all realized it was just as well that he leave.

Annie Jo had just been to the Biltmore House in Asheville with Uncle Lee and Aunt Lola. They'd stayed on to visit Lola's sister in Cashiers and Annie Jo had come back the day before. She kept rambling on about her trip, but no one seemed to want to hear any more details after she'd talked about it for half a day. Dexter and Shalene kept fussing with their little one and leaving the room to feed or change his diaper. The only redeeming relationship of the day was Vivian and Daisy who got along famously.

Laura Liz and I looked for things to talk about, but she didn't want to talk about Tommy and I didn't want to talk about the Faulkners. We both had seen Donnie's new girlfriend drive up to his house with her parents earlier in the day and watched her get out of the car with a Christmas present, but we both pretended we hadn't and didn't talk about that either.

All the time she'd been going steady with Donnie and we played Dot-to-Dot, she'd put "L²" for initials. We started a game after Christmas dinner and I noticed she'd gone back to "LL." We'd only played a few minutes before she said she didn't really feel like Dot-to-Dot and I agreed. We ended up pulling out the Ouija board and playing with Ansley, but even the Ouija was uninterested that day.

Daisy went home that night with Vivian for a few days, but the visit got cut short when Daisy fell out of their top bunk and broke her wrist and had to get a cast all the way to her elbow.

Tommy and his family had been to Wisconsin for Christmas. He came back with a candle shaped like a mushroom and a bottle of Jean Naté cologne for me. I gave him a St. Christopher's medal and some sand art that I'd made for his room.

For New Year's Eve, the Wilsons invited me to their house for a party. It was all adults, except for Tommy and Glenn and me, but it was a very fancy party and we mingled with the adults like we were grown up.

The food was set out on silver trays with tall candelabras and holly branches all around. They had hired Rubelle Jackson to help serve the food and her husband Isaac to be the bartender. I knew Rubelle because she worked five days a week as the Dalrymple's maid. They had a son, Isaac, Jr., they called Izzy, who had polio as a child. The Dalrymples had helped the Jacksons with Izzy's medical costs. I remembered Momma and Daddy talking about it. Their younger son, Bailey, was one of the Negro boys that came to my school in eighth grade.

Rubelle was wearing a black dress with a white lace collar. She was heavyset and the dress was tight around her breasts. She had on shoes that looked like nurses shoes, except they were black, and black stockings. She also had on a string of pearls that really made her look pretty. Her hair was curled, and you could still see where each one of her hair rollers had been. She was dressed as well as the guests, except that she wore a pair of pink Playtex gloves.

Isaac was really thin and wore black trousers, spit-shined black wingtips and a natty gray and black sports jacket. He had a wonderful deep voice and a contagious laugh. The men seemed to enjoy hanging out at the bar best of all so that they could cut up with Isaac.

I wore a pink jumpsuit that Momma had in her closet, plus some of her heels and hoop earrings. Tommy and I kissed (not French because we didn't want his parents or Glenn to see) at midnight, but Glenn didn't have anyone to kiss, so we made it really quick and I gave him a big hug. He kissed me on the head and then shook hands with Tommy.

Mr. Wilson drove me home about 12:30 and Ansley pitched a huge fuss the next day that I got to stay out so late.

"It's not fair. Why does Josie get to stay out until after midnight?" she whined.

"It was a special night, Ansley, and you'll get your chance soon enough," said Daddy.

I pursed my lips and cocked my head and added more detail about the stuffed mushroom caps.

"Josie's a constipated ape," Ansley screamed as she ran out the front door. I thought she'd get in trouble for that, but maybe because it was a holiday, neither Mother nor Daddy stood up to run after her.

Instead, Daddy spent most of New Year's Day working in the garage. He'd sawed off the toothbrush attachment of our electric toothbrush and attached a thin, bristled wire from an old bottle washer so that it could fit down Daisy's cast and scratch her arm when it itched.

Tommy came over and we played a game of gin rummy then watched the University of Southern California beat Indiana in the Rose Bowl. Except for Daisy buzzing the cast-scratcher every few minutes, it was a great game.

April 2003

"We found your prom dress."

"My prom dress? What do you mean?"

I think it was one you wore when you went to the prom with Tommy Wilson," said Ansley. "The pink one with the white piping."

"Tommy had already moved to Minnesota before I was old enough for the prom," I said holding back a grimace for my sister. "I wore that senior year when I went with Donnie."

"Well, whatever. We found it in a box at Annie Jo's. I gave it to Grace and it fits her perfectly."

"Good. How did the clear-out go?"

I picked up my pen and doodled "Josephine Grace Flint," "Josie Flint," "Josie Flint King" as I listened to my sister fill me in on the weekend.

"We made a lot of progress. I think you'll be pleased. We've got everything separated with a room for giveaway and a room of things that we still need to divide among the family, but we're getting very close. Allen is sorting all the estate documents, and we'll have to work on that with Mother and Doc next."

"Great news. And sorry I wasn't there to help. Houston was crazy — and wildly successful though. Did you see the 'Good Morning, America' segment with Charlie Gibson at the new museum in Houston?"

"I don't turn on a television until I've meditated for an hour in the morning. You know that."

"Never mind, but I am sorry I wasn't there for y'all. Any other interesting finds?"

"More marzipan."

"Yuck. What did you do with her recipe box?"

"Daisy is going to copy all the recipes and make a notebook for each of us."

"Great idea, but if no one else wants them, I'd really like to have the box and the cards when she's finished."

"Fine with me."

I thought of Annie Jo's perfect penmanship and the silk flowers she had taped to all of her ballpoint pens. She had a bouquet of pens she kept in vases in her kitchen, on her desk and in her foyer. I remembered sitting at her kitchen table while she practiced letters with Daisy as I showed Ansley how to write the same letters in cursive. The pink and yellow silk flowers bobbed as we went.

I listened to Ansley talk, as I thought about Annie Jo's recipe for homemade noodles written in perfect cursive with a 1 o'clock-slant on a card that was crusty with egg wash and flour. I'd written my name and two hearts on the back of that card.

"I'm driving to Auburn on Saturday to help the twins move out of the dorms for the summer," Ansley said. "Would you like to ride with me?"

I pulled my attention back to the present: Joe would be playing in a golf tournament and the kids would be doing their things. And I wasn't any help with Annie Jo's place when I was in Houston. And this was Ansley asking. We didn't typically seek out opportunities to spend time together. We were perfectly civil during our many family obligations, but she was asking for something outside of that, and I was touched.

"Sure. That sounds fun," I said. "Count me in."

March 1968

Tommy and I decided to break up when he got busy with base-ball. I was babysitting a lot and helping Mother with a flower arrang-ing business that she'd started on the weekends, so we both agreed it was for the best.

One day he came to school with a paper lunch sack with my name written in bubble letters on the outside. He walked me to the end of the science hall to present it. Inside was a gum wrapper chain he'd made that was more than four-feet long.

"I just want you to know I really want us to stay friends," he said.

"Thanks, Tommy. I do too."

I had the funny feeling he was about to kiss me, but I saw his eyes linger in the distance just a little too long.

"Is that Laura Liz?" he asked.

I turned toward the school's outside smoking area and saw her standing next to a pine tree with some kids I didn't know. She was smoking a cigarette like she'd been doing it forever.

She was wearing a yellow dress with fringe on the bottom that I'd never seen.

She turned and I know she saw us, but she turned back and pre-tended she didn't.

It wasn't long before we saw her drop the cigarette onto the ground and stomp it with her shoe. She walked the other direction toward the front of the school and never looked our way.

Soon after, LaDarla and I became official best friends.

Roger Saylor and Ansley celebrated their tenth month of going steady and Roger gave her a giant crepe paper flower that she pinned to her side of our bulletin board.

The next week they were nominated for the king and queen of the Vernal Equinox celebration at school. For the dance, Annie Jo made her a dress out of lavender organza with an empire waist. She wore my navy shoes from homecoming. Mother said that they weren't exactly right, and they were a little big, but all of Momma's heels were too high and we were afraid she'd trip and fall. Roger wore a navy sports jacket and tie, and Mrs. Saylor made buttonholes in one of his dress shirtsleeves so he could wear the cuff links that Ansley had given him. Momma dyed a carnation the exact same shade of lavender as Ansley's dress for Roger's coat.

The look would have been perfect, except Ansley insisted on having her hair done. I tried to talk her into keeping it long with a lavender ribbon as a headband, but she really wanted it fancy for the dance.

Momma took her to Kimmy's Kut-n-Kurl, and she came back with a beehive that stood a full eight inches off the top of her head. Kimmy had even added a few little polyester bees to the design. On the sides, she'd twirled and gelled pieces of hair to make sideburns that looked like miniature Slinkies.

I laughed, but Ansley actually liked it. She looked like she was completely uncomfortable and walked around like a statue as if her hairdo was going to break if she moved too fast. She'd move her head slowly and with tiny movements when someone spoke to her.

The hairdo and the heels made her taller than Roger by about five inches, but we took lots of pictures before the dance.

Wanda Jean Smith and Kenneth Dalrymple were named Mr. and Miss Vernal Equinox that year, but Ansley and Roger got runner up. The funny part was that some of the pictures for the school yearbook were destroyed when some kid's science experiment blew up and started a fire. The only photo that the staff had from the crowning that night was of Ansley and Roger. They had a full-page picture in the celebrations section of the school yearbook. The picture was taken from below the stage, so Ansley's beehive looked about two feet tall.

May 2003

$\mathcal{I}$ turned 50 on May 3. It was the first year as an adult that I hadn't celebrated my birthday with Annie Jo, who would have been 87 on May 9.

I overheard Grace and Joe talking weeks before about how they might pull off a surprise party, and I was grateful I had interceded before they got too far.

"No surprise party this year, please. Really," I said. "What I'd really love is if we could all just spend a quiet day together."

"But 50 is a big deal!"

"Not a big deal I care to shout to everyone I know, Grace."

I thought about celebrations with Annie Jo over the years, but the thought of a quiet day seemed so much more appealing. "Really. Not this year."

"You know what I'd really like? If the four of us could climb Stone Mountain, then come back down and go to dinner that evening. Quiet, perfect. I'd love that."

Joe and Grace looked at each other and I could see in their expressions that they had resigned to the new idea. It had been a difficult month for everyone.

Joe and I had spent the day there a few months earlier with a client of his who was in town from Boston. It was a cool winter day, but the skies had been clear and sunny and I longed for another day in the sunshine. We'd taken his client, Mitchell Moore, to visit the park's historical sites. A bas-relief sculpture of Confederate heroes of the Civil War is carved across one side of the mountain, and we watched a video of how it was made at the park's museum.

A curly haired woman with a little too much aqua eyeshadow and a "Hello, I'm Marge" nametag waved to the three of us as we walked inside and joined her tour already in progress.

"Not an actual mountain, Stone Mountain is the world's largest exposed mass of granite, though there are trees and vegetation over much of it," she recited.

"The carving was a project of the Daughters of the Confederacy in the early 1900s, but was left incomplete due to funding," Marge continued. "The artist took the drawings for the unfinished design and ended up carving Mount Rushmore instead."

I'd lived in Atlanta all my life, but so much of the information was new to me.

Marge pointed at the screen with a green laser as the video's narrator described the completed part of the carving that includes images of Jefferson Davis, President of the Confederate States, and Generals Robert E. Lee and Thomas "Stonewall" Jackson, each on their horses. "The Stone Mountain carving is actually larger than the Mount Rushmore carving," the narrator said as video showed how sculptors used drills and torches to sculpt the design, and showed footage of workers sitting on the ear of a horse and on the eyebrow of one of the soldiers to eat their lunches.

Some of the images sent chills down my back as we sat in the darkened room. The video we watched showed clips of the resurrection of the Ku Klux Klan at the base of Stone Mountain in 1915 through grainy images in a film, "Birth of a Nation." I knew many viewed the carving as a symbol of Atlanta's sordid history of race issues and the South's past with slavery.

Images of Izzy and Bailey Jackson, their parents Isaac and Rubelle, and that photo Laura Liz and I had once found in her attic kept playing through my head. I was grateful when Marge turned the lights back on and we all stood up to listen to her tell stories of today's park and test our attention with questions to the audience.

"Can anyone name any of the Confederate leaders' horses?" Marge asked.

I was surprised when I saw Joe's arm go up in the air.

"Lee's was Traveler, Jefferson Davis' was Blackjack and Stonewall Jackson's was Little Sorrel," he recited proudly.

"My goodness! That's the first time I've ever gotten a perfectly correct answer to that one!"

The crowd clapped and nodded at Joe as Mitchell slapped him gently on the back.

Marge awarded him with an accordion-style brochure filled with photos of Stone Mountain Park and its festivals. We teased and bragged on him the rest of the day.

"So the South shall rise again, huh, King?" teased Mitchell as we left the welcome center, his Boston accent adding a weird juxtaposition to his all-too-common stereotype.

"This is the twenty-first century, Mitch," said Joe flatly. "Atlanta's history is its history, but its future is so promising. Josie and I love the South and are proud to be Atlantans."

I was surprised at his sensitivity.

"Nothing personal, Joe. Just kidding around," Mitchell said.

The sky was its bluest blue and spring was already showing itself, despite it only being late February. Mitchell had noticed and commented on the beautiful day and amazing climate several times during the afternoon.

"Besides, next time you're in Massachusetts I'll take you to my witch's coven. We meet every Thursday night."

"Ha! I'll take you up on that. And a Sox game, too, buddy," Joe laughed.

Just one more difference between men and women.

The tension I feared would put a damper on the day was gone as quickly as my imagination had conjured it.

May 3 was an equally beautiful day. Tiny white sandwort flowers were in bloom along the edge of the walk-up path that was filled with climbers moving up and down the mountain. Some carried walking sticks, but others had children in umbrella strollers or babies in papoose backpacks. Some wore hiking boots, but most wore tennis shoes or even flip-flops.

The mountain was alive with happy people chatting as they enjoyed the spring day, none more than me as I celebrated my 50th year with my family. Once we got to the top, Joey opened his backpack and revealed Grace's carefully packed cupcakes and candles, along with three cards, a matchbook and a small package wrapped in white paper with a blue ribbon that I noted exactly matched the sky.

Grace put a candle in each of the four cupcakes, and we held them all together as Joey lit the candles and the three of them sang, "Happy Birthday." I opened each card. I could have picked out which one was from whom even before I saw their messages and signatures.

"This is the perfect day. I love spending it like this with you three," I said as Joe handed me the box.

"We have reservations for dinner at 7:30," he said. "We thought you'd like to wear this."

I opened the box and pulled out a string of pearls. I wasn't sure how to react: Joe had given me pearls for our first anniversary. I wore them all the time. These were a shorter length and would work well with many necklines, but they didn't look any nicer than the ones I already had. I looked at him, I'm sure he saw the question mark written across my face.

"Your mother wanted you to have them," he said. "She found them loose at the bottom of one of Annie Jo's dresser drawers and gave them to me. We had them restrung."

"And count them," Joey added. "There are exactly 50."

The pearls were a perfect gift. I hugged my children and husband and choked back tears as they welled in my head and chest.

"This is truly the perfect day," I said as I felt for the clip at the back of my neck and let the sun and blue sky clear my head of tears.

"Thank you all," I said smiling at each member of my family.

I hooked the pearls and imagined how much I would love them

with my favorite t-shirt and khaki shorts when I got the chance to look in a mirror.

Just as we were rising to make our way back down the mountain, a group of teenagers walked into view. They were laughing, and some of them were singing loudly and obnoxiously about flying in a beautiful balloon, no doubt fortified by alcohol.

They botched the lyrics and the tune, but I still recognized it easily.

I thought of Annie Jo's turntable and stack of Ray Conniff albums.

"That was one of Annie Jo's favorite songs," I mumbled, just as a pink and yellow hot air balloon came into view, no doubt precipitating the kids' song in the first place.

"Happy birthday to you, too, Annie Jo—a few days early, that is," said Joe as he saluted and extended his hand toward the balloon.

"Happy birthday, Annie Jo," the rest of us said together, waving and blowing kisses to the balloon.

I touched the pearls on my neck as I felt Joey's hand slip into mine as we traveled down the granite mountain.

"I love you, Mom," he said.

"I love you, too, Joey."

April 1, 1968

On a pretty spring Monday after getting dressed, I reviewed my note cards on the aquatic ecosystem for a first period test. Tommy and LaDarla and I had met at the Dalrymple's house Sunday afternoon to study together and we were certain we were ready. I was convinced I could make an A and cautiously optimistic for a 100.

Daddy had been working overtime and had some vacation days coming to him, so he left the day before to go fishing on Lake Lanier with Mr. Elliott. He'd planned to stay "until the fish quit biting" and sleep in the boat's hull. He told us to be ready for some fresh fish for dinner when he got home Monday night.

Mother was blowing smoke rings, and when I entered the kitchen to join Ansley and Daisy for breakfast, I noticed they perfectly circled the three lunch bags she had ready for us on the counter. I grabbed the one marked with a "J" and gobbled a few bites of Sugar Smacks. We heard the bus's brakes before it turned onto Duberry Street and Ansley and I screamed goodbye to Mother as we ran out the door.

On the bus, I saw Ansley whispering and laughing with Mary Ellen, and when I saw Mary Ellen crane her head and look at my lunch bag, I got curious and opened it up. I peered inside and instead of my usual lunch, I saw a box of orange Jell-O mix, no doubt for the weight, atop one of my bras. On the side was a note that I could see just enough of Ansley's handwriting to know it said, "April Fools!"

The bus stopped at the middle school. Ansley looked at me just long enough to let me know she'd seen me peek into the bag, but then turned and laughed with Mary Ellen while they stepped off the bus with Daisy behind them. They were still laughing when the bus pulled away.

I'd never hated her more. I vowed to spend the day figuring out how I'd get back at her.

The science test was multiple choice with one discussion question at the end. It was so much easier than I'd expected, and I couldn't wait for Ms. Preston to return the grades.

Tommy asked, "How did you answer that second discussion question on page 4?"

"Page 4! I only had three pages," I said.

I looked at LaDarla, and her eyes were as wide as mine. "What second discussion question?"

Tommy laughed and we groaned as he poked us both in the ribs with an annoying, "April Fools!"

Turns out he and LaDarla were equally confident that they'd aced the test.

I searched through my desk during homeroom to see if I could find enough change to buy lunch. I was 15 cents short, but was confident I could convince the lunch ladies to accept an IOU for the next day. The announcements came on the intercom with a message that all music classes would be canceled for the day and students that were scheduled for music should report to the gym for Bombardment. I groaned out loud.

Mrs. Byrd, the music teacher, opened the door and brought a stack of books to my homeroom teacher.

"They need me to sub over at Seaton Ferry Junior today," she told Ms. Preston as she scurried out the door.

We'd barely opened our books in social studies when Mr. Cook, the principal, came to our room and stood at the doorway. I'd always been friendly with the principal at Seaton Ferry Junior, but in high school so far, I'd had no real contact with Mr. Cook.

"Pardon the interruption, but I need to see a student from your class," he said. For one fleeting moment, the thought of another April Fools joke passed through my mind. Our other principals liked to tease the students once in a while. Our elementary school principal once dressed like a clown for an entire week because the students had met their book-reading challenge. Mr. Cook didn't seem to fit that though, I realized, as I heard him call my name.

"Please bring your belongings with you, Miss Flint."

My chest was solid and heavy as I looked around the room and saw all eyes on me. A million things ran through my mind as I gathered my books and pencil and tentatively stood and walked toward Mr. Cook.

Tommy stared at me until I met his eyes and he gave me a confident, "you're okay, you can handle this" kind of nod, but I couldn't for the life of me figure out what I'd done as I made the long walk to the front of the class and out the door with Mr. Cook.

"Everything is going to be fine, Miss Flint. You have done nothing wrong," he said as we walked down the hallway. "Do you have any other items you want to gather from your locker?"

"No, I don't think so," I stumbled. "Am I leaving school?"

"I'll let your mother fill you in. She's in the office with your grandmother."

I saw Annie Jo first. Her eyes were red and her hair looked like it hadn't been combed. Corkscrew curls — the kind she always combed smooth — circled her hairline. Conversely, though, she was standing tall and watching me carefully as I entered Mr. Cook's office. Mother was seated in a gold wing chair, but she lifted her head and then stood when I entered the room.

"Josie, there has been an accident," Mother said. Her dress was wrinkled and she had on a sweater that didn't match. "Annie Jo and I will take you home and we'll tell you what we know."

She walked across the room and hugged me tight. "We're all going to need to be strong, " she whispered as she kissed me on the head.

Then turning to the principal, she straightened her back and held out her hand.

"Mr. Cook, thank you for your assistance," she said with all the confidence of a woman greeting a guest at a dinner party. "Josie will be fine and we will provide an update to you and her teachers as soon as possible."

Her tone was stiffer than I'd ever remembered.

Annie Jo gave me a confident smile, but I saw it quiver on the side. She wrapped her arm around my neck as we headed out the door of Northbridge High School.

We walked in silence and my mind ran in thousands of places, but I couldn't stand it anymore.

"Is Daddy home?" I heard my voice crack as the words came out louder than I'd expected.

Mother looked at me sadly.

"What accident? What's happened?" I asked as Annie Jo opened the car door.

I got in the back seat behind Mother, and Annie Jo opened the right side back door and moved next to me with a big hug and a hand on my thigh. Mother turned around in the seat and looked at me carefully before she spoke.

"There was a boating accident, Josie. Early, probably around one this morning. A fisherman spotted Mr. Elliott's boat when the light came up. It had been hit by another boat and was filled almost halfway with water."

"Is Daddy okay?"

"No, Josie." She shook her head and swallowed. "He's not. The coast guard believes that both people on the boat died instantly. The police came to the house this morning and told me just after you girls left for school."

Annie Jo pulled me tighter.

She rubbed my head, and I sank deeper into the seat and tried to understand how to feel. I pictured Daddy, and my first vision was in the kitchen serving scrambled eggs to Ansley and Daisy and me. I thought of my View-Master as a picture in my head clicked into a new picture of him smiling at me as I presented my math test to him with a 99 and Mrs. Sanders' note about how to properly "dot an i."

I felt Annie Jo's soft hand on my head and I let out a wail.

I saw my mother wince at the sound that was coming from somewhere in a pocket of my chest that had never been heard before. Mother reached for my hand and her eyes filled with tears. My head felt like it was filled with concrete, and it was all I could do to keep it atop my shoulders.

I looked to Annie Jo for help, but despite the strength I could see her working to muster, she'd never looked smaller to me.

Mother turned back toward the front of the car and lifted her eyes to the rear view mirror as she looked at me sadly. I hadn't noticed before, but her eyes were red and swollen, and she didn't take them off of my reflection in the mirror.

"We are going to be okay, Josie. We are going to be just fine," she said. "Your daddy would want us to be strong, and that's what we're going to do."

"Let's get you home and get you both cozy under a blanket," suggested Annie Jo. "I'll make us all lunch, and we'll figure out what to do next."

The phone was ringing as we entered our home. Mother answered in the bedroom, while Annie Jo led me to the sofa and covered me with the black and white quilt and stepped into the kitchen to boil some eggs for egg salad.

I thought about my conversation with Daddy the day before, and visions of the day filled my memories: He'd quizzed me on the differences between lentic and lotic ecosystems on the way to church. Afterward, he asked me to describe the hydrologic cycle. Ansley had hummed a Beatles song as loud as she could to drown out my voice, so I added in a lot of detail to annoy her.

Daisy was skating with Vivian up and down the driveway and I was helping them tighten their skates when Daddy finished packing the car for his fishing trip. He hugged us tight, just like always, and threw Daisy and Vivian up in the air until they squealed just like he did with me when I was smaller. He was wearing his khaki shorts and an aqua shirt that looked nice with his eyes. He gave the horn a little toot like he always did when he drove down the street.

Mother had fixed spaghetti with salad and garlic bread for Sunday supper and had mentioned that Monday's dinner would probably be fish, if Daddy and Mr. Elliott got lucky on their trip.

We had watched a story about an orphan boy from Mexico on Walt Disney's "Wonderful World of Color" the night before, and I remembered thinking how much Daddy would have liked it. He would have been on the floor with us all surrounding a bowl of popcorn and would have asked us questions after the program to see how well we'd remembered silly little details.

Muffled sounds wafted from the bedroom. After a few minutes, I heard Mother hang up the phone and then close the bedroom door.

I tried to picture my father on that boat and wondered what he and Mr. Elliott were doing when the accident happened. Did they see the other boat approaching? Were their coolers filled with fresh-caught fish? Or were they asleep and hoping for good fishing in the morning?

How would we tell Daisy and Ansley? Why didn't Mother pick them up from school too when she got me? What will happen to our family without Daddy?

I wandered in to the kitchen as Annie Jo was cutting my egg salad sandwich into four triangles, just like she always did. I sat alone at the kitchen table as she brought me a glass of sweet tea. She kissed my head and then walked down the hall to Mother and Daddy's bedroom.

"Beverly? Can I come in?" she asked.

I jarred back to the present as I stared at the untouched egg salad sandwich.

My eyes welled with tears, and I looked at the chip on the side of our scalloped-edged dinner plate through glassy layers of tears. My shoulders felt numb, my bottom heavy and uncomfortable on the hard wood of the chair. Mindlessly I moved back to the living room with the sandwich untouched.

I burrowed under the quilt on the sofa as Mother answered one phone call after the next. I listened to her reassure one person after another that we would be okay. I could hear occasional quivers in her voice, but she'd quickly recover and it made me both proud and confused about how to feel. I looked at the clock at 4 o'clock and realized I'd fallen asleep for more than an hour.

I heard Mother talking in her bedroom, so I dragged the quilt down the hallway and peeked inside. She was sitting on the bed with Mrs. Baker, and her face was red and puffy. I didn't see Annie Jo.

Mrs. Baker walked over to me and wrapped the quilt over my shoulders and hugged me. "I'm so sorry, Josie," she said. "Your Daddy loved you so much, and he knew how much you loved him too."

Mother's skin was pale and her eyes were glassy. She had to steady herself against the bedside table as she stood. Straightening her skirt, she reached for her comb off the dressing table.

"Josie, honey, Mrs. Baker is going to stay with you for a few hours. Ansley and Daisy are at Annie Jo's. The police need to talk to me, and I'll need to start making plans with the church. Mr. Baker is going to drive me, and I should be back before bedtime."

She applied a fresh coat of lipstick and smiled at me. "We're going to be okay, sweetheart. You and I are going to have to be very strong for your sisters, but we're going to be just fine."

Mrs. Baker excused herself to finish dinner.

I didn't want to stay alone with Mrs. Baker, and I didn't want to face my sisters either. I wanted to turn back time and be back in the driveway with my Daddy quizzing me on the ecosystem.

I tried to imagine a scenario where the police might be mistaken. *Maybe Daddy and Mr. Elliott had found a terrific fishing hole on the other side of the lake and they were catching so many fish they didn't want to leave. Maybe it was a boat similar to Mr. Elliott's that had been in a wreck. Maybe Daddy swam to shore and he was trying to find a way to contact us. Maybe...*

I struggled to find any idea that seemed plausible.

Mother left the room and I opened Daddy's t-shirt drawer. A yellow one from our trip to Callaway Gardens the summer before was on top.

I pictured Daddy leading the line of Flints, each on our own bicycles, through the paths of the garden. He'd hold one or both legs or one arm at a time to the side, and we all followed like Monkey-See, Monkey-Do in a game we never planned or talked about after our bike ride. It was just a game, like so much of life with my Daddy.

I grabbed the shirt and held it to my face and stretched across his side of the bed as I sobbed, and sometimes wailed, until I saw Mrs. Baker standing at the door of the room.

"Are you getting hungry, sweetheart? Dinner is almost ready."

I couldn't bring myself to tell her the truth, so I lied and said, "A little."

Mrs. Baker had a chicken and noodle casserole cooking in our oven. She'd made enough for her family, so she called Donnie to come pick it up. She had the meal all packaged up and met him at the door when he arrived. I heard her tell him that I wasn't ready for company yet, so to put the casserole in the oven and make sure he and Dena cleaned up the kitchen after dinner.

I ate a bite and immediately felt sick. Mrs. Baker didn't push. I saw her scrape my plate into the garbage, and she offered to make me a cup of tea.

She put it in front of me and rubbed my back for a few minutes. I thought about the cup of tea Annie Jo had made for me the day I started my period and agreed that might be nice, but it just wasn't right either, and I sat at the table wishing this day could start over again.

I slept with Mother on Daddy's side of the bed that night, and Annie Jo kept Daisy and Ansley with her.

I woke the next morning to the smell of my father on the sheets. I was wearing his yellow shirt and clutching his pillow. Mother was already up. Shadows from the sheer curtains folded across the walls of my parents' room. Daddy had painted it "lavender mist" soon after we moved to Duberry Street. The sun filtering through the room was quiet and still, and it magnified the sounds of the birds chirping in the tree outside their window.

I found Mother in the kitchen drinking a cup of coffee and staring at the wall.

"Good morning, Josie. How did you sleep?"

"Okay, I guess. How about you?"

"Mmmm..." she said as she pulled me onto her lap.

I couldn't see her face as she said, "Josie there is something else I need to tell you. And this is especially hard."

My mind was reeling.

What's happening? Did Mother forget she had told me about the accident? What's harder than what I already know?

"It's Mr. Elliott, Josie," Mother said. "He didn't die in the accident."

"Will he be okay?" I asked. "Is Daddy going to be okay too?"

"No, Josie," she said firmly. "Your father died on impact. His body is at the funeral home, and we'll go there today. The police say the other boat was going almost 40 miles an hour when it hit the Elliott's boat."

"They think both people died on impact," she continued. "But Mr. Elliott wasn't on the boat when it happened. Someone else was."

I tried to process what she was telling me, but my mind was racing. I was having trouble guessing what she was trying to say, but my mind wouldn't even allow me to focus.

I was about to choke out a question when I heard my mother say, "It was Miss Paulk."

My heart stopped with a thud while a world of uncertainty filled my head.

How could that be? My Miss Paulk? How...

"Miss Paulk? On the boat with Daddy?"

I began to realize how naïve I sounded just as I spit out my next question, "Where was Mr. Elliott?"

"Josie, Daddy *told* us that he was going fishing with Mr. Elliott, but in truth, he *borrowed* Mr. Elliott's boat. He had *invited* Miss Paulk to go with him. She was supposed to be at school yesterday, but when she didn't arrive, the school called in a substitute. The police confirmed that the other body on the boat was hers."

I felt the heat of my heart bore through my body and shoot through the earth's crust. Donnie Baker's science project — a cross-section of the earth made from plaster of Paris — came to mind as I felt my heart drilling through the crust, the mantle, the outer core and the inner core.

Daddy and Miss Paulk?

What are we supposed to do now? What will happen to the Flints? Will everyone know? How could Daddy do this?

The reality hit quickly: Of course, everyone will know that Daddy and Miss Paulk were together. They probably already do.

Miss Paulk will never be at school again, and everyone will know why. An affair? Just once or many times? Did they know the other boat was coming toward them before it hit? Did they feel the impact of the wreck? Did they have on clothes when their bodies were found?

I turned to face Mother, and she looked pitifully sad. And small. Nothing like my mother Beverly Flint. She couldn't hold back any more and cried like I'd never seen her cry before, while I held her head and her shoulders as tight as I could.

My thoughts went to Daisy and Ansley.

That's why they're with Annie Jo. Momma is trusting me with this information first. Will she tell them too? Will Daisy understand? Can Momma and I keep this a secret from them? Should we? Does Annie Jo know this new information?

She calmed down and pulled a handful of napkins from the Tupperware napkin holder on the other side of the table to wipe her eyes and nose. I felt a will growing within her as she met my eyes, and I knew she was going to forge through this. She trusted me with the truth, and that somehow steadied me.

My mother was strong. How difficult this must be for her to share this with me. She was trying hard to treat me like an adult. Her honesty and solidness touched me.

How could this happen! How would we go on without Daddy? I want a Mulligan! I want to go back to the peace of Sunday morning.

I want my Daddy.

Mother stood up and poured herself a cup of coffee and a glass of orange juice for me and set it on the table. I thought about our drive to church and my science test note cards. It all felt so insignificant. And my heart so heavy.

I pulled the black and white quilt off the floor and wrapped it around my shoulders and arms.

"We'll need to get dressed soon and go pick up your sisters and Annie Jo," said Mother. "They want us at the church at 11:30 to talk about the service."

I picked up the juice and wandered into the garage.

Daddy's tools were neatly hung on the pegboard where they always were. I looked at the ceiling and noted for the first time just how methodical the yellow hooks he'd installed in the ceiling for our bicycles were. Clearly he'd measured the length of each bike so that when hung they were in a parallel line with just inches separating one from the next.

The cast scratcher he'd made for Daisy was hanging on a peg. Our old record player was sitting in a metal box on the counter between his small and large vices — no doubt in wait for its next inspired purpose, just like the old shower curtain pole that lay aside the metal box.

Three of his six fishing poles were lined up to the right of the window — each with its own set of perfectly lined hooks. He had kept his tackle boxes on hooks underneath, and both were gone.

There was a double picture frame resting at the shelf above his table saw. Mother's photo from their wedding was on the left. A photo of Ansley, Daisy and me was on the right. Daisy was just a baby. I was seated Indian-style with my legs crossed, and she was on my lap. Ansley was on her stomach with her patent leather shoes swinging in the back.

On the inside of the garage door was one of the posters Ansley had made when she ran for student council in sixth grade. The edges were warped, and the tape that held it to the door was turning yellow.

And over in the corner was a neat stack of the Georgia stadium seats that he still had left. I counted seven as I thought about how proud I was when he built the reading benches for my classroom. Just to the left I saw the scrap plywood that he'd cut the storyboard from for the theater.

An image of Miss Paulk and my father on the boat while he handed her an already-baited fishing pole filled my mind, and I was grateful when I heard the door open and saw Ansley walk in followed by Daisy and Annie Jo.

"We decided to come on over instead of waiting for you and your mother to pick us up," said Annie Jo. "Figured we could all use the walk."

Their eyes were red, and their faces were swollen. I knew Annie Jo would have told them, but I wondered if they also knew about the Miss Paulk part.

The situation was so personal, yet it was weighing on me that all my friends and teachers would know that Miss Paulk died while on a boat with my father. And, in fact, this was a school day, so my friends and all my teachers were at school and the rumors — the facts, actually — were already buzzing.

I could almost hear my View-Master click as an image popped into my head:

Mrs. Byrd standing at Mrs. Preston's desk. ""They need me to sub over at the Seaton Ferry Junior today," she'd said.

I ran to Annie Jo, and she opened her arms and waved for Daisy and Ansley to join us. I cried harder than I had to that point and just couldn't let go. By the time Mother came into the garage, the four of us were wailing uncontrollably. She picked up the quilt and put it around the four of us and then crawled right in the middle with her arms around us. We howled and cried — each of us louder than the next — for what seemed like ten minutes until our wails turned to wet sniffs.

Mother pulled out of the circle first and pinched her cheeks and swept her long fingers across her eyes.

"It's time to be strong, ladies," she said. "We are Lady Bug Flint Muffins." She looked deep into each of our eyes and lingered until we each looked back. "We are going to do this and we are going to be fine."

She carefully stretched her lips — with just the slight hint of faded "Blood Rose" by Mary Kay lipstick — into a smile, but I saw it quiver a bit on the side and hoped that my sisters hadn't noticed.

"Get dressed, Josie, and the rest of you freshen up, and I'll meet you in the car."

We all looked to Annie Jo as Mother lifted her shoulders and walked purposefully back into the house.

As we were coming out the front door to leave for the church, Mrs. Dean was walking across her lawn. She was carrying a bowl of tuna salad and a box of Ritz crackers and had a grocery bag under her arm. I thought about all of the meals Daddy had cooked for her and dropped off at her house and realized for the first time that she'd never done the same for us. In fact, though her head was lowered and she looked frightened, it was the first time she didn't seem crabby and mean to me.

"I made you and the girls some tuna fish salad, Beverly," she said. "I do hope you like it. I put sweet pickles in mine. I don't know if you do yours that way."

"Why, thank you, Gloria," my mother said. "You are *so* kind."

Momma pulled back her shoulders and turned both ways to look at us all behind her, as if to indicate we all were united in our pleasure of the tuna salad.

"Well, I really loved that Cooper, and I just can't tell you how sorry I am that this happened."

I looked up at Annie Jo and saw tears streaming down her face. She saw me look at her and blinked hard and smiled. She hugged Mrs. Dean and thanked her for the tuna salad.

"Oh, and there is some of your Tupperware in the bag," Mrs. Dean added. "From the beef and rice Cooper brought over last week. It was delicious," she added quietly.

Ansley took Mother's keys and the tuna salad and crackers into the house and then relocked the door as the rest of us waved to Mrs. Dean and then got inside the Rambler. Ansley got in beside me, and I moved to the middle, and we headed toward the church.

Gloria. I never knew that was Mrs. Dean's first name. I didn't like tuna fish, but I knew that she would miss Daddy too.

May 2003

Since Annie Jo's will had not been updated since Papa Ray's death, the attorneys had to file some extra papers. In reality, however, other than the equity in her duplex, her other assets offered little more than what would cover the funeral and hospital expenses.

I just felt fortunate that Allen was willing to take on all the filing and executor's duties.

Annie Jo's death had brought my sisters and me back together in a way that made me very happy. Daisy and I were talking daily, and Ansley and I, and sometimes Mother, were meeting for dinner at least once a week.

Like so many families, we had become a bit fractured with our own individual families over the past few years. Our gatherings were fun and social, but had become less meaty with lots of surface talk and niceties, but not a lot of deep discussions or honest soul-searching. Suddenly we were really interested in one another and were catching up on years of shallow talk and turning them into honest, caring relationships.

Ansley and I had a great visit to Auburn and climbed the dormitory stairs at least 25 times with Carly and Chip and filled the cars with boxes and books and blankets and clothes.

She called me on Monday to see if my thighs were throbbing as badly as hers were from all the stair climbing.

"Yes, they're killing me, but I figured with all your tennis, you wouldn't be feeling a thing."

"A different set of muscles," she answered.

"But here's why I'm really calling, Josie. You won't believe who I have a date with…"

"Who? Tell me."

"Kenneth Dalrymple!"

"Okay, that's weird. How did you finagle that?"

"He and his girlfriend broke up. I overheard him telling Doc. So I conveniently parked myself in the lobby of his office building this morning. I was all dressed up and told him I had an appointment with an accountant. That's why I just happened to be there."

"Nothing like giving him a little time after a break up, Ansley. Not to mention starting off a relationship with honesty…"

"Well, there's no time like the present. And, besides, it's not like we're related."

"Technically no. Still…"

"Plus, he asked me. Sounds to me like he's ready."

My mind went to LaDarla. We were the best of friends for four years. Inseparable for junior and senior years, but we drifted apart when she followed her brother, Winston, to Duke and I went to Georgia State.

"So I'm wondering if you have a copy of the Seaton Ferry yearbook from the year we were in the Vernal Equinox pageant. I want to bring it on our date."

"This date is getting weirder by the minute," I said.

"Do you have it? I wouldn't know where to look at Mother's."

"Yes, I think I know where it might be," I said.

"Will you look and let me know?"

"Yes, and Mother's birthday is next month. Let's talk about whether we want to all go in on a gift."

"Sure. That would be great. Call me about the yearbook."

I thought about the Polaroid photo of LaDarla and me in our caps and gowns with our heads tilted together so that both of our mortarboards were sitting catawampus on our heads. I'd just had my bangs cut and they were way too short. LaDarla had braces on her teeth that year, so she was trying to smile with her lips closed, but the shiny silver made a funny starburst reflection from the side of her mouth where her teeth were showing.

In another photo we were posing with Annie Jo and Mother standing next to me and Mr. and Mrs. Dalrymple next to LaDarla.

I wondered if that photo had been among Annie Jo's things and thought about the boxes I'd brought home from her place the first weekend we'd sorted.

I could picture the photograph perfectly, but wanted to look at it again. I wanted to examine the faces to see if there was any hint of the future in them.

I poured myself a glass of wine and carried it to the hall closet where I immediately eyed the boxes from Annie Jo's and on just one shelf up, a row of yearbooks from Seaton Ferry Junior, Northbridge High and from Joe's high school and college in North Carolina.

I praised myself on my Type A organizational skills as I pulled out a stack of the thinner books from Seaton Ferry Junior High School and settled into the comfortable chair in our guest room.

I opened the book to the teacher's page and quickly flipped to pass it by. The next page I opened was the one with Ansley's beehive.

April 4, 1968

Mr. and Mrs. Elliott were at the funeral parlor when we arrived. They spoke with Mother in the corner of the room in front of a large painting of a ship and I noticed how small my mother looked. They both hugged her and then nodded with an uncomfortable smile at each of the rest of us before rounding the room for a quick hug for each of us girls.

I wondered if he knew Daddy wouldn't be fishing alone when he asked to borrow the boat.

"It's going to be okay," Mrs. Elliott said kissing my head.

Annie Jo wore a pink jacket and black skirt I'd never seen. She signaled for me to stand beside her as the first groups of friends, neighbors and members of the church arrived.

The Grogans, our party line partners, greeted us as I moved to her and Annie Jo took my hand.

"I am full of fret to tell you this, Annie Jo, but I always thought you were Beverly's mother, not Cooper's," said Mrs. Grogan.

Mr. Grogan gave her a healthy nudge in the arm, and she quickly stammered, "Oh, I probably shouldn't have said that. I'm sorry. I always seem to say the wrong thing. What I really meant to say..."

"Never you mind, Mabel," said Annie Jo. "Beverly is my daughter just as much as Cooper is my son. I've loved her like a daughter since the day Cooper brought her home. And we are so pleased you came today to pay your respects."

I saw Mrs. Grogan cock her head toward Mr. Grogan and imagined her saying, "See?" She looked pleased with herself.

Mr. Grogan ignored the show and said, "Well, we are indeed sorry for your loss, Mrs. Flint. You have a fine family."

Then he bent his knees to be closer to my height and put his thumb under my chin to lift my face until I was looking straight into his eyes. "Josie you be strong for your momma and your sisters."

I nodded and he put his arm around Mrs. Grogan and looked back to Annie Jo.

"And I want you to know that I have made arrangements with the manager of the Piggly Wiggly to bring home a nice cut of beef roast for your family this week. May I drop it off at Beverly's?"

"That would be so kind of you, Mr. Grogan," drawled Mother as she approached the conversation. "And Mabel, thank you for coming. You look so pretty in *thaaat collaahhh.*"

Mrs. Grogan's dress was the color of the goldish brown tiles in our hall bathroom. It definitely wasn't my favorite color. I wondered if Momma really meant what she'd said.

Hank and Rita were there with Laura Liz. She hugged me but it was awkward. Tommy's family was there. So were a lot of people from the church, Mrs. Dean, the Bakers, the Faulkners and several teachers from the school including Mrs. Sanders. She was wearing a scarf fashioned into a headband, which I didn't think worked for her.

Across the room, I saw Mrs. Baker talking with Ansley's dance teacher, Miss Kate. I could tell that they were whispering. I was certain that they were talking about Daddy and Miss Paulk, and I felt ashamed.

I looked around and spotted Mother. She was talking with the Grogans again, but I saw her look toward the conversation and knew she also sensed their topic.

I watched her gracefully hug Mr. and Mrs. Grogan, excuse herself and walk straight to Miss Kate and Mrs. Baker. They looked at her nervously as she put her arms around the two of them.

"My girls are going to need a lot of support in the coming months," I heard her say. "I just want you two ladies to know how grateful I am that they have strong women in their lives like the two of you to help them."

"Of course, Beverly! Please, whatever you need..."

Mother smiled at them individually and then lifted her eyes to see the Dalrymples entering the room.

"If you will excuse me," she said and gracefully moved on.

It seemed nearly 300 times I heard that my Daddy "was in a better place." It confused and annoyed me, but I worked hard to let it go. I didn't want to give any more thought to what my Daddy was feeling than was already coming to the surface of my thoughts. Instead, I did my best to follow my Mother and grandmother's lead and stood tall as I greeted the guests that I'd hugged, shook hands with and nodded politely with over the course of the day.

Mr. Elliott spoke at the service on behalf of those who knew Daddy in a business way, but he didn't mention his boat or the accident at all.

Dexter was supposed to speak on behalf of the family, but at the last minute he gave his notes to Reverend Yates to read, claiming he just couldn't do it. He said that he was too upset, but I think he was also afraid of public speaking.

Reverend Yates talked about life in the hereafter and beauty beyond the pearly gates, but my head was swimming with new thoughts about Daddy and Miss Paulk and I found it hard to follow and pay attention. I held Daisy's hand for most of the service, but at one point she just let go and lay across Mother's lap.

Reverend Yates had a lot of nice things to say about Mother and her work with the suicide hotline. He introduced Ansley, Daisy and me, but it seemed like he changed the subject to something he was more comfortable with every time he mentioned Daddy. Afterward, Annie Jo's friend Anabelle Levy stood and thanked the ladies of the church for making a *beee-autiful* luncheon spread and invited everyone to join for a reception in the fellowship hall.

Mrs. Grogan grabbed my hand as we walked in the fellowship hall.

"I'm so sorry, Josie," she said sweetly. "I saved our copy of the *At-*

lanta Constitution this morning with your father's obituary. I know your Momma will want to have some extra copies." She tucked the newspaper under my arm, and I thanked her.

There was a crowd at the burial, and we spent more than an hour after the service talking among the tombstones. Daisy wanted to stand beside me every minute and asked several times if she could walk alone to the car, but Mother said no.

As we lingered there, Miss Paulk's family was holding a funeral for her in Mississippi. Several teachers and the principal had driven together to attend, I heard that the school couldn't find enough substitute teachers and had to bring four classes into the gym for Bombardment for part of the day.

LaDarla Dalrymple came to the burial site with her parents. She put an envelope in my hand as she was leaving and asked that I read it later at home.

After the reception at church, Anabelle and Annie Jo packed all of the leftover Jell-O squares, pimento cheese sandwiches and ham salad and brought it to our house. Dexter and Shalene and their kids came, and most of our neighbors stopped by.

"You Flint girls are going to be just fine," I heard over and over.

How? How would we be just fine?

The words grew more and more hollow to me as the afternoon passed and the Flints' new reality began.

I slipped into my room and placed LaDarla's note in my top drawer to read after everyone was gone. I walked in to Mother and Daddy's room and placed the newspaper Mrs. Grogan had given me on the nightstand.

Shalene had called the newspaper for the obituary for Daddy, so I'd heard it read several times. It said that he had died in a boating accident, but there was no mention of another victim.

I heard Reverend Yates in the front room speaking to everyone and closed the bedroom door and sat on the edge of the bed to read it again.

Pam Paulk's obituary ran the same day and on the same page. Pamela Jane Paulk was 28 when she died. She had the same birthday as Tommy Wilson. She'd been the Delta Delta Delta pledge trainer at the University of Mississippi and a sweetheart for the Phi Delta Thetas. It said that she was a beloved teacher at Seaton Ferry Junior High and that in addition to her parents, an older brother Peter, a younger sister Paige and a two-year-old nephew survived her. There was no mention of how she died.

I wondered if we would save the whole newspaper page, cut out both obituaries or just cut out Daddy's.

I wandered out of the bedroom and found Annie Jo in the living room chair talking with some ladies from the neighborhood and the church. I sat on the floor and leaned against her legs as they talked.

In the late afternoon, Mother made a pitcher of lemonade, which I helped her bring to each guest who was still at the house.

Daisy and Vivian were playing in Daisy's room with the door closed. I heard them giggling as I walked down the hall and wondered how I would maneuver the doorknob while holding both cups of lemonade when a sharp, ear-piercing bang roared from inside the room.

My heart dropped.

What was that?

A gunshot?

The lemonade slapped across the hallway wall and my feet as I dove for the door.

May 2003

"I think you should talk about it," Joe pleaded.

"My memories spill out like lava, and so many — most really— are so wonderful, but somehow it just doesn't feel right to praise him. He may have been the greatest father up until that point, but what he did was so wrong that I feel guilty remembering the good things."

I knew that what I was saying didn't really make sense, but I'd been handling my feelings this way for 35 years, and it was what I knew how to do.

I'd spent more than a week before in the guest bedroom looking through the yearbooks and photo albums and boxes of notes and treasures, even my fourth-grade diary. I had to cut the strap because I didn't have the key. Joe had found me there crying and even bawling and heaving on more than one occasion since I'd started my trip down memory lane.

"Tell me just one favorite story about your father," Joe said. "Just one. Just between you and me."

I smiled. Joe King was a good man. A good father. A man who truly cared about me. A man who found me interesting and had made that clear from the day I sat next to him in Piedmont Park. Thank God, my sandal strap broke when it did and put us on the same bench with an obvious conversation starter (my shoe), or who knows where I would have ended up or who I would have ended up with. What could have been a quick toss of the shoe into the trash can and a barefoot trek back to the car turned out to be dinner that night, a whirlwind romance of dancing, picnics in the park and a weekend trip to St. Simons, then a wedding, two children and 26 years of mostly solid marriage.

"Well, once he made this really cool bird feeder for my mother's birthday," I said. "It was shaped like our house, and it had a secret opening where he had hidden a tape player with bird calls he had recorded. Some of the sounds were his duck call, and some of them were Ansley and Daisy and me recording sounds we thought sounded like birds. It had a remote control so she could play the bird sounds from inside the house. When birds would sit on the feeder and start eating the birdseed, we'd turn on the sounds. They would stop and look around, but after a while they just stayed and ate and listened to our crazy sounds. Later they pecked at the recorder until it broke."

"I like that story," Joe said, hugging me and kissing my head. "Maybe tomorrow you will tell me another one."

"He loved to tinker," I said mindlessly. "And his inventions were wonderful. Maybe tomorrow I'll tell you about the cast scratcher."

"When you're ready, Josie. I'd like to hear all your stories about your father and what it was like growing up Flint."

"I'll tell you the cast scratcher story. But first let me show you this hysterical picture of Ansley and her beehive in the school's Vernal Equinox celebration."

"I almost forgot the best part," I said after pointing out how the camera angle exaggerated it even more. "She kept the beehive hairdo for school the next day, and when she got home, we found two pencils stuck in her hair. Some kid probably poked them in there, and she didn't even feel it!"

Joe and I laughed about Ansley's beehive hairdo and the cast scratcher, and I showed him pictures of LaDarla and all my friends. I even found the courage to turn to the teacher's page and show him Miss Paulk's photo. She looked exactly like the picture I had in my mind from all those years ago. I lingered just a moment, then turned the page.

One of the books showed a picture of Mrs. Jacobs' class and you could see the reading benches, so I told Joe about those. I showed him Laura Liz's picture and told him about the Faulkners' sons, Mason and Dixon. I set the yearbook aside to drop off at Ansley's before her date with Kenneth.

I found the picture from graduation in one of my albums and put it aside to show LaDarla. I looked at each face carefully, but I couldn't see any clue that the future might tie us together in a whole new way.

April 4, 1968

There was, in fact, a gunshot, but that's not the sound we heard. Instead, the sound from Daisy's room was a shelf breaking loose from the castle-shaped bookcase Daddy had built as it slammed to the bottom shelf while Vivian and Daisy climbed it to reach the Ouija board on the top shelf. They had already cleared the bottom shelf while playing with the Light Bright. When they stepped on the second shelf, their combined weights broke the shelf loose, slamming it against the bottom shelf. It sounded just like a gunshot.

Mother, Annie Jo, Dexter and Shalene came flying into the room. Vivian and Daisy thought they were in trouble for breaking the shelf, but Mother handed them the Ouija board and assured them that they were free to play. The adults traveled back into the living room with mutterings mixed between relief and sorrow.

I found Ansley, and the four of us sat on the bedroom floor and tried to think of a question for the board. Questions I couldn't say out loud kept pushing through my head. *Could bugs get inside the coffin? Could Daddy see us? Was he cold? Did Daddy love Momma or Miss Paulk more?*

I suspect the other girls couldn't find a question they wanted to verbalize to the Ouija either because we quickly switched to the Petticoat Junction game and then to Rummy.

The gunshot though — possibly at the exact same moment — was in Memphis, Tennessee. And it killed Dr. Martin Luther King, Jr., who had delivered the "I Have a Dream" speech that Mrs. Sanders had played for us on her tape recorder the year before.

Reverend King was a preacher at the church Bailey Jackson and his family went to. Rubelle and Isaac Jackson credited Reverend King and the people of Ebenezer Baptist Church with saving Bailey's older brother Izzy from childhood polio. Isaac was an Elder there, and Rubelle sang in the choir. I remember her praising the work of Reverend King at the Wilsons' New Year's Eve party when one of the guests asked about her church.

"*Lawwd*, God bless Martin Luther King, Jr., and God bless us all!" she said a bit louder than she'd meant to. Mrs. Wilson quickly stepped in and reminded Rubelle that the oyster tray needed to be refilled.

Mrs. Dean — Gloria, as I now thought of her — came across the street to tell Mother the news. Annie Jo, Dexter and Shalene, the only adults still at the house, were putting together a salad and warming a casserole that Mrs. Baker had dropped off when she came to the door.

"Turn on your television set, Beverly," she said. "Dr. King has been killed. He was shot on a balcony in Memphis."

The four of us ran from Daisy's room to see what the commotion was about as Dexter turned on the television. Turns out, the news was on every channel:

"At 6:01 p.m. tonight, civil rights leader Dr. Martin Luther King, Jr., was hit by a sniper's bullet. King had been standing on the balcony in front of his room at the Lorraine Motel in Memphis, Tennessee, when, without warning, he was shot. He was taken to a nearby hospital, but was pronounced dead just minutes ago."

"Dexter, go pick up Luke." Shalene said of her son who had been with a sitter during the services. Her voice was shaking.

From the corner of my eye, I saw Annie Jo lock the back door.

Mother picked up the phone. I'm not even sure whom she had intended to call, but the Grogans were using the party line.

"Oh, excuse me Mabel... Yes, I can wait, please pardon.... Yes, we did hear the news. So sad... Yes, I do appreciate your concern, and the pie you sent over too... Thank you, Mabel... Yes, Tuesday week would be wonderful for the beef roast... Thank you sweetie. Bye-bye."

I studied my mother's face and the faces of Annie Jo, Gloria, Dexter and Shalene, trying to understand why this news of Dr. King would affect us so personally. Why were we afraid here at our home in Atlanta? Were we supposed to feel sadness or panic? Why did everyone look so scared?

How could this be any worse than what had already happened?

I wanted my Daddy.

May 2003

"*Y*ou are one hot chick in this photo, Josie!"

I heard Joe calling me from the guest room and peeked around the doorway to find him looking at one of the photo albums I had pulled from the closet. It touched me to see him looking at them unsolicited, sharing my family memories as if they were his own. And made me proud of my family and my memories and to have brought my handsome husband Joe King into our Flint family fold.

Joe had little family. His mother died when he was just 8, and his father died in a nursing home when he was still in college. Long before I met him, he had lost his brother to a drug overdose and lost touch with his sister, whose last-known address was a commune in New Mexico.

We took a vacation to Italy in 1978 to meet his favorite uncle and aunt. He was proud to introduce me to his mother's brother, Uncle Leon, who lived in a farming village about 50 miles northeast of Rome. Leon had not seen his sister for more than 10 years before she died and had never met Joe's father but Uncle Leon had sent the family Christmas cards every year with a long, newsy letter about life in Italy, and I think Joe always felt like it was the home that loved him in a way that his own really never could.

Uncle Leon and his wife Gertie were gregarious, full of life, and were wonderful hosts. They introduced us to everyone in their village — the baker, the fishmonger, the innkeeper and the man at the post office who spoke no English at all — and, of course, to all the relatives Joe had never met or perhaps heard of. They wanted us to feel part of the family and despite the language limitations, we did. We drank wonderful wine, toured the countryside in Umbria and made a weekend trip to Florence, ate cheese and breads and pastas and gnocchi. We toured the museums and churches and took more than 1,200 pictures. We left after ten glorious days in the country with promises to go back, but despite grand plans to make it happen, it never did. The last letter from Uncle Leon included the sad news that Aunt Gertie had fallen over dead while hanging out laundry.

There are a couple of cousins from his father's side in North Carolina, but my big family was definitely a plus for Joe who loved the big family gatherings as much as I did. My mother loved him. He and Trey were great friends before Trey and Ansley divorced, and he's a loving uncle to both Charlie and to Ansley's twins. He warmed up to Annie Jo the day they met.

Joe's one-man commercial development business was so successful that he was swooped up by Atlanta's oldest and largest commercial development firm after just six years in the business. He was named a vice-president, has a corner office on the penthouse of the city's tallest building and gets to wine and dine investors one night and be wined and dined by architects, materials vendors and large-scale construction teams the next.

Our marriage has been strong — with exception of a seven-year itch that lasted almost two and a half years, but counseling and a date night ritual we really stuck to for at least a year pulled us out.

Photo albums were in neat stacks around him as I sat down to join him.

"What picture are you talking about?" I asked.

"This one. You are rocking some serious bellbottoms!"

He held up a black and white photograph that had been taken outside a restaurant in the Jellico Mountains. Snapped during a weekend trip to Tennessee with Mother, Daddy, Annie Jo, Ansley, Daisy and me, so I'm not sure who had taken the photo as we were all accounted for in the two-tiered line up.

Annie Jo taught me to sew, and we started with the bellbottom pants suit in the photo. We had picked out a Simplicity pants suit pattern at J.C. Penney and the loudest floral print fabric that the store carried in bright blues and reds and yellows. We spread the fabric, folded with wrong-sides together, across her living room floor and she showed me how to line the pattern's arrows against the grain of the fabric and pin and cut.

She had me practice on scrap fabric adjusting the sewing machine's speed and reversing to lock a stitch, but I was too anxious to put the pants suit together and didn't practice long.

We began with the tunic that had darts. Annie Jo showed me how to mark the dart with a metal wheel and stitch. I caught a piece of the bodice inside one of the darts for a few stitches so I had to take out one of the darts with a seam ripper, but Annie Jo said that knowing how to undo mistakes was a big part of successful sewing. Once that was fixed, I stitched the sides together, and we pinned up the hem and turned to the pants before starting on the hand sewing.

"Annie Jo, do you think we could change the pattern of these pants to make them have a wider bellbottom?" I asked.

"Of course, we can! This is your creation, Josie!"

I wasn't expecting that, even from Annie Jo. After all, it was my first attempt at sewing.

"We could even make a wedge from a coordinating piece of fabric to make the bell of the pants," she added.

Visions sharpened and colors intensified as my mind filled with possibilities in a life-changing moment.

We found a remnant of fabric that matched the yellow in the flower print, measured my leg from the knee to the ground and made our own triangular-shaped pattern piece to cut out of the yellow fabric. Then we pinned the outside leg seam to the knee and instead of taking the seam all the way to the bottom, we stopped and I sewed the yellow wedge — right sides together — to the pants seam.

I loved it.

And there was enough extra yellow fabric that we made our own pattern for a sash to tie around my hips.

It was the greatest outfit ever.

Ansley was insanely jealous of it and begged Annie Jo to teach her to sew too. She did, of course, but her creation just wasn't as wonderful as mine. I wore it until the bellbottoms were well above my ankles and the tunic darts became somewhat pertinent to my finally budding boobs.

And my adoration of Annie Jo Flint...

"Oh God, I miss her, Joe!"

I fell into his arms and cried uncontrollably. We both laughed when an exceptionally loud snort came from deep in my throat and I finally gained control. I fingered the photograph from his hand and stared at it through my tear-filled eyes.

"I did look good, didn't I?" I admitted. "Let me tell you about this outfit..."

April 1968

The Dalrymples gave Rubelle Jackson a week off with pay after Martin Luther King, Jr. was assassinated. She and Isaac took their boys, Izzy and Bailey, to stand among the mourners that lined Atlanta's downtown streets from Ebenezer Baptist Church to his alma mater, Morehouse College, for a three-and-a-half-mile procession after the church funeral. King's casket was carried on a wooden wagon pulled by two mules.

Reverend King delivered his own eulogy. His family had a tape recording of a sermon he'd given earlier in the year that played at the service. In that sermon, King had described his funeral wishes and requested that there be no mention of his awards and honors, but rather his work toward human rights.

"Yes, if you want to, say that I was a drum major. Say that I was a drum major for justice. Say that I was a drum major for peace. I was a drum major for righteousness. And all of the other shallow things will not matter."

The news had pictures of his wife, Coretta Scott King, and of their children at the funeral. Their little girl, Bernice, had just turned 5 years old. She was lying across her mother's lap wearing a beautiful little white dress just like Daisy lay across Mother's lap at Daddy's funeral.

Later a man who had escaped from a prison in Missouri a year before was identified as the killer. Police found a rifle and the fingerprints of James Earl Ray in a boardinghouse that had a view of the Lorraine Motel. He wasn't found until mid-summer at a hotel in London where he had been staying.

Riots broke out all over the country — Tallahassee, Chicago, Boston, Detroit — but newscasters noted Atlanta was relatively quiet.

Still, all of the neighborhood families huddled in their own houses and parents insisted their children stay inside. The weather was
turning warm and azaleas were blooming all over the neighborhood,
but no one was playing kickball or Bloody Tiger.

Annie Jo stayed at our house and slept in Daisy's room. Daisy slept
with Momma for a long time even after Annie Jo went back home.

Watching the television coverage with Momma and Annie Jo took
our minds off thinking about Daddy, but it also kept us at home
longer. Mother had originally told Mr. Cook that I would be back to
school the Monday after Daddy's funeral, but the school was closed for
several days after Reverend King was killed, and many people didn't go
back to school for days even after it reopened.

I always thought about Daddy when Momma or Annie Jo would
call us for dinner because I knew it wouldn't be Daddy's shish kabobs,
fried toast or barbecue. The casseroles that kept coming from neighbors and ladies at the church were all beginning to taste the same.

The note that LaDarla had given me at the funeral included a little
silver ring.

*Dear Josie, I just want you to know that I thought your Daddy was the
most handsome and sweetest father I've ever met. He always made me smile
and he was so proud of you and your sisters. I don't know what I would do if
something ever happened to my father. I guess I just wanted you to know that
I'm thinking about you and saying my prayers that your family will be O.K.
I'm enclosing a ring. I have two of them and I'd like to wear one and if you
would like to wear the other one, it will be my way of showing you that you are
a very special friend to me and that I am so sorry for you because I know you
will really miss him. Love, LaDarla*

I slipped the ring on my pinkie. It was a little too tight for any
other finger and I tucked her note away in a treasure box I kept inside
my closet.

I hadn't seen LaDarla or Tommy or any of my friends since the
funeral — and since Martin Luther King's assassination — and I wondered if they were staying inside their houses too. No one had called

me either, and I wondered if they just didn't know what to say.

I thought about Miss Paulk and tried hard to push the visions of the night on the boat out of my head. But I knew they would never stop threatening. And I knew that there was little doubt that my friends, all the teachers, all the parents were talking about my father and Miss Paulk and the tragedy that had put a mark on my heart and torn my family apart.

I wondered what happened to her yellow Mustang with the Ole Miss and Tri Delt decals on the back. Had her parents known about my father? Did they know he was married and had three daughters?

Miss Paulk definitely knew. In fact, one of them was one of her favorite students, or at least she'd told me so. I thought about the night Daddy kissed her hand at the school's open house.

"Please, call me Cooper," he'd said.

June 2003

"Your grandmother's lease with the current tenant is more than three years old," Trey's email said. "The street is ripe for a tear-down. I'd recommend trying to sell it as-is. And according to Allen, it looks like the current tenant has missed at least four payments over the past 18 months. Probably best to give him notice and put it on the market."

Joe, Allen and Trey had remained good friends even after Trey and Ansley had divorced. I'd asked Trey for his help when it came time to figure out what to do with Annie Jo's duplex because he had been working in residential real estate since the twins were early teenagers.

Annie Jo's current tenant was a retired bus driver whom we rarely saw. He had lived in the left-side duplex for easily five years, but it seemed Annie Jo had slackened with her paperwork and had just let him remain without an updated lease. Tank Andrews was his name. He was the only tenant I can remember that hadn't become a great friend of Annie Jo's. Nice enough man, just very quiet and to himself.

"Can you help with the letter? Do we need to have an attorney write it?" I typed back to him, hit send and turned off my laptop assuming he was busy and I'd check his response later.

Trey Parker and Ansley met at the University of Georgia when she was starting as a freshman and he was an orientation leader. They began dating within weeks of her first class and were together for her first two years. His last name is the same as her middle name and mother's maiden name — Parker — so when they reunited a few years after college and eloped to Las Vegas, she became Ansley Parker Flint Parker.

According to Ansley, the coincidence was proof that they were "meant to be" for quite a while, but then she grew sick of people talking about it and would snap at anyone who mentioned it. Her hot and cold temper was a lot like Mother's when Mother was younger, but with an unforgiving sting. Her temper and his lack of tolerance for it turned out to be the end of their relationship and she and Trey divorced before Chip and Carly finished high school.

Ansley had not worked since the day they got married, but her divorce settlement provided a lifestyle that was barely different from the one she had enjoyed before, so when her short-lived stints working at a boutique and serving as a receptionist scheduling appointments at a fancy spa didn't work out, she just reverted to her tennis, massage, lunch-with-friends, mani-pedi routine.

They had sold their house and split the assets so she was now in a two-bedroom townhouse. The space was tight when the twins were at home, but Trey was close by and they had kept an amicable relationship, so often Chip would stay at his place and Carly would stay with Ansley.

I dialed Daisy's number just as Grant Greystone walked into my office. I was afraid to have him hear me discussing more personal business.

"Hello. This is Josie King," I said as soon as I heard her say "hello." "Would you mind if I called you back in an hour or so? This isn't a good time to talk after all."

I didn't even wait for her response before I hung up the phone. I knew I would have to apologize for that crazy call soon, but I turned my immediate attention to Mr. Greystone. Bud had been a great cover for my distractions, but I was feeling the guilt.

Mr. Greystone wrinkled his eyebrows and looked at me sideways, no doubt suspecting my poorly executed cover.

"Josie, I want you to put your concentration on a new project for the next few months or so," he said. "A pitch for the city. The mayor is interested in a re-brand of Atlanta and we have the chance to pitch the work."

Very exciting project. Very time-consuming project too. I was going to have to focus on work. Maybe this new project was just what I needed to force me out of the family's affairs a bit. After all, there were plenty of us to share responsibility for the family business and Annie Jo's estate.

Our firm was well suited for the work. We coordinated media for The King Center — the Martin Luther King Center for Nonviolent Social Change — and the production of many of its events. Also, the city's convention director came from our firm.

"Interesting project!" I said.

"I'd like to partner with Holland Cathcart for the broadcast media end of the project, and I'd like you to head up the proposal," Greystone continued.

"I'd love to, Grant. Thank you for your confidence. We would be perfect for this project. Do we have a scope of work or RFP I can look at?"

"The city is holding a query session downtown on Friday. The proposals will be due August 15. I'll have the details forwarded to you and Bud. See if you can get together with our contacts at Holland Cathcart in advance."

"By the way," he said as he stood in the door frame of my office. "How is everything going at home? Since your grandmother died and all."

"The estate is almost wrapped up. We're all doing fine. Thanks for asking."

Bud stepped behind him, and the two of them nearly danced as Grant turned to move away and head back to his office. Bud was holding a slip from the receptionist's desk carbonless message book.

"Your sister Daisy called," he said. "She just said to tell you, 'What the... ?' She said, 'Just write a big question mark.'"

"I know what that's about," I said. "Give me a few minutes to call her back and then let's go downstairs for a coffee. I need to fill you in on what you and I are going to be very busy with the next month or so."

"Sounds good," he said.

"I want to hear about your plans with Jill too..." I started, but then nodded, held up one finger and waved him on as I heard Daisy pick up the phone again. He understood and gave me a thumbs-up as he rounded the door frame.

"Okay, Josie King," Daisy said. "What was that all about? Are you Queen Josie King now?"

"Sorry. Really," I dropped my voice despite the solid walls of our well-soundproofed offices. "My boss walked in just as you picked up and I've been feeling guilty about all the time I've been spending on non-work work, if you know what I mean."

"I do. I've been feeling bad about all the time Allen's been putting into it too," she said.

"Well, here's a little more. Trey says that Annie Jo didn't have a current lease with Mr. Andrews. I don't know if that complicates things or makes it easier — or if Allen already knows that, but he's recommending we sell the duplex as-is. He thinks a developer will want to tear it down and start with something new."

"No lease with Tank? Why is his name 'Tank' anyway?"

"No, and no idea. Just wanted to let you know."

"Kidding. I think Allen knows that. He and Trey spoke last night. We should be able to finish clearing her side with one more visit. Then assuming we can get Tank out, we should be able to get it on the market within the month."

"Perfect," I said. "I'm sure I can make another day of it this weekend or next."

"What's the process for getting Tank to move, though?"

"I've asked Trey for advice on that. I'll let you know when I hear. How's Charlie?"

"Actually, it's almost time for his bus, Josie. I'd better run. Let's talk soon!"

I hung up the phone and worked to pull my mind back to the next thing on my list: *Ahh, the Atlanta branding proposal, of course.* I grabbed my wallet and headed to Bud's desk, ready for some coffee.

April 1968

$\mathcal{I}$ wore the silver ring that LaDarla had given me when we finally went back to school after the Easter holiday. She hugged me when she saw it and put her arm around my shoulders as we walked down the hall, though neither of us knew what to say.

The reaction from my friends was mixed. Some hugged me and some told me how sorry they were to hear about my daddy. Others dropped their eyes and pretended not to see me when I walked down the hall or entered the lunchroom.

The teachers did the same. Mrs. Preston asked me to stay after science class. "Josie, I just wanted to let you know that I would love to talk with you as you deal with all you're going through," she said. "Please let me know if you need someone to talk to. I actually have experienced a situation not a lot different from yours and I'd love to help."

I hurriedly thanked her and ran out the door, my face on fire from embarrassment. My father had died and in and of itself, that was impossible to fathom and excruciating to bear. But the stigma he left us with was written all over the faces of everyone I saw: *They were embarrassed for me. Or they felt sorry for me. Or they knew. Or they had heard.*

Some even snickered. I saw Belinda and Candy whispering. When they saw me, they both looked embarrassed and then started giggling.

I hadn't seen or heard from Laura Liz since the funeral until I saw her staring at me from across the lunchroom. She didn't wave or even smile, but she followed me when I got up to walk out a few minutes later.

"Josie," she whispered and when I turned around, "I just wanted you to know that I'm really sorry."

"Thank you, Laura Liz. I appreciate that."

She managed a pitiful smile, turned toward her locker and that was that.

Momma, on the other hand, was standing tall, smiling and doing everything she could do to keep some normalcy in our home. She cooked dinner — or reheated neighbor's casseroles — every night, and tucked us into bed spending an extra amount of time with each of us, just stroking our hair or holding our hands. But the bags under her eyes had starkly altered her normal beauty, and I often heard her crying in her room after she thought we were asleep.

Mrs. Baker often came over in the evenings just to talk or help her prepare dinner. Reverend Yates or someone from the church called our house several times a week. And Shalene and my mother became closer. She would bring a pie or a casserole over at least once a week, and she and Momma would sit in lawn chairs sipping iced tea and talking for hours.

Annie Jo met the school bus when Ansley and Daisy got off every day. The three of them would be working on homework, talking and having a snack when my bus dropped me off 40 minutes later. She worked hard to keep us busy on the weekends too and would invite us over to her house for cooking or a craft or some kind of outing every Saturday morning.

Just before school let out for the summer, Shalene invited Momma and Mrs. Baker for a "girls weekend" at the lake at her trailer on Lake Sinclair.

Annie Jo had planned to stay with Ansley and Daisy and me, but I got home from school the day before Mother was leaving and Annie Jo wasn't there.

Mother was packing her bags for the trip and Ansley and Daisy were watching television.

"Josie, there's been a change of plans," she said. "Annie Jo isn't going to be able to stay with you and your sisters. The doctor thinks she has a case of shingles."

"Shingles? Who will stay instead?"

"She's had a painful rash, and it appears to be blistering. The doctor wants her to rest and stay home for a while," she said. "But she's made other arrangements for each of you so I can still go with Shalene to the lake."

"What arrangements?" I was feeling panicked.

"Well, Daisy will stay at Dexter and Shalene's so she can play with Vivian and help take care of Luke. Ansley has been invited to stay with Mary Ellen's family. Annie Jo has made arrangements for you to stay with Laura Liz at the Roberts' house."

"The Roberts!" I screamed. "You know I'm hardly even friends with Laura Liz anymore! No way, Momma. I'm not going!"

"Josie! Rita was thrilled for you to stay with them this weekend. She's really wanted you and Laura Liz to mend whatever it is that has torn you two apart."

"No! I can't go there, Mother," I screamed.

"Josie, you and Laura Liz were closer than sisters! There is no reason you can't stay friends, even if you grow apart."

"Why can't I stay with the Dalrymples? Or I could stay here by myself," I offered. "I'm in high school. Please Momma!"

I noticed again the dark circles under her eyes. She was really looking forward to this getaway.

"Annie Jo has this all arranged, Josie..."

Tears filled her eyes and I could see that she was trying hard to find a solution.

"Maybe Shalene could postpone..." she said quietly.

My initial thrill at the thought of postponing gave way to guilt.

"No. No, it's okay. I'll stay with Laura Liz." I ran to my room, trying to imagine how awkward the Roberts' house was as Laura Liz was hearing this same news.

Momma came to my door and leaned against the frame. "Josie," she said.

"I don't want you to miss this trip, Momma. It's fine. Really."

The telephone rang before I could rewind the whininess. Rita told Mother that it was all arranged and that I should walk home from school with Laura Liz. She would meet me in front of the school after sixth period. She even told Mother that she'd bought a used car since Butch had been driving their truck, and that she'd be happy to drive us to the movies or the Dairy Queen while I was there.

Weird. Our mothers are arranging our schedules like they did when we were in elementary school. I assumed Laura Liz was as upset as I was.

July 2003

The Atlanta branding proposal requested creative development from the five firms pitching, culminating with back-to-back one-hour presentations on a single day.

The preparation schedule was grueling — we had barely more than six weeks — and had it not been such a high-profile project, MHG would have likely passed on it entirely. Requiring up-front creative is frowned upon in the industry. There was more than 125 years of combined experience between the five firms pitching, but when Bud and I met with the principals at Holland Cathcart, we all agreed that the effort required was worth the prize.

We set up a meeting schedule of 90-minute meetings three times a week for initial brainstorming and "blueprinting" and then put together our team of designers, copywriters and videographers between our companies' resources.

Joe and I passed on a weekend invitation to LaDarla and Greg's beach house in St. Mary's, Georgia, because the pitch preparation filled the last few weekends as well as almost 90 percent of the rest of our billable time toward other clients. I was confident with our ideas, but concerned about the amount of time, effort and talent we were putting into the speculative account.

Bud canceled his reservation at Atmosphere and postponed his proposal to Jill for the second time.

I was grateful that my children were old enough not to feel the strain that my summer work schedule would have made on them had they been younger, but I was feeling no less guilty about the time I was spending away from them, from Joe and from the final stages of clearing Annie Jo's estate and getting her duplex on the market.

Tank Andrews agreed to move out of Annie Jo's duplex and in with a daughter in Macon, but did not come current with the four months of rent he owed. According to Trey, Tank's daughter picked him up in a beat-up sedan and they carried away only a few suitcases and an old television. They left the apartment in shambles and full of hand-me-down furniture, and old electronics like CB radios and reel-to-reel projectors. We discussed the options of suing for the back rent but in the end, opted to drop it entirely.

Joey found a friend who paid $400 for all the electronic equipment. Mother found a shelter that was willing to pick up the furniture and she, Joey and Chip spent a Saturday clearing his side of the duplex and hauling the trash to the street. Annie Jo made many decent business decisions on her own, but had definitely faltered in the past few years. We opted to move on to get the estate settled and on with our lives. I was proud of how each of us pitched in without a lot of disagreement. Whatever additional money we might recover was simply not worth the time and effort.

It occurred to me, though, that the guilt was inescapable. When I wasn't feeling bad about the time I was spending on personal business, I was feeling guilty that I wasn't being as helpful to my family as I should. I made it to the first half of the final cleanup day at Annie Jo's, but I had to meet the videographer to direct some footage for the pitch in Olympic Park in the afternoon. Ansley and Kenneth, who ended up running the Peachtree Road Race together, had become inseparable and took up the slack.

The weeks passed, and we were all getting back to our individual routines. I was grateful for the break, but missing the closeness we had enjoyed when we were speaking daily.

May 1968

$\mathcal{M}$other agreed to drop off my suitcase for the weekend with Laura Liz at Annie Jo's as she and Shalene left town. I assured her it would be a good idea for me to check in on Annie Jo after school before I walked over to the Roberts' house. She'd already talked to the doctor who said that shingles would rarely be contagious except to those who had not had the chicken pox, and all three of us kids had them the year before we moved to Duberry Street, so she didn't refuse.

I saw Laura Liz at school and passed her a note to let her know that I would be walking with my bags from Annie Jo's before dark. Mother told me I should go directly after school, but I lied in my note and told Laura Liz that I needed to get Annie Jo her dinner before I could come over.

I packed my pajamas and toothbrush, my bathrobe, underwear and a bra, two pairs of shorts and two shirts in one of Daddy's University of Georgia duffel bags, and it was sitting on the front porch when I got to Annie Jo's door.

The front door was unlocked, as usual, so I pulled the bag in, set it inside the door with my books and went inside to check on Annie Jo.

Annie Jo was asleep under her covers and had drooled a huge wet spot on the pillowcase. She didn't hear me come in, so I walked back into the living room and picked up a magazine. When I'd finished and she still hadn't woken, I turned the television on with the volume very low and quietly closed her bedroom door. She didn't even stir.

I was watching "The Match Game" when she finally opened her door. Her arms were blotched with a deep red rash, her face was flushed and she still had flaky, dried drool on the left side of her face.

"Hi, Sweetheart," she said in a voice that clearly needed some warm-up.

"How are you feeling?" I asked. "Did the TV wake you up?"

"No, of course not. I've been asleep for hours, I'm afraid. I'll never sleep tonight if I don't get up."

She offered to fix me a snack, but I saw her struggling to pull open the refrigerator door and assured her I was there to take care of her. I poured a glass of milk and pulled some cookies from the cookie jar, but Annie Jo said she'd really like a cup of coffee, so she gave me instructions from the kitchen chair and I made a small pot.

We watched the rest of "The Match Game" and 'The Art Linkletter Show" and then went out on the back porch swing. I could tell she was in a lot of pain.

"I'll fix your dinner before I leave, then you can go back to sleep if you'd like," I said.

"Anabelle brought some vegetable soup by and a carton of the most beautiful strawberries you've ever seen," she said. "If you wouldn't mind heating up the soup, I think I would like to lie back down after I eat it."

I heated the soup and cut the strawberries into a bowl and watched her eat half-heartedly until she finally admitted she would just like to rest.

"Your Momma said you'd be walking to Laura Liz's house, so best get going before it starts to get dark, Josie. I'll be just fine here."

"Maybe I should stay here with you after all, Annie Jo. I'm sure the Roberts would understand."

"No, no. I just need to sleep and you don't need to watch me do that," she said. "You and Laura Liz should be having some fun. I'm glad you're going to get to spend some time with her."

I took the long way to Laura Liz's house dreading the weekend that was sure to be awkward.

Hank was in the living room smoking a cigarette and watching a western show when I got there. He called Laura Liz and she came out of her room and mumbled, "Hi. You want to come to my room?" with a vague enthusiasm.

We sat on her bed and she showed me some drawings that Dixon had made for her. One was a heart with some tiger claws wrapped around the sides with a sun rising from the top. He'd drawn her name in a fancy script inside the heart. Most of the others were of cars or cats.

"He really is sweet, Josie. I wish you knew him better," she said.

I was trying to think of how to respond when she added, "And I wish we were still best friends."

Tears felt like they might be building behind my eyes, but instead of letting it happen, I asked her about her plans for the summer, her dog Amos, and finally added, "I do like Dixon's drawings. That's really sweet that he gave these to you."

The ice was broken and we talked about school, summer, boys and parents like we'd never stopped.

"You know the Faulkner twins live right across from Annie Jo, right? And across from Butch too, for that matter."

"I know, but I've only seen them there a few times," I said. "You know Annie Jo is sick with shingles, right?"

"My momma told me. Maybe we can go visit her while you're here and make sure she's got food and things," she said. "I miss her so much."

"She'd love to see you too."

Rita opened the front door and hollered for us to help her with groceries.

"You've already had your supper, Josie?"

I lied and told her I'd eaten vegetable soup with Annie Jo, but I saw Laura Liz wrinkle her eyes a bit when she heard me say that. She knew I hated vegetable soup.

"Well, I thought I'd make you girls some popcorn later tonight if you'd like."

"That sounds great," I said realizing I was starved.

We unloaded the sacks of groceries — mostly frozen foods, chips and four six-packs of Coca-Cola — and put them away before heading back to Laura Liz's room.

We spent Saturday walking to the convenience store and the dirt hill, playing cards and washing Rita's car.

Laura Liz was still asleep when I woke up on Sunday morning. It was already past 10 a.m. I was listening to the birds from her opened window and enjoying the quiet when I heard Butch's truck pull through the gravel that made up their driveway.

I could hear the high-pitched squeak of the screen door even over his "Momma? Momma?" Then, "Rita!" in a much meaner tone. "Are you home?"

"Shut the racket, boy," came from Rita and Hank's room, and I heard rustling and Hank cussing under his breath. Their dog Amos started barking in the backyard and ran through the back door's dog-gie opening that Hank had cut himself and then covered by screwing strips of thick plastic to the top of the opening.

Laura Liz pulled herself out of bed and groaned. I pulled on my bathrobe, and we followed Butch's voice to the kitchen.

We found him looking at a note in Rita's handwriting: *Gone to the fruit stand. Be right back.* Underneath, she had drawn a heart with an arrow sticking partly through.

Hank emerged wearing a pair of sweat pants and no shirt. Laura Liz looked at me, clearly embarrassed, and suggested we go back to her room.

When Rita returned, she made scrambled eggs and cut up a water-melon. We made ourselves a plate, but took it to the backyard while Butch argued with Hank and then with Rita. Finally I packed my duf-fel bag, and Laura Liz and I announced that we were going to check on Annie Jo.

She was awake when we arrived and had showered and dressed. She was wearing a house dress, and I could see that her legs were cov-ered in the rash too. She unbuttoned her dress to show us her chest and stomach and described the pain as "little tiny knives cutting all over my skin."

"But I do feel somewhat better," she added.

She took us into the back yard where we staked some of her tomato plants, and then we all ate Popsicles while sitting on the porch. Mason Faulkner walked out the front door of his house, and Laura Liz jumped up. She looked back at me with a big cherry Kool-Aid Popsicle stain around her mouth, but I didn't stop her when she said, "Let's go say 'Hi.'"

Annie Jo handed me the dishtowel she had in her hand and I wiped my mouth roughly, knowing that my mouth was no doubt just as stained. Annie Jo looked at my mouth, nodded, and I followed Laura Liz across the street.

Mason was surprised to see us running across the street. After Laura Liz introduced us, he barely mumbled, "Yeah, I know Josie from school," before dropping his eyes to his feet.

"Is Dixon here?" she asked.

"I think he's in his room. I'll go see."

By the time Dixon came out, Laura Liz had already come up with a plan.

"Do y'all want to walk to the 7-11 with us? We're getting Slurpees and one for Josie's grandmother because she's sick."

Lame, I thought to myself, but Dixon agreed. He went back in the house to get some money and came out with his twin brother. I walked to the edge of the lawn and yelled to Annie Jo that we were walking to the 7-11 and would be back in less than an hour. She nodded and waved as the four of us took off.

Mason lit a cigarette and then bumped my elbow as we walked along. I looked over at him and he asked, "Do you want a drag?" and nodded toward the cigarette.

"No. Thank you," I managed.

I could feel my face burning and stared at the sidewalk as I walked. When we got to a streetlight I managed a peek behind me and saw Laura Liz taking a drag and handing the cigarette back to Mason. Then I saw her clenched jaw slowly let out a long, thin puff of smoke.

I shot my head back to the street and didn't say another word.

We each bought Slurpees and an extra one for Annie Jo and some rock candy. I spied a Maple Bun candy bar as I was paying — Annie Jo's favorite —and added that, too.

As we walked back, Mason walked beside me as Laura Liz and Dixon walked a few steps ahead.

I couldn't think of anything to say, until I finally managed, "Do you like our school?"

"It's okay," he said.

I counted 16 seams in the concrete as we walked in awkward silence and I tried to think of something else to say.

Mason came through with, "My mother knows your grandmother."

"Yeah. She told me," I offered. "She said your parents were nice."

Again, silence.

Annie Jo's duplex was only a few houses away. I counted another 16 sidewalk sections and surprised everyone, including myself, when I darted through the neighbor's lawn and headed for her front door shouting, "Well, bye! Better get this Slurpee inside before it melts!"

"Josie!" Laura Liz called. "Are you coming back to my house? What about your duffel bag?"

I hugged one of the Slurpees against my chest as I reached for the screen door and my heart skipped a beat when I felt a cold rush of Slurpee ooze against my neck and chest.

"I'll have Momma bring me by to pick it up. She should be back in an hour or so!"

The screen door hit my heel as it swung back and forth with a screech and I darted safely inside.

I looked out the front window and saw Laura Liz shrug. The three of them headed toward the Faulkner's house.

Annie Jo had crawled back in bed, and I could see her sleeping as

I walked through the living room and into the kitchen to unload the Slurpees and wipe off my cherry-stained shirt. I put her Slurpee in the refrigerator and her Maple Bun candy bar on the counter and sat down in the living room to wait for her to wake up.

I thought about the weekend. Laura Liz and I had fallen right back into our familiar friendship, but somehow I didn't expect it to last through the end of the school year, especially through the summer. Laura Liz and I had talked a little about what had happened with my Dad and Miss Paulk, but I never got the impression that she judged me or thought of it every time she saw me like I felt Belinda and even Dena did. LaDarla had given me the ring and the note and was probably my closest friend, but I realized I had been avoiding my friends and instead been staying close to home or with Annie Jo since the funeral.

Laura Liz was right about the Faulkner twins. They were cute. I just couldn't picture being friends, though. They were both nice. I'd taken a good look at the mole on Mason's neck and at Dixon's crooked front tooth, so I was sure I could tell them apart the next time. Gratefully, I was distracted from my uncertainty when I heard Annie Jo stirring.

Her face was flushed and her eyes were glassy as she appeared in the door frame. She held onto the door and then the wall as she walked weakly into the living room.

"Hi, sweetheart," she said softly.

"Oh, Annie Jo! You look terrible!"

"Well, mercy me. I suppose I've had nicer compliments than that Miss Josephine Grace Flint," she said with a half smile, clearly the best she could muster.

"I just mean... Let me make you a spot on the sofa. I got you a Slurpee. Maybe that will make you feel better."

"Well, I bet it would at that," she said as she slowly bent to sit at the edge of the sofa.

I pulled her legs up, put a pillow behind her back, covered her legs with the green afghan and got the Slurpee out of the refrigerator.

"I got you a Maple Bun, too. I know it's your favorite."

The shingles blisters covered her neck and chest. She bent her head to show me the back of her neck that was particularly bothering her. I told her about the weekend at the Roberts and about the walk to the 7-11 with the Faulkner twins.

She'd only had a few sips of the Slurpee and said she'd save the Maple Bun for when she was feeling better and could really enjoy it, when we heard Mother's heels clicking up the walk.

"I knew I'd find you here," she said brightly. "I stopped by the Roberts to pick you up and Rita said you were here."

"I wanted to check on Annie Jo..."

She took one look at Annie Jo and said, "Oh my, you have a fever, don't you?" She stepped across the room to place her hand on Annie Jo's forehead.

"I suppose I do," said Annie Jo. I'd never seen her look so spiritless. "I dropped the thermometer in the bathroom sink though and it shattered all over the counter."

"I want you to come home with me for a few days," said Mother. "The girls and I can take care of you. We'll set you up in the downstairs bedroom and I can bring you meals there if you don't feel like coming to the table. Plus, I want to see how high your fever is."

I expected her to say she would be just fine, but she didn't argue. "Well, I suppose I could leave a note for Barry to bring in my mail."

"It's all settled then. Let's pack you a bag and we'll pick up Ansley and Daisy on the way," said Mother. "I picked up your duffel bag from the Roberts' house, Josie. It's in the car. Where's Laura Liz?"

"She's hanging out with some kids on the street. She'll walk home."

"Rita said you two got along beautifully."

It was a statement but I heard the question at the end, and I didn't want to turn it into a full-blown conversation. The weekend had been okay.

"We did," I said. "It was good, but she knows I wanted to see Annie

Jo. She'll be fine."

"How about you, Beverly? Did you have a nice time at the lake?" asked Annie Jo.

"Very relaxing, thank you. But I'm happy to get back to my family," she said and pulled us both into a group hug.

Once we were all home, Mother gave us each our marching orders: Ansley and I were to put clean sheets on the guest bed and add two extra afghans. Daisy was to gather magazines that Annie Jo might enjoy and fill a pitcher with water and place it on the bed stand with a cup, a towel and washcloth. Mother found the thermometer and took Annie Jo's temperature — 100.5°.

"We'll monitor it and if it goes up any more, I'm going to call the doctor," she said. "In the meantime why don't you take a shower and put on some warm pajamas."

"Girls, I want of each of you to take a bath or shower after that and get ready for the last week of school," she added.

Mother made grilled cheese and tomato soup for dinner, and we all prepared for an early bedtime.

I was the last to shower. I pulled my bathrobe out of the duffel bag that Mother had picked up from Rita and put it on. The belt had come out of the loops. I searched through the bag and it wasn't there.

"Momma, my belt is missing!" I yelled as I headed toward the kitchen.

She wasn't there and I yelled again.

"What's that, sugahhhhrrr?" I heard coming from the basement.

I walked down the steps and saw Mother talking softly with Annie Jo and tucking in a blanket around her shoulders.

It was just we Flint women now. Daddy was gone, and that wasn't going to change. But Momma and Annie Jo were still there. And Momma was right: We all needed to be strong for one another. I'd never seen Annie Jo so weak, and I didn't want to fuss in front of her.

"Nothing. It's just the belt to my bathrobe. I'll ask Laura Liz about it tomorrow at school."

I kissed Annie Jo and hugged Momma and headed off to bed. We were going to be okay.

August 2003

"Sorry, I can't. Grandmother is taking me shopping," said Grace.

I'd called to invite her to dinner. Joe and I had barely seen her since she was back in school and living in a garage apartment near campus for the summer. She had started dating a fraternity boy from her summer economics class and was going to a homecoming formal with him in the fall.

"She is? For your dress for the formal?"

"Yes, we had lunch yesterday and I told her all about Todd. She wants to buy my dress. We're meeting at Lenox tonight and having dinner after we shop."

"You had lunch yesterday?"

"Yes, Mother. I'll come home one day this week. I need to pick up some jewelry and a bag and some things."

Memories of shopping with Annie Jo came flooding back. I thought about the navy shoes and powder blue dress I wore to the Seaton Ferry Junior dance with Tommy Wilson. I thought about Laura Liz's light yellow dress with Swiss dots and her white shoes that were just like my navy ones. We'd celebrated our purchases with ice cream cones. Annie Jo got Cherry Almond, her favorite. Laura Liz and I got Rocky Road.

Somehow I had always thought of Annie Jo as the grandmother — everyone's rock, just like she was mine— even to our children. How is it that I never really thought of my own mother in the same kind of relationship with my kids?

I thought about the last morning I'd been at Annie Jo's place for the cleanup, and pictures of Mother from that day filled my mind: Sipping lemonade on the back swing deep in conversation with Chip; laughter from the back bedroom and seeing Mother, Grace and Carly emerge suppressing chuckles over a joke that they refused to share; Mother closing her eyes while she kissed Charlie's head as they left to return to Charlotte; Mother and Doc arriving with their hands filled with trays of homemade cookies.

"I just didn't know you two had been to lunch..."

"Of course!"

"Well, let me know when you will be by so I can be sure to see you, Grace. And good luck with the shopping."

"Grandmother has the greatest taste. I know we'll find something perfect," she said. "Love you, Mom. Bye."

She had already hung up before I'd finished, "Love you, too!"

I struggled to put definition to the thoughts that were stirring in the back of my mind: My father had been my hero until the day he died. Annie Jo had been my rock since the day I was born.

My mother...

My mother was strong. She was beautiful. She was smart. But perhaps she's played second fiddle to the heroes of my life so long that I'd discounted her impact.

She'd sweetened over the years. Everything changed after Daddy's death. Her quick tongue had mellowed.

My mind flew to a conversation she'd had years before with her sister Pauline when I was 9 or 10. Mother and Aunt Pauline were watching a television show about a book called "The Feminine Mystique" that many people were reading. Daisy and I were coloring in one of her coloring books on the floor nearby.

"If a woman can't be happy with her own husband in her own home, she shouldn't be allowed to have a husband or a family," said Pauline.

"First of all, my dear sister," my mother said. "We live in a country that quite fortunately does not have such rules about what a woman is and is not *al-lowwed* to do."

Her tone was precise and deliberate as she clucked along like I'd heard her do so many times before.

"And secondly, Pauline, this is not about happiness, it is about fulfillment. And every woman should indeed have the right to find fulfillment whether it be by work outside the home or otherwise. Using one's brain, stimulating one's talents, finding one's spiritual calling is every bit as important as cooking for a husband, cleaning a home and changing diapers. You have a daughter. I have three. It is my full intention to have my girls grow up knowing that they can be happy and successful with or without a man and that they be able to sustain a lifestyle for themselves financially with or without a man."

"Oh, for heaven's sake, Beverly Parker Flint. Are you going to burn your bra now too?" clucked Aunt Pauline.

Daisy's eyes darted to mine.

"Absolutely not," she said. "Cooper loves my brassiere. He especially loves the see-through lace and the little butterfly with tiny silver wings." And then without skipping a beat, she added, "Josie, honey, why don't you and Daisy go see what Ansley is up to."

Aunt Pauline stood up, grabbed her purse and stomped toward the door.

"Ladies," she said looking at Daisy and me, "you two are growing up as pretty as you please. Please give my love to your sister."

Then she turned to Mother and just made a humpfing sound as she pushed open the screened door and walked out.

Mother just looked at us and smiled, her dimples as deep and as perfect as ever. Then she walked to the door and called, "Toodle-ooo, Pauline. My love to your family, honey!" to no one as Aunt Pauline had already slammed her car door.

"We Flints are strong," I'd heard her say a million times. "We are going to be just fine. Let others say and think what they will. We control our own hearts and minds, and if there is goodness and truth there, then you've got what you need."

Mother's posture was always perfect, and I subconsciously straightened my back when I was around her.

"Hold your head high," she said. "And know that you have the support of everyone in this family. And when it all comes down to it, that is all that matters."

I thought about the day she'd married Doc.

She wore a pink lace suit with three-quarter length sleeves, pearls, white gloves and a pillbox hat. Her hair was pulled back in a French twist. She wore tiny pink pumps and had big round sunglasses in most of the photos because the flash bulbs failed inside the judge's chambers and only those taken on the street outside the courthouse turned out.

Mother had always been fascinated with the Dalrymples. She'd wanted to know everything about their house when LaDarla and I had first become friends. She knew Dr. Dalrymple and his wife CeCe from church and from our schools.

When I was a senior in high school, their oldest son Winston was taken as a prisoner of war in Vietnam. LaDarla and one of Winston's friends from Duke coordinated an effort to distribute POW bracelets — 500 of them with Winston's name — through the church, Northbridge High School and the community. The silver bracelets were engraved with the prisoner's name, rank and the date of capture: Winston's read "PFC Winston George Dalrymple 7-17-71."

Just a few weeks after the bracelets had been delivered, there was an explosion in the prison and Winston and four other American soldiers were killed. The Dalrymples divorced a year later.

A year after that, Doc and Mother sat next to one another at the high school graduation ceremony for Ansley and Kenneth. CeCe was there too, so they all just spoke casually. A few months later, Doc sent Mother flowers with an invitation to join him for dinner. They married at the Justice of the Peace just two months after that. The only guests at the wedding were the three Flint girls, LaDarla and Kenneth

Dalrymple and Annie Jo. Aunt Pauline had planned to come, but she called the morning of the wedding and said she'd come down with a bad cold and was having chills.

I thought about Mother's work at the church. She'd run the bereavement committee, volunteered at a depression and suicide hotline and had designed flower arrangements, corsages and bouquets for many of the weddings there.

She came to most all of Joey's basketball games, Chip's football games, Carly's soccer games, Grace's dance recitals and had even traveled to Charlotte for some of Charlie's sports and Boy Scout events.

Doc retired from his periodontal practice in 2000 and they had enjoyed traveling, the country club, entertaining and their grandchildren ever since.

The conversation with Grace rolled over and over in my mind.

Odd how I'd always considered Annie Jo as our family's matriarch and rarely thought of Mother the same way.

I opened my jewelry box to pull some necklaces and earrings Grace might want to wear for the formal.

June 1968

The summer wasn't the start of a healing season for our family like we'd hoped.

First off, Laura Liz said she had not found the belt to my bathrobe at her house. I asked her three times at school if she'd looked under her bed or maybe on the bathroom door knob, and she said she'd keep looking, but she didn't think it was there.

Then, I woke up late on the first day school was out and found Mother crying in the living room.

"Another assassination," she said through tears. "Senator Kennedy was killed last night. Bobby Kennedy, president Kennedy's younger brother. He was hoping to be our new president."

I turned up the volume to hear the news she had been watching. It had happened in California in a hotel just moments after he had won two states for the Democratic nomination. A man, only 24 years old, was being questioned for the murder.

"Our country just can't take more of this senseless killing," she said. "This is so sad."

Ansley walked out of the bedroom just as the phone rang.

"Hi, Annie Jo. Yes, I'm watching the news right now. The girls are just waking up," Mother drawled.

"What's the matter?" asked Ansley. I told her what I knew. She pulled a blanket over her shoulders and stretched out on the couch.

Annie Jo had gone back home a few days before. The blisters were fading a bit, but the doctor said it might take another month before the pain was completely gone.

"I know. It just doesn't make sense," Mother continued. "How are you feeling today, by the way?"

By the time Daisy got up, the news coverage was just repeating itself.

From the window, I saw Mrs. Dean scuffing across the street wearing a jacket over pajamas and bathroom slippers.

"Good morning, Gloria," Mother called as she held open the door.

"Yes, we've heard the news. It's so heartbreaking," she said as Mrs. Dean pushed passed her and entered our living room.

"Well, I just wanted to check on you then," said Mrs. Dean looking at the three of us girls. Daisy and I were each scrunched uncomfortably on either end of the sofa, while Ansley was stretched out across the rest under a blanket with nothing but her head showing.

"I'm glad you stopped by, Gloria," said Mother. "I made some ham salad last night and I thought you might enjoy a little for your lunch today."

"Well, that sounds mighty nice," she said as she followed Momma into the kitchen. I heard her telling Mother about a hotel bus boy who had held the senator's head after he'd been shot.

"Well, I just wanted to make sure you had heard the news," she reiterated as she held her container of ham salad by the door.

"Thank you for checking on us, Mrs. Dean," I said. I glanced at Ansley to see if she noticed how mature that sounded.

"Well, since you're okay, I'll mosey on back."

"She's so lonely," said Mother as she closed the door and watched Mrs. Dean scuff back across the street through the window.

Daddy, then Martin Luther King, Jr., and now Bobby Kennedy, all dead. I realized that only Daddy's death affected my family and me directly, but somehow they felt connected. Somehow each death felt very personal. And each intensified the deflation we were feeling. Worse, I felt like a million eyes were on us to see if we would make it through each new storm.

The senator's body was moved to New York. Mother watched every minute of coverage of the funeral. The black lace veil that Mabel

Grogan, the butcher's wife, had given to Mother to wear to Daddy's funeral was very similar to the one that the former first lady Jackie Kennedy was wearing. Mother held it throughout the coverage of the service and used it to wipe tears as we listened to his brother Ted Kennedy's voice shake and crack during his eulogy. We watched the personal and political stories of the senator's life, but I think Momma was thinking about Daddy too, just like me.

The following Monday, though, she started back to work at the Frito Lay plant. She knew it was going to be difficult while we were away from school for the summer, but she said we'd make it all work.

The Bakers' niece from Cincinnati, Debbie, was spending the summer with them before she started at the University of Georgia in the fall, so Mother offered to pay her $50 a week to come over to our house in the mornings and stay with us through lunch and early afternoon. I was in charge in the mornings before Debbie arrived and was to get everyone breakfast. Then at 3 o'clock, she would walk us half way to Annie Jo's. Annie Jo would meet us or watch for us as we walked to her house, where we'd stay until Mother picked us up after work. Mother assured me that I would be in charge the next summer, but since Debbie was available and Daisy was not quite 10, this year we would have her help.

I didn't mind. I liked Debbie. She brought her transistor radio and we'd sing along to all the songs on WQXI. We played games with Ansley and Daisy. Once a week Mother would leave a cake mix or a cookie recipe for us to make. Debbie was a really good artist, too, so she'd draw a picture of a cat, a clown or a ballerina, and we'd all try to copy it.

Debbie wore braces and had to find an orthodontist that could work on her teeth while she was away from Cincinnati. Since she didn't have a car, Mrs. Baker drove all four of us to the appointments every other week while we waited on Debbie to get her adjustments. I looked forward to it because they had "Seventeen" magazine in the waiting room. She said she couldn't eat after the adjustments because her teeth would be so tender, so we stopped at McDonald's after every appointment and were all allowed to get a milkshake.

"Would it be okay if Dena came with me tomorrow?" Debbie asked me one morning.

"Sure, why wouldn't it be?" I asked.

"She said you two haven't seen much of each other since your Dad was killed."

"Well, that's true," I said, trying to imagine what else Dena might have told her.

"I think she'd like that. Donnie's kind of getting on her nerves since school's been out."

Daddy had died more than two months before, and I hadn't spent time with any of my friends. I was ready. LaDarla was spending the first six weeks of summer in Cape Cod with her family. She called to tell me she'd send postcards.

"Sure. If she wants."

I tried to act like it didn't matter to me, but I was hopeful. It was my first summer without a best friend since I'd met Laura Liz.

August 2003

After more than 700 hours of non-billable time — not counting those of the Holland Cathcart creative team—MHG/Holland Cathcart took second place in the quest for re-branding the city of Atlanta. And, of course, second place meant nothing, so missing the selection by a miniscule margin was almost worse than the fact that we lost the project to our strongest competitor.

"Excellent effort by you and Bud and your team, Josie," Greystone said. "This is a blow, for sure, but we'll recover."

By the Labor Day weekend, I was over the sting, back on my regular client projects and happy to be helping Grace with setting up her new apartment on the Georgia State campus where she was now determined to finish her degree in management.

The downtown commuter campus I had received my degree from 28 years before had changed a lot since I'd been a student. Once called the "concrete campus," Georgia State had added green space around its buildings and acquired land in every direction to add administrative buildings, additional classrooms and student life spaces. Plans for the university's first dormitories were in the works, but Grace had found a new spot in an apartment building that was used mostly by students. She'd be living in a three-bedroom apartment and sharing a bathroom with one roommate.

We picked up a shower curtain, sheets and a comforter at Target during our first visit. By the end of the day, we had returned twice more and come back with a shower curtain rod, extension cords, double-sided tape and a framed poster and then snacks, toilet paper, cleaners, paper towels, a set of cereal bowls and a printer.

We hung curtains in her bedroom, set up her computer and printer, decorated the bathroom and bedroom with photos she'd brought from home, a bouquet of flowers from our sunroom and a white board wall calendar.

She surprised me when she pulled a bottle of wine from the refrigerator and asked if I'd like to have a glass to toast a successful day. She had turned 21 in February, but it still felt a little awkward. I agreed, though, and we sat down on the futon and mismatched chair supplied by one of the roommates to toast our handiwork.

"We should have thought about drapes for this room," I said looking at the large picture window that overlooked Mitchell Street. "You won't want to be in here at night without something to cover this big window."

"True. As soon as it starts getting dark out, we will be illuminating for all to see," she said. "What about blinds?"

"Well that's an idea, but I think I have some drapery panels that will work. Why don't you come home tonight, and we'll come back in the morning with a plan. I think I have a curtain rod that will fit this window, too."

I called Joe and asked him to order an extra large pizza, and we headed home.

The next morning I found the drapery panels in the hall closet just where I thought they would be. There were two panels. They had hung in Mother and Doc's guest room before they redecorated it. The color was a cream and taupe buffalo check, but the contrast in color was subtle enough to work as a neutral with Grace's room. The width was perfect, but I wasn't sure about the length, until I remembered some trim I had in the laundry room that I could sew to the bottom and add up to another four inches.

Grace came out of her room wearing one of Joey's shirts from football camp. Her hair was in a day-old ponytail. I noted how long and tanned her legs had become. She had reaped all the beauty benefits of Joe's Italian heritage, despite my insistence that she looked just like a Flint.

"These are the drapes I was thinking of," I said holding up a panel above my head and peeking around the side to see her reaction.

"Sure. I like that," she said hoarsely.

"Why don't you look in the basket in the laundry room closet and pull out the off-white trim that's in there. You should also find the curtain rod I was thinking of leaning against the inside of the closet. I'll fix some pancakes in a bit," I added.

As I folded up the panels, I spied the boxes I had brought back from Annie Jo's duplex on the bottom two shelves. I pulled out the first one and headed to the guest room chair.

A cigar box was on the top filled with black and white pictures. They were old, mostly of Annie Jo, Papa Ray and Daddy when he was young. There was a photo of Daddy, at about 8 or 9, in a pair of knickers that I'd never seen. There was a cute one of Annie Jo, Papa Ray, Uncle Lee and Aunt Lola sitting around a table playing cards and another one of them standing in front of a lake. Dexter and Daddy were standing in front of them, each holding a string of fish. Their arms strained under the weight, but their smiles were priceless. Dexter was missing all four of his top front teeth.

I found a lot of photos of Daddy and Dexter — sitting together on a hobby horse, standing by the entrance sign to Walford Grammar School, and one where they were each holding cookies over their eyes. Neither had any siblings, and Annie Jo had mentioned several times that they had been raised like brothers.

"Is this what you're looking for?" asked Grace, holding up the remnant of bullion fringe that I had used on the edge of an ottoman years before.

"Oh, perfect. I think the color will be great. Let's see if there is enough to trim out both panels," I said, pointing to the folded drapes.

We pulled the fringe across the width of the drape, and then held that measurement to one side and did it again. There was another 1/3 yard to spare.

"Perfect. If these are too short, we'll add the fringe to the bottom."

"All right," she said half-heartedly. Then, "What's all this?" as she pulled a stack of photos from the cigar box.

"Boxes I brought home one of the days we cleaned at Annie Jo's. I'd almost forgotten about going through them."

We laughed at the pictures, admired Annie Jo's thin calves and toothy smile and noted how much Joey looked like Daddy when they were the same age. I pulled out a few of my favorites, but decided to divide the rest between Dexter, Ansley and Daisy.

Grace pulled out a tissue-paper covered package that held a Christening dress. There was no indication of who wore it, but I made a mental note to look through the photos carefully to see if I could match it up.

"What in the world is this?" exclaimed Grace as she pulled out an old-fashioned looking toaster from the box. From inside the toaster, she pulled out a wooden board shaped like a piece of sliced bread with writing all over it.

"Oh my gosh! That's the toaster alarm clock that Daddy made for Ansley's birthday one year!"

"A toaster alarm clock? What?"

I explained how it worked. We dug through the box and found five more pieces of "toast" with the morning messages and the Georgia Bulldog statistics painted on the sides.

My heart filled with the weight of lead as I looked at the toaster for the first time in close to 40 years. My throat filled with what felt like a rubber ball.

Grace grew quiet, too, as she turned each slice of toast to read its message.

"That might be the craziest — and the sweetest — thing I've ever seen," she said quietly.

She looked up at me, and our eyes caught for a moment before I looked away. I knew she knew I was going to cry.

"Mom, you hardly ever talk about your father," Grace said. "I'd like to know more about him."

I dropped my head as I thought about Cooper Leon Flint. I pictured his smiling blue eyes that perfectly matched the blue shirt he wore the night he stood in the front row at the Vernal Equinox Pageant to cheer for Ansley and Roger. I pictured us together under a Georgia Bulldog blanket watching the Johnny Carson show while we shared a bowl of popcorn.

The sound of his voice filled my head: "Suppertime! Where's my Jaybird?"

"I'm the luckiest man in the world to be a daddy to you pretty Lady Bug Flint Muffins."

And then, "Please, call me Cooper."

Grace and Joey knew enough about my father's death to know it was a subject I didn't want to talk about. But Grace was right: I didn't ever share my memories of him with them. For that matter, I pushed the thoughts out of my own head too.

My love for my father was endless when he was alive. And yet I always assumed that love had ended on the day he died. Maybe it was simply hurt that I couldn't stop feeling.

"He loved to tinker with things in our garage," I said. "And if something broke, he always wanted to fix it in a new way. Make something totally different out of it."

I told her about Mother's bird feeder.

"Annie Jo showed me a pair of earrings he had made for her from old fishing lures when he was a boy," I laughed. "He glued a seashell to an old pair of her clip-on earrings and dangled the lure from underneath the shell."

"He liked to call the three of us, 'Lady Bug Flint Muffins.' It was such a dumb name, really, but I loved it. And, of course, he called me 'Jaybird.' And I loved that too."

"Mom, you should write down all these stories," Grace said sincerely.

"Hmmm," was all I could muster. "Let's go make some breakfast.

Your dad has some coffee brewing; I can smell it."

"Oh, and Grace," I said as we walked down the stairs. "He had the Georgia fight song hooked up to speakers in his car. Every kid in the neighborhood knew when they heard his truck coming down the street with the fight song playing, it meant we were all going to Dairy Queen."

She smiled.

Maybe it was simply the hurt that I couldn't stop feeling. Maybe I still loved him, and it was time to forgive.

August 1968

"They call these the 'dog days of summer,'" said Annie Jo as we sat on her front stoop and she passed us all a homemade Popsicle from her Tupperware mold.

She'd invited all six of us — Ansley, Daisy and me, plus one friend each — to a spend-the-night/paint the picket fence party before we all headed back to school at the end of the month.

It was hot.

I'd invited Dena. We'd been stuck like glue for weeks, and it was wonderful to be around a friend again. Ansley had invited Mary Ellen, and Daisy had invited Vivian. The six of us sat sucking on the Popsicles in our terrycloth shorts and old t-shirts, covered with white paint, sweat and sunburn.

"Why dog days?" asked Vivian.

"Don't know for sure, Vivian," said Annie Jo. "But I'd guess it's because it's so hot that we all walk around panting with our tongues hanging out, just like a dog."

Vivian stuck out her tongue. It was bright orange from the Popsicle, so we all joined her and stuck out our tongues and looked at one another. Three were orange, three were green.

We still had four sections of fence to finish, but were thrilled to be trusted with a paintbrush. We'd started the afternoon before and then spent the night in sleeping bags on her screened porch. Annie Jo made herself a bed on a reclining lawn chair and slept right in the middle of us.

We'd made pizza and then popcorn and told ghost stories, sang songs and cut pictures out of magazines for 'a poster of our favorite things' before we fell asleep listening to the cicadas and bullfrogs chirping at the heat.

After our Popsicles, we made way to finish the fence — one friend on either side so we could cover both sides of the fence at the same time as we scooted along from section to section, each set of friends at a side-by-side section. We each carried a pickle jar filled with paint as we scooted along the patchy grass.

Annie Jo painted the tops of the posts and followed us with her brush to catch any drips or "holidays," as she called missed areas.

I was just thinking about what a great weekend it had been when Butch Roberts drove up.

"How you doing, Annie Jo?" he said, though he was looking at each of us girls one at a time and lingering his eyes just a little too long.

"Ugh, what a creep," I thought. *And she's not your Annie Jo!*

I had to think back a few seconds to make sure I hadn't said that out loud.

"I've got some leftover pizza in the fridge, if you'd like some Butch," Annie Jo said cheerfully.

I cut my eyes to Ansley. I figured she would be the most likely to understand why a friendship between Annie Jo and Butch Roberts would be so annoying, but she didn't seem to notice. She was terrorizing a preying mantis that had landed on the grass next to her by dripping paint all around it.

"That sounds good," he said, shifting a paper grocery sack to his other arm. "Barry's off duty tonight so I'm meeting him later down at Otto's Bar. Pizza would hold me over. So, don't mind if I do."

He walked right through Annie Jo's back door to help himself.

I was still seething when he came out the door, holding a slice of pizza in one hand and a can of Coke in the other.

"Nice work," he yelled toward us as he lingered between the two screened doors.

I watched him as he walked to the duplex door just a few feet away.

His t-shirt had brown stains under the armpits and his hair was dirty and long.

"Jaybird's looks a little sloppy though," I heard him laugh as he disappeared into the other side of the duplex and the door creaked into position.

A sour taste filled my mouth as I balanced my paintbrush across the lid of the pickle jar to go inside for some water.

On the counter, I saw the grocery sack he'd been carrying, now empty and folded next to the kitchen sink. I looked inside Annie Jo's pantry to see if he had filled her pantry with any groceries, but I couldn't tell. I looked in the refrigerator and noticed he'd left the pizza box empty inside.

October 2003

"So, can you bring an appetizer?" asked Ansley. "But try to make something in the theme."

"Like it has to be something orange?"

"Something Halloweenish! I'm making deviled eggs but adding an olive slice and sriracha sauce to make them look like bloodshot eyeballs."

"Yum," I said into my cell phone as I sat impatiently at my third red light of my four-mile commute home from work.

"And little hotdogs wrapped in crescent rolls to look like mummies," she said excitedly. "Oh, and I have Rhodes Bakery making cookies to look like tombstones. Mother is bringing Bloody Marys, but she's going to serve it in her punch bowl and add something to make it look creepy."

Ansley was almost breathless with her enthusiasm for the party.

"And of course, you have to come in costume," she said. "Kenneth is going to be Captain Jack Sparrow and I'm going to be Elizabeth Swann."

"Who?" I was finally at my driveway.

"Oh for God's sake, Josie. From Pirates of the Caribbean! Curse of the Black Pearl?"

"Oh, right, okay. I'll think of something ghoulish to bring and we'll be there in costume."

"Tell Grace and Joey too! Carly and Chip both promised they'd be here."

After hanging up, I felt a little guilty that I hadn't matched Ansley's enthusiasm. She and Kenneth had been together for more than three months, and both were as giddy as I've ever seen either of them. The party was the first for her in a long time.

Doc and Mother came to the party dressed as Peter Pan and Tinker Bell. She had placed a fake bloody hand in the punch bowl with premixed Bloody Marys all around it to look like a bowl of blood. It didn't stop the young adults from enjoying it.

Joe wore a puffy sleeved shirt and a long violet-colored vest that I found at the Goodwill store. He taped on a thick, fake mustache and went as Sonny Bono. I wore a sequined evening dress that had been in the back of my closet for more than a decade. I cut off the sleeves and slit the dress up one leg, wore a black wig and went as Cher.

Grace and I had spent the morning baking cheese straws with almonds on each end to look like fingers, and then arranged them around a pumpkin with a large butcher's knife stuck through the center.

She wore an old uniform of Joey's and came as a football player. Joey dressed as Severus Snape from Harry Potter.

"So, what do you think of my brother and your sister?" asked LaDarla. Her face was a bright green under the black witch's hat. She and Greg had just returned from New York City, where they had seen the premier of "Wicked."

"I'm Elphaba," she'd explained to me earlier.

"I think they think this is pretty serious," I said. "Or at least Ansley does."

"Oh, I think Kenneth is just as serious," she said. "Our connections just keep getting closer and closer, Josie! Next thing you know, Matt and Grace will be dating!"

She nodded toward the food table where Grace and Matt were talking with Joey and Chip, but Matt was three years younger and at least six inches shorter than Grace. I didn't see that happening.

Besides family, Ansley had invited women from her tennis team, a few neighbors and three college friends. She'd actually invited Trey, but he was out of town for the weekend. Kenneth had invited several fraternity brothers and friends from work.

About halfway through the party, Doc tapped his wine glass to get the crowd's attention.

His mustache and cane were funny complements to his Peter Pan hat, green tunic and short pants. Mother had made him some felt "boots" to fit over his shoes, and he had a rope tied around his waist.

"A toast," he said. "To a fine evening hosted by a fine couple and a fine blending of these two families — the Dalrymples and the Flints — that began the lucky day I married this woman, my beautiful wife Beverly." He held up Mother's hand and everyone cheered. "Now Kenneth never wanted to become a periodontist, as I'd once hoped, but perhaps he's made an even smarter way to follow my lead, and that is to court this lovely woman I am proud to call my stepdaughter."

He held his hand toward Ansley, and the crowd cheered again. "Ansley and Kenneth, many thanks for a beautiful party, and may the courting continue! Then, before he let go of the spotlight, he nodded to each of us, "And to LaDarla, Daisy, Josie, their husbands and kids, Carly and Chip: I love you all."

I just smiled and said a prayer of thanks as I watched that adorable man in the funny green hat lean over to give his Tinker Bell a kiss.

I'd thought many times that I was happy that everyone had always called Dr. Dalrymple "Doc" because I couldn't imagine ever being comfortable calling him "Dad" or "Daddy." Nevertheless, he was a father to me - proud of my kids as if they were his own grandchildren and a lifesaver for my mother.

"Winston rescued me," Mother drawled. It was rare that anyone used Doc's real first name since he'd retired. "Like a ship in the sea he carried me away."

"No, Beverly, you were the beacon that brought this ship to shore," he said. His green tunic stretched across his ample mid-section like Peter Pan's never did.

"I might still be lost at sea if I hadn't found you."

August 1968

"It's the dog days of summer," was the line from the 6 o'clock news that caught my attention as I walked through our empty living room.

I stopped and listened as the newscaster described an event from the night before on Luckie Street, not far from the offices of the *Atlanta Journal and Atlanta Constitution*. I remembered the street from our sixth-grade field trip to the newspaper because Tommy Wilson had gotten lost from our group and a policeman had found him wandering around on Luckie Street looking for our bus.

"Luckie Street is lucky for you!" we'd all chanted after he was found.

"An unidentified Negro man, approximately 20 to 25 years old, was found badly beaten and unconscious behind a dumpster this morning. Because of the nature of his injuries, police speculate that he might have been dragged behind a vehicle before being left for dead near the intersection of Luckie and Forsyth streets."

I picked at the white paint from Annie Jo's fence that was still stuck to my fingernails as I listened.

"The identity of the young man is unknown."

Pictures of the dumpster and the intersection signs were shown, but nothing more before the newscaster moved on to the next story.

The next story was about a cat that had been found more than 30-feet high in a pine tree and had been rescued by a brave firefighter. It struck me how the cat story got as much time and photos as the Negro man that was dragged behind a car and left for dead.

But it wasn't until the next day when I overheard Mother on the telephone that I thought about it again.

"Oh, my heavens," I heard her say. "Yes, I know who you mean. I think Josie knows the boys and their parents too."

I sat down at the kitchen table to listen to her side of the conversation.

"I think that would be a lovely idea," she continued. And then, "Yes, please do. Thank you so much for calling," she said as she looked at me and shook her head and hung up the phone.

"That was CeCe Dalrymple," she said.

I knew Mother had met Mrs. Dalrymple only a few times. Once when she picked up LaDarla at our house, and at the funeral, but I was surprised to hear that she would be on the telephone with Mother.

She hung up the phone and motioned for me to sit down.

"The Jacksons' son Izzy is in a coma. You know his brother Bailey, I think?"

"Yes. And Rubelle and Isaac are his parents. Remember I met them at Tommy's parents' New Year's Eve party?" I said. "Rubelle is LaDarla's family's maid. What happened?"

"They aren't sure, but he was found unconscious downtown yesterday. He's at Grady Hospital."

My heart felt like it was filling with liquid lead as I listened to her words.

"I saw that on the news," I said quietly. "They said it was an unidentified man..."

"His mother works for the Dalrymples,"

"Momma, I know Rubelle. I've met her at LaDarla's house and at the Wilson's party. Is Izzy going to be all right?"

"He's in serious condition, Josie. The Dalrymples have set up a fund for his care at Grady. CeCe was asking if I would consider using some of the extra flowers from the church and making an arrangement for the Jacksons' church in Izzy's name for the next few weeks.

"The news said he might have been tied to a car and dragged behind it," I said.

"CeCe said that the police think maybe so," she said quietly. I saw a deep wrinkle between her eyes that I'd never seen before.

"But this flower arrangement idea will be a good project for you and your sisters and me," she said brightly. The falseness of Mother's always-positive spirit was becoming clearer to me as the months passed. I wasn't sure if I should be happy for her trying— I knew it was for me and Ansley and Daisy. Or if I should be sad that she wasn't fooling me any longer.

Or, I thought, sad that she was really so sad.

We did spend that Saturday, though, helping her make arrangements for the Jacksons' church. They were members of Ebenezer Baptist Church, the church where Rev. Martin Luther King, Jr., had been pastor.

Reverend Yates sat in a cafeteria chair in the church activities room chatting with us as we cut flowers and wire and handed them to Mother as she arranged two identical arrangements, one for either side of the altar.

"Girls, save a few of the carnations and baby's breath," said Mother. "I want to make a corsage for Rubelle, too."

"I don't think it's wise for you to deliver these arrangements, though Beverly," he said. "I can have Walter take them for you in the church van. There is still too much unrest downtown. I don't want you and the girls to get caught up in anything."

"No, Reverend. Thank you just the same," she clucked in a rhythm that was familiar enough for me to guess her next words. "We are doing something good for someone else, and we are going to hold our heads high as we take these arrangements to Ebenezer. I don't want my girls to be afraid of such things."

And we did. We put the arrangements in the back of our station wagon, and the four of us pulled up in front of Ebenezer Church. We did get a lot of stares. We were the only white people on the street, but Mother just nodded, "How do you do?" at each person that walked near us. She held her pink handbag at the crook of her elbow as she pulled the arrangements and stands and the corsage from the back of the car, handing us each something to carry. Then she gathered us just like ducklings as we paraded with our hands full into the church, empty but for a few people praying near the back.

We walked quietly behind the communion table and set up the flowers. Mother stood looking from about three rows back as she silently directed Ansley and me to move and turn the arrangements until they were perfect. Then we found a small refrigerator in a side room where she put the corsage. She wrote a note about where to find the corsage and that it should be given to Rubelle Jackson with love and wishes for Izzy's recovery. We walked back into the church where she quietly and carefully laid it on the pulpit. Then we marched in silence right back out the door.

We did the same routine the next Saturday and for three Saturdays after that, but in late September, the doctors pulled the life support from Izzy Jackson. He had never regained consciousness.

November 2003

I put on my pajamas and then poured myself a glass of wine. I sipped it slowly as I walked around from room to room of my house taking note of how little time I'd spent enjoying it the past year.

I'd thrown myself back into my work. We'd been extra busy with a new account for a national restaurant chain, and Bud had been out for ten days because just two weeks after he'd finally proposed to Jill, they decided to elope in Las Vegas and then fly to Mexico for a week-long honeymoon.

I had been looking forward to the long Thanksgiving holiday weekend. We took Doc and Mother up on the offer to have turkey, dressing and pumpkin pie at the country club instead of cooking, and I had my shoes off and the belt of my dress undone before Joe was able to drive us home.

Joe and Joey were leaving the next morning to go to Auburn, Alabama, for Saturday's Alabama vs. Auburn game with Trey and Chip, and the four were planning to stay overnight to fish on Sougahatchee Lake on Sunday. Grace had left directly from the country club to spend the rest of the weekend with a friend in Athens.

With three full days to be on my own, I sat down with a pad of paper to jot some ideas of what I might want to accomplish during that time.

First submission: *Sleep as late as I feel like it tomorrow.* I drew a square to the left of the to-do, to fill with a check mark later — the way I've always done my to-do lists.

Next, I decided: *Pull out Christmas decorations from attic space.* I wanted to look through the boxes enough to separate them by rooms, but

I wanted to wait for when the family was back in town before actual decorating.

Three: *Address Christmas cards.*

Four: *Take a long bath with candles, a glass of wine and great music.* I would pull the portable CD player into the bathroom and play my Norah Jones CD all the way through before getting out of the tub.

I made squares for three more entries, but decided to add to the list later when I heard Joe calling from upstairs.

"Coming," I said as I rinsed out my wine glass and set it next to the sink. I was ready to go to bed anyway. I'd wait for a fresh mind after my "Sleep as late as I feel like it" to-do was checked off.

"I was looking for that navy blue duffel bag," Joe said. "I'm just taking an extra shirt and another pair of jeans and a windbreaker."

"Hall closet, I think," I said as I opened the closet door. "Yep, here it is."

I handed him the bag as my mind registered the two additional boxes from Annie Jo's I had never sorted.

Number Five: *Go through Annie Jo's boxes.*

"Sexy pajamas, Josie," Joe said as he tossed the bag to the bed and wrapped his arms around me and grabbed both butt cheeks through my flannel Blackwatch plaid pajama bottoms.

"Sexy you, Mr. King. I felt you playing footsies with me under the table today while you talked so calmly with my mother and sisters and your own children. And while eating pumpkin pie, to boot!"

"Ah hah, guilty as charged, Mrs. King. Footsies, indeed."

He kissed my neck and nuzzled his nose into my ear and I barely noticed my Blackwatch plaid bottoms slip down as we climbed across our king-sized bed. He slipped my pajama top over my head and tossed it. I saw it land on the navy duffel bag as I settled in for a great, relaxing weekend ahead.

August 1968

Ansley's side of our bulletin board always bugged me.

She put a construction paper border around all her photographs, and she looked so grown up in her recent dance recital pictures.

She had pinned her sash from the Miss Vernal Equinox contest diagonally across her side of the bulletin board and then neatly arranged her photos, birthday cards and awards around it, careful to keep all edges parallel to the sides of the board.

By contrast, my side was layered with years of papers and pictures, Tommy's gum wrapper chain, ticket stubs, Georgia football schedules and notes all piled on top of one another.

I was less careful because Ansley was so neat and careful. She fussed about my side sometimes, but I ignored her, rarely ever took anything down, just added to the top and never tried to be neat. It was an intentional jab. That, and I couldn't have out-neated her even if I had wanted to.

A photo of Daddy posing with Ansley in front of the gold velvet drapes caught my eye. She was wearing one of my hand-me-down dresses and platform heels and her hair was long and pulled back from her forehead with a wide stretchy headband. Daddy was wearing a long-sleeved shirt with a tie loose around his neck. He had on black pants and shiny dress shoes. The photo was probably taken after church one day. I unpinned it and studied it more closely.

Daddy was looking straight into the camera when the photo was taken. His eyes were clear. As clear as if he were standing right in front of me.

I couldn't take my eyes away. It wasn't until I realized that tears were running down my face that I pulled my eyes away from his.

I studied the rest of the bulletin board. A picture of our whole family on the Elliott's boat from four years earlier was partially showing. Daddy had on a red bathing suit and an Atlanta Braves ball cap.

I pulled it down and unpinned another: A picture of Daddy with Dexter and Dexter's dog. He was looking right into the camera and smiling that smile I loved.

I unpinned six more photos of Daddy from both sides of the bulletin board and lined them across the desk Ansley and I shared.

My anger grew with each image. Daddy at the barbecue grill. Daddy and Mother dressed for New Year's Eve and standing in front of the velvet drapes. Daddy blowing out birthday candles.

In every picture, Daddy was looking right into the camera and smiling. That same smile that had always made me feel so safe and so loved. So special.

I picked up a straight pin from the corkboard and pierced a hole through both of his eyes. Then I picked up the next photo, and the next and punched right through his eyes in each one.

I heard the back door open and the voices of my sisters and mother when it occurred to me that I was sobbing out loud. I ran to the bathroom and locked myself in to try to get control of my tears.

I heard Mother calling for me but I didn't answer right away. I was hoping she wouldn't catch me crying.

It was Ansley's screams that sobered me right up.

"Mother! Josie messed up my side of the bulletin board!" she screamed. "Mother!" Then I heard her go quiet. I knew why. I stayed quiet in the bathroom knowing I'd be in trouble.

I heard her footsteps as she ran down the hallway outside of the bathroom.

"Mother! Mother, you need to see what Josie did..."

November 2003

Once Joe and Joey had left for Auburn and the house was empty, I fell back to sleep and slept until 9:20. Not bad, I thought as I ground a fresh batch of coffee beans and placed them in the copper canister. I looked over my to-do list as I watched a couple of red birds play in the backyard trees and then decided to start with a long walk around the neighborhood.

"Pace yourself," I told myself as I laced my fairly new Nike shoes. I hadn't had a weekend alone in months and knew that the opportunity for a perfect balance of accomplishment and relaxation was just what I needed.

The answering machine was blinking when I got back into the house.

"Josie! I have been thinking about you! Let's get together!"

It was LaDarla's voice. She and Greg had missed Thanksgiving at the country club because Matt had come down with strep throat.

"Matt's antibiotics have finally kicked in and I'm so ready to get out of this house!" she continued. "I know the guys have gone to the game today and so hopefully you have some free time. Can you meet me for lunch or dinner? Tomorrow could work too. Call me. Love you."

I picked up my to-do list and realized my ambitious plans were indeed ambitious. A lot to accomplish in one free weekend.

Then I thought about my circle of friends: Fortunately my sisters and I had grown closer over the past year because I'd been pretty wrapped up in family and work since the kids were born. Bud didn't really count as a friend, though we probably knew more about each other's business than anyone else in our lives other than my husband

and Bud's new wife Jill. My bridge club friends were friends, but not outside of bridge, and some were a little too serious about the game. A few neighbor friends, but Joe and I typically interacted with them as couple friends, not as girlfriends for me.

Without question, LaDarla was my closest friend, yet I was certain there had been times we hadn't been in contact over the years other than our Christmas card exchanges.

She and Kenneth spent a lot of holidays with CeCe and her new husband, or at their beach home. Mother and Doc went to many of Matt's school and sports activities, and Matt was just like a real cousin to our kids, but we'd never gotten in the habit of including one another in everyday activities.

LaDarla had been great when Annie Jo died. We'd seen them at Easter and at the Halloween party, but it had been forever since we'd really spent any time just talking.

My children had their own friends and were doing their own things and rarely needed me. Joe had his work and occasional poker friends...

I picked up the phone and dialed.

"Josie! I was hoping you'd call right back!"

"I just got your message. I'm so glad that Matt's feeling better."

"God, me too! I am so ready to get out of this house. I feel like I've been working in sickbay for a week! Do you have time to get together?"

"Well, yeah. I made a pretty aggressive to-do list yesterday, but so far the only thing I've checked off of it is to sleep late. I'd really like to get my Christmas things out and address a few cards today, but how about we meet for dinner?'

"Oh, I'd love that, Josie," she said. "Do you like sushi?"

"Sure. How about the new Thai place near the mall? Joey took a date there and says they have a great sushi bar."

"Oh, I'm so excited. How about 7:15? I'll meet you there."

"Can't wait, LaDarla. Thanks for thinking of me. I'm so excited to catch up."

I finished my coffee and headed straight to the attic for the Christmas boxes.

By noon I had delivered each box of Christmas decorations to the appropriate room and had sorted several of them to create a box for Goodwill. Better idea: I'll let the kids look through them first, since they both have their own places now. I added a few of my nicer things to the box knowing that they'd enjoy decorating their own places this year.

I had planned to wait for the family to actually decorate, but I got too excited and hung our stockings and decorated our mantle with some tall candles and garland and a gold metal angel that Grace had given me the year before.

After lunch I put on a Norah Jones CD and pulled out the cards I had picked up the week before and my favorite pen and had completed more than 30 cards with addresses and personal notes inside before the CD was complete.

After cleaning out the refrigerator and kitchen junk drawer, I returned to my list and decided it was time for a long bubble bath. I opted to forgo the glass of wine I'd promised myself with the bath, but found a Barry White CD that seemed to fit the bill for soulful sounds and carried it into the bathroom with the old boom box from Joey's room.

I added hot water until the tub was teetering toward overflow. The CD had long-stopped before I finally pulled myself out of the tub and into my pink fluffy bathrobe.

I felt like I was going on a date as I lazily played with my makeup and hair before selecting a red turtleneck, black slacks, a print scarf and my favorite black heels to meet LaDarla for dinner.

The restaurant was crowded when I arrived: No doubt, people looking for a change from turkey leftovers. I spotted LaDarla at the bar.

"Wow. Maybe we should have thought about making reservations," I said as she jumped out of her chair with a wonderful bear hug.

"I know. I never expected this crowd, but I'm in no hurry! Greg and Matt were watching the first movie from the Star Wars trilogy when I left, and they have plans to go see "Attack of the Clones" tomorrow afternoon," she said. "I'm free as a bird!"

"Me too! Let's have a glass of wine!"

The bartender acknowledged us just as he lifted up two martinis to deliver to a couple across the bar from us.

"On second thought..." I started.

"Maybe it's a martini night!" LaDarla said brightly.

"Exactly! Let's do it!"

We were as giddy as I could remember ever being. We toasted to our friendship when our martinis arrived and did a quick calculation to add, "of more than 37 years!" and clinked our glasses again.

By the time the hostess brought us to a table, we had already brought each other up to speed on our jobs, kids, husbands and her mother and were covering our Christmas shopping lists.

"What are you getting for the parents? Your mom and my dad, that is," she asked.

"Good question. Any ideas?" I asked.

"I was thinking of sending them on a trip somewhere," she offered. "Do you think we could get Daisy and Ansley to go in on something? I could talk to Kenneth."

"Oh my God! We haven't even talked about my sister and your brother! How much weirder can the connections get with our families?"

"I know, but somehow they really seem to work, don't they?"

"They really do. Ansley's almost tolerable. Kenneth is a really good match for her."

Over bowls of miso, sashimi and a shared spicy tuna roll, we decided on a trip to Asheville for Mother and Doc. They would enjoy touring the Biltmore House when it was decorated for Christmas, and we made plans to check reservations at the Grove Park Inn.

The waiter asked if we'd like a third round of martinis. I looked at LaDarla.

"I'm thinking maybe coffee?"

"Good idea. One for me too," she said to our waiter, before we jumped to our next topic of discussion.

The hot coffee set the tone for another hour of non-stop talking.

"You know Monday would have been Winston's 56th birthday," she said as the evening grew mellower and the restaurant cleared of other patrons.

"Really? I know that's still tough."

"Yeah, it is. My mother still hasn't truly dealt with his death," she said.

"Trust me. I'm finding new feelings to feel about my father every single day and Joe is on me all the time to open up. I'm in the same boat, I think."

That choice of words smacked, but LaDarla didn't seem to notice and we moved on.

"When you think about it, I think we've had more than our share, Josie," she said sadly. "Your father, Winston, Izzy..."

Her addition of Izzy Jackson to the list surprised me as my head filled with the reminder. Izzy Jackson. Brutally murdered and the crime was never solved.

"Mother is still in touch with Isaac," said LaDarla. "Rubelle passed away about six years ago. Mother said it was a heart attack. I would love to see Bailey. Isaac says he's married and living in Valdosta. Working for a cable company there."

"So odd that the murder was never solved."

"Anything from Laura Liz?" she asked.

"Not since her mother died. And that's been at least 15 years. She was living in Tennessee at the time. She was married and had gone back to school. I think someone said it might have been for a law degree."

"Donnie?"

"Still in Manhattan making the big bucks on Wall Street. His son got married this summer, but Joe and I couldn't make the wedding. I called him on his birthday and we've talked about going up to stay with them for a long weekend."

"Oh Donnie Baker... Good for him."

"Do you remember that girlfriend Winston brought to the beach that year?" I laughed. "With the pink and green bikinis?"

"Lorna!" LaDarla spewed. "Ugh, Delta Zeta with a different pink and green bikini for each day! She was so full of herself! Gag, I couldn't stand her!"

"Were they still together when Winston was killed?" I asked.

"Lord, no," she replied. "Winston was dating a wonderful girl we all loved when he left for the service. I still get cards from her occasionally. And she tells me she still wears Winston's POW bracelet."

"I still have mine," I said.

"Me too. I look at it every day when I put on my jewelry. I close my eyes for just a few seconds and think of him," she said. "It's a constant reminder."

"I know it's still tough for Doc, too," I said.

"Well, Winston's death was the beginning of the end of their marriage, for sure," she said. "But it was probably inevitable anyway. Besides, your mother is much more attentive to him than mine ever was. Beverly has been good for him."

"Agreed," I said. "They've been good for each other. And I think we better call it a night before we get entirely too melancholy to want to do this again!"

"Second. But let's do it again. I've really missed you."

We gathered our things, hugged and headed for the door still chatting all the way to our cars.

September 1968

*M*y second year at Northbridge High school started off much differently from freshman year.

LaDarla's family had practically been keeping vigil alongside Rubelle and Isaac at Grady Hospital for weeks by the time school started. CeCe was spending days at the hospital and nights writing letters and calling everyone she could think of to try to get some progress in leads and an arrest. LaDarla made flyers with Izzy's photo and a description of where he was found. She and her father and brothers distributed them throughout the shops downtown and tacked them to utility poles. In social studies, our teacher gave LaDarla the chance to tell the story, and we had a full-hour discussion about it.

But Izzy died. And so did the efforts to find who killed him.

"It's like it never happened," LaDarla cried one day at the lunch table. "My mother says that the district attorney tells her that they have no leads in the case. The police log says that evidence was received when Izzy's body was found, but they can't actually come up with any of it. They can't even find photos that were supposedly taken. Nothing!"

I grabbed her hand from across the table as Karen patted her back.

Bailey hadn't come back to school that year, and just a few weeks after Izzy died, the Jacksons moved to be near family in south Georgia near Valdosta.

CeCe pushed for action for months even after they'd left, but she finally slowed down too.

As LaDarla's focus on Izzy waned, we started getting back into a more normal high school routine. Dena, LaDarla and I called ourselves "The Three Musketeers," and I found myself with two Cs at midterms, my first Cs ever.

The sophomores won the homecoming float competition after spending three full weeks after school with crepe paper and chicken wire to make a ten-foot eagle carrying a trophy and soaring over our flat-bottomed trailer that we'd covered with more chicken wire and crepe paper.

I rarely saw Laura Liz. I never had to wonder again if I wanted to be friends with Mason Faulkner or his twin brother, because the opportunity never came up. They just all faded deeper and deeper into a darker crowd at school, and our paths very seldom crossed at all.

November 2003

*I*t was raining Sunday morning when I woke. I ambled down the stairs to make a pot of coffee and picked up my to-do list from the day before.

LaDarla had mentioned her Christmas china the night before, and it occurred to me that starting Grace on a pattern would be a great gift idea that I could add to every year. Maybe for Carly, too.

I added, "Shop for china" to the list next to one of my empty squares that beckoned for a check mark to increase the productivity of the weekend.

"Drop off heels for new taps" went in the next slot, though I realized the shoe repair would likely be closed until Monday.

I looked at the newly decorated mantle and decided to embellish a bit more. So, I rambled through a couple of the Christmas boxes and found a tall, sleek tree made from silvery disks that resembled fish scales and added that to one side and another candle to the other.

I put some Christmas CDs into the CD player before pouring myself another cup of coffee and heading upstairs to tackle Annie Jo's boxes.

I took another look at the photo of LaDarla and me at graduation that was atop the boxes. We were happy and proud. Her braces made her mouth seem small. I tried to remember if I'd thought that at the time. I realized Donnie was in profile in the crowd behind us and it looked like he might have been talking to Belinda Roach. I hadn't even noticed them the last time I'd looked at the photo.

We were two young, happy faces with no clue that we might be stepsisters 35 years later sipping martinis and eating sushi while we enjoyed a quick, well-deserved retreat from our respective families.

A second cigar box revealed even more photos from Duberry Street, a church pageant where Daisy was dressed like a giant bell, and even one of Ansley, Roger Saylor and Mary Ellen working on the paper maché beaver project. There was a second boy in the background, whose name I couldn't remember, but I noticed he was wearing the exact same short-sleeved plaid shirt as Roger. There was also a letter I had sent Annie Jo from our beach trip with the Dalrymples.

I added it to my pile of photos to show to Ansley, Daisy and LaDarla when my cell phone rang.

"I just wanted to tell you how much I enjoyed catching up with you last night," LaDarla said before I could even finish my greeting.

"Me too. So needed and so fun. I was going to call you anyway because I have found some photos you really need to see. You will love them!"

"Oh, I want to."

"And a letter I'd sent Annie Jo from our trip to the beach with your family and Lorna!" I put a nice dose of eye-rolling emphasis on Lorna's name.

"Oh my God. I hope you told her how annoying Lorna was!"

"I was a little benign with my description, but you've got to see it. You'll scream! Oh, and thanks for that china pattern idea. I'm going to do a little shopping this afternoon."

"Macy's is having a big sale."

"Macy's was on my list. In fact, why don't you stop by later tonight. We can have a glass of wine and see these pictures."

"Better yet, let's meet at the mall and then come back to your house for the wine and pics!" she exclaimed excitedly as if we were 15 again.

"I love it! Yes!"

We made plans to meet in the afternoon. I hung up the phone and opened the box again to pore through the next stack of contents.

A file folder wrapped with rubber bands both horizontally and vertically revealed documentation from the purchase of the duplex. They'd paid just $26,800 for it with a 30-year mortgage. I put it aside to show to Joe.

I also found receipts for appliances that had long-been replaced, warranty information for the Buick she drove back in the early '80s, a copy of Daddy's death certificate and a savings bond for $50.

I emptied both boxes on the floor so that I could separate what should be thrown-away and kept, and I made a small pile of things I knew we'd never need that would probably be better to shred.

Each new item brought back another flood of memories. She'd tucked recipes into files — most of which I didn't recognize at all. Plus more photos — a beautiful black and white headshot of Annie Jo when she must have been about 18. She wore a crew neck sweater and strand of pearls and her hair was longer than I'd ever seen in any other picture. Wavy and pinned at the top with a tiny star bobby pin. I searched her face and saw a lot of Ansley and even Carly and Joey, but I couldn't really identify features that reminded me of Daddy or Daisy or me.

The next file contained programs from school functions —the program from my band performance in fourth grade, a couple of Ansley's dance recital programs.

I found a photo from our Winter Dance at Seaton Ferry Junior High when Annie Jo took Laura Liz and me shopping for dresses. I thought the powder blue spaghetti-strapped dress to be a lot more flattering than the photo indicated.

A mimeographed program from Daddy's high school graduation. I found his name and Dexter's too. Clipped to the back was his senior picture with "1946" written in fine gold pen across the bottom corner.

I stared at the photo. His eyes were looking right into the camera, his smile as mesmerizing as I'd remembered.

I'm still having trouble forgiving you.

I listened for a response, but nothing came.

I looked deeply into the photo again and then placed it in the pile of photos to share with Ansley and Daisy.

I pulled out a large padded envelope sealed with packaging tape. It had a large water stain across the front and it looked like a sticker had been torn off the envelope after the stain was made because the stain was missing in the rectangular areas where the sticker had been.

Scissors were not in reach, so I tossed it aside and revisited the stack of photographs. I separated the pictures in piles for my mother, sisters and a few for LaDarla of the two of us. Feeling good about all I'd accomplished, I did a time check and realized I still had time to peruse the boxes before I had to meet LaDarla.

There were scissors in the bathroom. The ones I trimmed my bangs with. I grabbed them out of the drawer, grateful that I didn't have to tackle the stairs as I was on a roll with my final big to-do item. The box I had filled with stuff that could be tossed was almost full.

I cut the top edge of the envelope and pulled out a stack of 8" x 10" black and white photographs. A plastic envelope had some miscellaneous items mostly separated in separate clear bags.

I thumbed through the photographs and a sinking feeling filled my heart. The photos were nondescript, but eerie. Most showed various angles of an alley. A large dumpster. Photos of a street with a few parked cars, a large postal cart, several overflowing trashcans. No people in any of the photos. I noted one of the doors in the alley was marked Shoe Repair, but it looked like a back door and there was no other name or means of identifying where the photos were taken.

A musty attic smell filled my head. I picked up the plastic bags one at a time, each one was sealed with yellowing tape. One held a ballpoint pen, one a partial pack of gum, one looked like a house key but it had no markings. There was a folded piece of paper in one, a plastic card in another and a mud-crusted piece of fabric in the last one.

What in the world is this?

I checked out the outside envelope again for another clue. The remaining sections of the sticker had markings, but parts were torn and others were smeared. None of it legible enough for me to read.

I opened the bag and unfolded the paper inside. It ripped along the folds as I did.

It was a cash receipt for peanuts and Bayer aspirin from Harmon's Drug Store. The total bill of $7.91 was marked as paid in full. There was a name at the top, but the only section that was still legible looked like the name "Jack," though much of the rest was clearly written quickly and looked more like haphazard scribble.

I studied the key through the plastic bag, but could tell it had no identifying marks. There were two pieces of hardened Juicy Fruit left in the open pack of gum. The plastic card was a Fulton County library card. It had a membership number but no name.

I opened the plastic bag with the cloth and the smell of dried mud and mold filled my head. I tepidly pulled out the mud-stained cloth now brittle with age and decomposition. The shape was deceptive. As the crusts of mud broke away, I realized it was much longer and narrower than I had expected. A fray of familiarity tickled my mind as I listened to the beat of my heart getting louder and louder threatening to implode my chest, my world.

March 1969

*E*ven a year after Daddy's death, I still had tinges of feelings that everyone around me was looking at, whispering about or judging me.

Dexter and Shalene surprised Daisy with a puppy on Valentine's Day. Mother was unhappy at first, but she quickly warmed up to the idea, and in a lot of ways "Cupie" brought some of the calmness and laughter back to our home.

Not because Cupie — Cupid Valentine Flint Superdog —was calm. She was anything but. But the squealing, ball-chasing and bows we'd dress her in all helped to take the uneasy edge off our home that we felt since Daddy died.

Dexter thought she was probably a cocker spaniel and Maltese mix. She stayed little, and we loved walking her around the neighborhood and bathing her in Mother's Styrofoam ice cooler with the water hose.

Mother saved a plate from almost every night's meal for Gloria, and she baked cookies or made her favorite tuna salad with pickles for us at least once a week. She finally learned our names and even taught us all to crochet. She helped us each make a headband, and Daisy crocheted a little blanket for Cupie.

Mr. Cook invited me to help out in the principal's office during the mornings and during my study hall break fourth period. I filled out attendance reports, brought messages to classroom teachers and even gave Governor Lester Maddox a tour of our school when he came to visit for an assembly.

Probably the most surprising event of sophomore year though, was that Donnie Baker and I became close friends. We'd meet at the dirt hill almost every day after school to sit on our "conversation rock" to talk. His annoying behaviors gave way to someone that I really came to trust and depend on. I told him things I never said to anyone else about how I felt about Daddy's death, his betrayal of us, the embarrassing legacy he left. He told me about his secret crushes — Belinda Roach was number one —plus the book with graphic descriptions and drawings of sexual positions he'd found behind the Ben Franklin store and about his dreams to become a pilot.

Twice we tried kissing. The first time we'd just gotten started when we heard a loud tire screech and jumped up to run to the top of the hill to see what was going on. An older guy from our school was turning wheelies in his truck in front of the Bakers' house. I saw the Faulkner twins in the flatbed of the truck, but they drove away quickly when Donnie's mother came out the door hollering and waving her dishtowel at them. The second time was more complete, but we both agreed that we were best as just friends.

Sometimes Dena joined us at the conversation rock, but mostly it was just Donnie and me.

Once he brought a folded paper cootie catcher that he'd made at school. He snapped it with his thumbs and forefingers to the top and sides while asking to pick numbers and colors. He finally asked, "Who is Josie's best friend for life?" He asked me to pick one more number.

"Four," I said.

He snapped the cootie catcher four more times then ceremoniously lifted the tab to see who the answer would be: "Donnie Baker! Donnie Baker will be your best friend for life!"

I laughed and grabbed the cootie catcher. Sure enough, he'd written his name under all eight spots.

"Well I guess that settles it then," I said. "We'll be best friends for life!"

November 2003

I picked up my cell phone to call LaDarla, but then put the phone back down to think.

There was something about the photograph scene. Something that brought me back to the television news report that I had seen so many years before that reminded me

Izzy.

I dug for the courage to pull the cloth out of the bag to its full length. It was frayed thin in spots. The loops of the fabric were flattened and worn. I had known from the second I'd opened the bag, but my mind continued to fight it....

The belt to my bathrobe.

I felt sick. My mouth filled with thick, sour saliva and my stomach gave way before I could make it across the bedroom carpet and into the bathroom.

Afterward, I lay on the cold tile of the bathroom for a long time before pulling out old towels to clean up the mess.

I crawled back into bed and covered my head with the covers trying to make sense of what I'd found.

What does this have to do with Annie Jo?

The package was sealed with lots of packaging tape. *Did Annie Jo tape it shut or did someone give it to her that way? Did she know what was inside?*

What was on the sticker? Why is the envelope stained?

My heart beat filled the tiny space between my bed and the blankets on top of me until the resounding pulse made me feel sick again. I threw off the covers and ran into the bathroom.

I washed my face and brushed my teeth and changed out of my pajamas and into a sweater and pair of sweat pants.

I found my cell phone under the stack of photographs and quickly searched my recent calls.

"Hello?"

"I really need to talk to you. Can you come over right away?"

I hung up the phone and a cold sweat enveloped my face and chest. I sat down next to the photos I'd put aside and noted my father's graduation photo at the top of the pile.

I'm sorry, Jaybird.

I picked up the photo, looked into his eyes and answered back.

"I'm afraid, Daddy."

April 1969

$\mathcal{I}$ came home from school and was surprised to find Mother already home.

Her shift at Frito Lay was 8 a.m. to 4 p.m., so I was usually home alone after school until Ansley and Daisy got off the bus and then Mother got home by 4:30.

"Well, hello, Josie," she said just a little louder than seemed necessary since we were in the same room.

I dropped my books into the wingback chair nearest the front door.

"Hi. Why are you home?"

"Actually Arlene Simpson covered my shift today. She's trying to get in some extra hours before she has to have a hysterectomy next month."

I was about to ask my next question when she added, "I spent the morning taking care of banking and other errands," and then nodding toward the hallway, "and Reverend Yates was kind enough to stop by for a visit this afternoon."

Reverend Yates turned the corner, wiping his hands with one of our hand towels.

"Hello, Josie," he said. "I was just using your 'little boys room.'"

He made an odd gesture, an awkward point with his head and both arms toward our hallway bathroom.

Are you pointing to our 'little boys room?'

"I've been praying a lot about you and your sisters and mother," he said.

I stayed quiet as he talked, but my mind was reeling. *We actually don't have a "little boys room," and something about this entire scene feels a little off. And for that matter, the lavender hand towels are usually in Mother's bathroom.*

"Please share with me," he said. His forehead was wrinkled, and his eyes were squinty as he shook his head and put his hand on my shoulder. "How are you feeling these days?"

"I'm fine, Reverend Yates. How are you?"

"Well, I'm fine too, Josie. But we don't get to see as much of you Flint ladies since your Mother is no longer working the telephones at church, and I've been thinking about you and your family. I wanted you and your mother and sisters to know that the church is here for you."

Cupie walked out of the kitchen and into the living room.

"Your mother tells me you girls are doing well at school and she tells me you are enjoying the family's new puppy," he said excitedly.

I wanted to be rude, but I was too afraid. All I could muster was to counter his enthusiasm with a teenager's dose of apathy.

"Well, it's really Daisy's dog."

"The death of a father can be devastating on children and can manifest itself in many kinds of feelings and behavior," he said trying a new tone. "Do you have someone you can share your feelings with, Josie? I say again, the church is always there for you."

"Well, there is a counselor at school that I talk to a lot."

I glanced toward Mother and could tell she knew I was lying.

"And Annie Jo helps me a lot too."

I glanced toward Mother again. I wondered if the insinuation in the poison dart lie I'd just thrown was obvious.

"Annie Jo Flint. Such a lovely woman," he nodded as he folded the lavender towel and walked it down the hallway and placed it on the counter of the hall bathroom.

"Well, Beverly, I enjoyed our chat today," he said as he picked up a sweater that had been hanging on the coat rack near the door.

Then looking at me, "Josie, it was a pleasure to see you. Please give my best to your sisters. You are growing into a lovely young woman. Please let me know if I can be of service in any way."

"Will do, Reverend," I managed flippantly as he walked out the door, knowing that I was going to get away with it.

"I'm surprised you didn't mention that you were taking the day off, Mother," I said as I watched him greet Ansley and Daisy, who were walking toward the house across from the bus stop.

"Oh, I thought I did, Josie. Poor Arlene is worried about her finances because she will be away from work for six to eight weeks after her surgery," she said. "Wasn't that kind of Reverend Yates to stop by to check on us, though?"

"It sure was," I said more sarcastically than I expected and headed toward the hallway bathroom and closed the door.

I heard Mother greet Daisy and Ansley as I sat on the toilet thinking about what had transpired. I washed my hands and dried them on the green hand towel that was hanging on the hook and picked up the lavender one and walked it through Mother's room and placed it on the sink in her bathroom.

Her bed wasn't made, but that wasn't really unusual. She hadn't been nagging us about our own beds very often since Daddy died. Her makeup bag was just where it always was next to the sink. Her bathrobe was lying across the bedroom chair where it always was. Her closet door was closed, and the book I'd seen her reading earlier in the week was lying on the nightstand.

I heard Daisy calling for Cupie, so I followed the voices and joined my mother and sisters in the kitchen.

"What's for dinner tonight, Momma?" Ansley asked.

"I have some pork chops thawed. And I'll make a salad," she said. "I think we still have some of Annie Jo's apple sauce too."

"Can we put them on the grill like Daddy used to do?" Ansley pleaded. We hadn't even tried the barbecue grill since Daddy died. Mother used the oven or stove or a crockpot to cook all our meat.

"I suppose it's time we gave that a try," Mother said tentatively.

"Can we make a cake too?" shouted Daisy.

I put the visit from Reverend Yates out of my mind as we settled in on the dinner project. Daisy and I made a strawberry cake from a box we had in the cabinet. We made homemade icing from a recipe on a box of powdered sugar and we had enough fresh strawberries to decorate the top. Daisy insisted on adding red sugar sprinkles left over from the last time we'd made sugar cookies.

When it was time to start the barbecue grill, Mother found lighter fluid and a partial bag of charcoal in the garage.

"Why don't you call Annie Jo and see if she'd like to come for dinner," Mother said.

I shrugged my shoulders pretending not to care if Annie Jo came or not.

"Josie," Mother said as she steered me toward the back door and away from the tree swing where Ansley was pushing Daisy. "People need to deal with their grief in many different ways."

I noted an unusually long hesitation before she continued.

"I know how much time with Annie Jo means to you. And she needs you too. Please call her and see if she's prepared dinner yet. Besides, I'm feeling confident that these pork chops are going to be delicious."

I shrugged again and then went to the phone and dialed her number suddenly eager to see her. I wanted to tell her about the découpage project we had started in art class. She picked up right away.

"Oh that would be lovely Josie, but I've already got chicken and noodles made," she said.

Chicken and noodles were my favorite. Ansley's too.

"Well maybe you could save them for tomorrow?" I asked hopefully.

"Actually sweetheart, I've invited Butch and Barry over to eat with me tonight."

Barry? The horrible guy with the caterpillar on his lip? And Butch? Oh God. My heart sank.

"Well, another time then," my voice cracked, so I quickly said, "Bye, Annie Jo," and hung up the receiver.

I heard the phone ring a few minutes later when I was outside watching Mother spread the charcoal. Ansley answered, and I heard her say, "No, everything is fine, Annie Jo. She's outside with Mother. There's nothing wrong with her."

I didn't offer to help with the grill. I thought the pork chops were dry at dinner, but I went along with the celebration when my mother and sisters celebrated our first big grilling attempt.

That night I watched the big hand on the toaster clock between our beds make a full circle before I fell asleep. I must have flipped my pillow ten times trying to find a dry spot as tears spilled from my eyes.

November 2003

I watched her from the window as she got out of her car and walked up the steps.

I'd already called LaDarla to beg off of the Macy's trip and our photo show and tell with a story about a sudden stomach ache.

I wasn't certain I'd made the right choice, but she was the only one I could imagine telling what I'd found.

"You look like you've seen a ghost, Josie. What happened?" she asked sincerely as I opened the door.

Ansley put her arm around my waist as we ducked out of the wet, chilly air and into my living room.

"I found something in Annie Jo's things. I need to tell someone because I can't figure out what to do or think."

"Is Joe home?"

"You're the only person I've talked to. And he and Joey should be getting home in an hour or so."

"Well, what... You're scaring me."

"It's upstairs. I made some coffee. Grab a cup and I'll show you."

"No coffee for me. It stains my teeth," she said. "But tell me what's going on..."

I gazed steadily and wordlessly at my sister hoping against hope that I had made the right decision to call her. I nodded toward the stairs, and she followed me without more questions.

I handed her the photos first and then the sealed bag with the key and miscellaneous items.

"I'm not sure what I'm looking at here, Josie. These are obviously old photos of something but I don't recognize what I'm seeing."

I handed her the plastic bag with the belt. She opened the bag and timidly tugged at the belt with perfectly manicured nails.

"Seriously, Josie. Clue me in. I don't know what this stuff is."

"I'm pretty sure it's the belt from the bathrobe I won at the school carnival. The bathrobe that CeCe donated to the Go Fish booth."

She looked at me with confusion but no sign of concern.

"I lost that belt. I left it at Laura Liz's house and she could never find it."

"Okay..."

"I think all this is related to Izzy's murder."

"Izzy's murder?"

Her head dropped back to the photos, and she looked at each of them again carefully.

She held up the one from the alley and looked at me questioningly.

"Do you remember where Izzy's body was found? This looks a lot like the alley behind Jennings Five and Ten."

"I know it was in that area of town, but no, I don't think I ever knew exactly where."

She looked back at the photos and studied the key, then asked, "So what's the significance of your belt?"

"Ansley. Really? Don't you know how he died?"

"Well, what was I, 12? 13? It seems like I remember he was dragged from behind a car... Oh, you think... Ansley grabbed the edge of the belt and pulled it out letting the muddy fabric flap across our knees. Her face was fearful.

I picked up the drug store receipt. "This could be part of the word "Jackson," and there is enough room in front of it that it could have said Izzy Jackson. See what I mean?"

"Oh, God, Josie. What does Annie Jo have to do with this?"

"That's what I'm so afraid of..."

"Where did you find it?"

I showed her the padded envelope.

"It was all sealed inside this. Taped shut with packaging tape."

She looked around the room. "Just mixed in with all these photos and things?"

I nodded.

She picked up the plastic bags with the paper, the key, gum and ballpoint pen. Her face held a question.

"Annie Jo, though?"

"Maybe she never knew what was inside," I offered. I reminded her about Barry Hazelip, the police officer that lived next to Annie Jo. "Butch Roberts lived with him for a while, and they got close with Annie Jo. Maybe one of them gave this to her to hold and she had no idea what was inside. I guess there's nothing here to prove it's related to Izzy, but I just have a feeling... And if I'm right, I think it's clear that Butch has something to do with his murder."

"What about Barry?"

"Maybe Barry too. All I know is, that belt was at Butch's house."

She picked up the outer envelope. "You cut the tape on this. Maybe she was told to hold it and never knew what was inside. What about this sticker?"

She pulled the envelope close and worked to make out anything from what was left of the sticker.

"No idea," I said. My mind was spinning. "What I do know though, is that CeCe has stayed in touch with the Jacksons all these years. She's never given up on the fact that Izzy's murder was never solved. Rubelle passed away a while back, but CeCe has stayed in touch with Isaac and Bailey. I'm sure LaDarla would know a lot of the details and that this stuff would make some sense to her."

"Actually, Kenneth mentioned the murder the other day. His mother checks in with the police every year to see if there have been any breaks in the case," Ansley said. "But you haven't told LaDarla yet, right?"

"I'm afraid to. I'm afraid all this will somehow implicate Annie Jo."

"Maybe she didn't know what was inside..." she said.

I heard the front door open and the happy voices of Joey and Joe calling to me up the stairs. I quickly shoved all of the photos and the belt back into the plastic bag and covered them with a box lid.

Ansley beat me to the top of the stairs.

"We're up here," she called.

Despite the November weather, they were sunburned across their noses. I could tell that they both had been wearing sunglasses because the burn followed the shape along both of their cheeks. They were both wearing ball caps backward and looked as much like brothers as they did father and son.

"By the looks on your faces, I'm guessing it was a good weekend," I called from over the banister.

"28-23 Auburn over Alabama and 28 fish between the four us today," said Joe as he wrapped his arm around Joey's shoulders. "What are you two up to?"

"Just laughing at old pictures." I pressed my thumb into Ansley's back as I lied.

"For now, our secret," she said under her breath.

May 1969

Annie Jo and I were picking out laundry detergent at the Piggly Wiggly when we heard a familiar voice from the next aisle over. Or at least a familiar subject. I couldn't immediately place the voice.

"She's the one whose husband was cheating with the teacher last year," said the voice in a loud whisper. "The husband and teacher were killed on the boat. I looked at Annie Jo and could tell she'd heard it too.

"I know who you mean. My son had Pam Paulk for English last year," said another. "They had to have a long-term substitute for the last two months and she ended up giving my son a C-minus."

"Tragic."

The C-minus or that they were killed on the boat? Which did this woman consider tragic?

"So Beverly is working at the Frito Lay plant..."

Annie Jo took my arm. We abandoned our cart and marched to the end of the aisle and did two right angle snaps to head down the next aisle.

Ansley's dance teacher, Miss Kate, was talking with a woman I didn't recognize, and their heads bobbed like two bees swarming to be the first to enter a beehive. She didn't even look up until Annie Jo cleared her throat and pushed her arm straight toward the aluminum foil that was in front of Miss Kate's head.

She looked at both of us before she made the connection, but still pretended not to recognize us.

"Yes, Carol. I do like this toilet paper," she said, picking up a four-pack of Charmin from her cart, but covering poorly. "George the Grocer is right," she added lamely.

Annie Jo made a loud "Hmmpphh" noise and roughly grabbed a roll of aluminum foil just inches from behind her head.

Then, still arm-in-arm, she snapped me back in the other direction. She put the aluminum foil on the top of a display of cakes as we walked straight out the front door of the Piggly Wiggly without the groceries we came in for.

Annie Jo never mentioned what happened to Momma, and she and I never spoke of it again either.

December 2003

Ansley and I went through all of the remaining boxes from Annie Jo's things, but we didn't find anything more. Trey had already listed the duplex for sale, but we went back and double-checked all closets and the attic storage.

"We have to take this to the police, Josie," Ansley said for the fifth or sixth time since I'd shown her the photos and the plastic bags the Saturday after Thanksgiving.

"I just wonder if it will mean anything since there's no obvious connection to Izzy. Or worse, what if it is connected to his murder and the police think Annie Jo knew something."

My reasoning was feeling weaker and my arguments less and less valid as the days went on. And Ansley— not me— as the voice of reason nagged deeply.

I finally got the courage to confide in Joe and immediately wished I had done it sooner.

"It's clear what you need to do here, Josie," he said.

"You're right," I said. It felt odd that there had ever been any question.

We called a family meeting and asked Daisy, Mother, Doc, LaDarla and Kenneth to come. Daisy drove in with her family from Charlotte and Allen and Joe joined us for the meeting while Charlie watched a movie in the basement.

I felt bad that we hadn't told Mother before that day because she was visibly shaken, as was Doc. Once we decided that LaDarla, Ansley and I would take it to the police the next week, Doc asked if we would mind if he called CeCe to let her know.

"I'll do that if you'd like, Dad," said LaDarla.

"I suspect she'd love to be a part of that meeting with the police," he said as he put his arm around Mother's shoulders. "She's hounded them for years to solve Izzy's murder, and she could probably be very helpful. If for no other reason, to instill some urgency. Isaac Jackson deserves to know what happened to his son."

"Please let your mother know, LaDarla, honey," Mother added. "She's suffered with this tragedy just as the Jacksons have."

The officer we met with from the Fulton County police department gave no indication of whether or not he thought the photos and materials could be part of police evidence. He confirmed that Barry Hazelip had left the department in 1975, but shared nothing more. He made a lot of notes and asked a lot of questions about where the envelope had been and about why I was so certain that the terrycloth belt had been mine and where I'd last seen it. We gave him Butch's name and details about the Roberts' home.

"Tell me more about your grandmother," he referred to his notebook. "Annie Jo Flint. Is that short for Annette?"

"It's actually Josephine. Josephine Louise Flint," I said. "Her maiden name was Walcott, but she married in 1933 and used Flint since that time. Everyone called her Annie Jo, but there was no Ann or Annie. Or Annette. In her name, I mean."

I wondered if the others could hear my heart pounding.

"And her husband?"

"Raymond James Flint. He died in 1959," Ansley's voice questioned the date and she glanced at me. I nodded. "I was four," she added.

"Annie Jo made friends with everyone." I felt the conversation moving in the wrong direction and my voice was fitful. "Barry Hazelip was her tenant in the duplex where she lived, but they weren't really friends."

The officer stared at me from over his wire-framed glasses. I wasn't sure whether he was giving me a signal to wait for his questions or to elaborate, so I chose to elaborate.

"Annie Jo had lots of friends from church, but Barry was just her tenant," I added. "And the last time I saw this belt it was in Butch Roberts' house."

He questioned my relationship to the Roberts family, why was I certain it was a belt from the same bathrobe, and asked me to repeat the story about losing the belt. With all of it, though, he gave no indication of whether he had interest in our answers or was just appeasing us.

"My mother knows a lot about the Izzy Jackson case," said LaDarla. I could tell she was also feeling that we'd made a mistake. "Her name is CeCe Dalrymple. I'm sure you'll find notes from her in your files. She was rather close to the Jacksons and she has been an advocate of sorts for keeping this case alive. She couldn't come today, but she'd be happy to fill you in on the notes she's made on the murder. She has notebooks full of notes... I could have her contact you..."

"That won't be necessary," he said standing. "Ladies, thank you for your information. We'll contact you if we need anything further.

We left not knowing if we'd done the right thing. We left not knowing if we'd inadvertently pointed a finger at Annie Jo. And we left not knowing if the police even cared.

"So, how do you think that went?" Ansley asked carefully as our elevator descended toward the ground floor.

"Not feeling good about it," said LaDarla.

They both looked at me and tears filled my eyes.

"I've got to get back to work, but I'm going to call Mother from the car on my way," said LaDarla. "It's going to be okay so let's not worry. We did the right thing."

She hugged my neck and kissed the side of my face as she wiped off a stray tear rolling down my cheek. She hugged Ansley too as the three of us got into our separate cars we'd confidently left in front of the police station just an hour before.

I dialed Joe's number as I started my car, and my heart fell again when I heard his cheerful "Hi, babe" greeting.

"Joe," my words paced with the loud beats of my heart. "I think we've made a big mistake."

June 1969

*D*addy's garage had been untouched for more than a year. Mother had boxed up some shirts from the closet to make more room for her hanging clothes, but the three drawers on the right of their dresser were still filled with his underwear, socks and t-shirts.

Then over Memorial Day she filled bags with his pants, shirts, ties and suit jackets and dropped them off at the church for a thrift store some of the members were organizing.

"Do you think we could do a garage sale, Annie Jo," she asked one night at dinner.

"Of course, we can, Beverly. If you're ready for that, I'll be happy to help you. We'll all help, won't we girls?"

We all nodded.

"I want to help," said Daisy.

We spent the first two weeks of summer break sorting through our own closets and toys to find items for the sale. We put Daisy in charge of inventorying all puzzles and games and attaching a note to the outside of the boxes to let buyers know if all the parts were intact or if something was missing.

Mother pulled the lawn mower, a small toolbox of wrenches, screwdrivers and hammers aside and called Dexter to come over and pick out tools he'd like from Daddy's collection, but he only took a chain saw, some wood veneer and a few cans of nails and screws.

We spent all day Thursday pulling the rest to the front of the driveway and setting up the tools, lumber, remaining UGA cushions, boxes of nails and washers and bolts on our kitchen table and card tables we'd borrowed from the Bakers. We filled in the sale with old games, Daddy's shoes, books and some of Mother's jewelry. Ansley was in charge of signage and merchandising and I made the price tags.

We covered the tables with tarps we'd found in the garage. Mother agreed to let us pitch the tent in the front yard and sleep outside in the tent that night. Annie Jo brought over her pajamas, a flashlight and some cupcakes and joined us in the tent.

The next morning Annie Jo picked up some dollar bills and rolls of quarters and dimes from the bank, and we set up a checkout table. She was in charge of all money. Daisy set up a lemonade stand next to Annie Jo. Mother walked around talking to customers, while Ansley and I moved the items around to keep the displays fresh as crowds of neighbors and strangers pillaged and purchased what was left of my Daddy.

We had a steady crowd until past 2 o'clock, when we finally looked around and realized our sale had been a huge success. Customers trickled in until about 4:30 when Mother called it done and we started filling boxes that Mr. Grogan had dropped off from the Piggly Wiggly. We filled the trunk of Mother's car with the boxes, and she made plans to drop them off at the church before we went inside to count the money.

Mother made sandwiches and filled five glasses with lemonade as we pulled out $45 for Annie Jo to cover the change she'd started with and the rest of us counted and recounted our bounty. After checking our totals three times, Annie Jo made the announcement: We'd cleared $405.65. Mother gave each of us girls $20, then tucked some folded bills into Annie Jo's hand with a "thank you so much, Annie Jo. This is going to make a big difference for me."

Then she announced we'd all celebrate our work with a trip to Six Flags the next day.

Ansley, Daisy and I screamed with delight. Annie Jo and Mother smiled and looked at one another. I realized I hadn't seen either of them that happy in almost 15 months.

We were on the tram from the parking lot into the Six Flags park when I overheard the family next to us mention that it was Father's Day.

I looked around at the four women that now made up my family.

Today was Father's Day and I no longer had a father. Moreover, it hadn't even occurred to me that this was the day to celebrate fathers.

I looked at the father in the family next to us on the tram and wondered if he liked the Georgia Bulldogs. If he like to tinker in his garage.

I saw him notice me looking at him, and I dropped my eyes to my lap.

I wondered if he ever lied to his family.

February 2004

"Josie, my mom just called me," LaDarla's voice was frantic. "They've got Butch! Murder!"

"What? You're kidding!" I dropped my pen as I spun around in my desk chair and looked out the window. "I thought she felt they were dropping the case. It's been so long since we've heard anything!"

The sky was crisp and extra blue as I looked across the Atlanta skyline and listened to LaDarla's account of the phone call she'd received.

"Wait, what about Barry?" I interrupted.

"They've charged him too."

"Oh my God, LaDarla! This is such great news. How can we learn more?"

"Mother has a pretty good relationship with the investigator. Now that they've made an arrest, she feels he will be more open about what's happening. She's going to call me as soon as she knows more."

The police had interviewed Mother in December, but she was far less concerned than I was that fingers would be pointed at Annie Jo.

"Josie, their questions were very routine," she tried to convince me for the millionth time. "No one that knew Annie Jo would think for a minute that she knew what was in that envelope. I'm sure she just thought she was doing a favor for a friend and forgot the envelope was in her closet. You've done the right thing, sweetheart."

After two and a half months of silence, I'd relaxed a bit, but the growing concern that the murder would stay unsolved kept nagging at me. LaDarla's call crushed my concentration for the PR campaign I was working on. So, I packed up my laptop and bag and told Bud I'd be taking the rest of the afternoon off from work.

"You look pretty happy, Josie. Care to share?" he asked.

"Yes, but not yet," I said. My fear of implicating my grandmother had kept me quiet about the envelope to all but my family. "But you're right. There's some good news."

I called Joe from the car.

"Joe, the police have arrested Butch."

"For murder?" he asked.

"Yes, but that's all I know. Do you know anyone that might be able to find out more?"

"That's wonderful, babe. You've got to feel great about that," he said. "And, maybe... There's a guy in my office that might have some connections. I'll ask."

"I'm taking the rest of the day off, by the way," I said. "Meet me for a date?"

"Well, that's tempting. I'm swamped right now though. Why don't you make reservations for dinner somewhere and let me know when and where to meet you. We'll start there," he added flirtatiously.

"I like that," I said.

"What about the Hazelip guy?" he asked.

"He's been charged too, LaDarla thinks it might have been for tampering with evidence. CeCe's information was very limited, but I hope you can learn more from your friend."

"On it, Josie. I love you," he said. "And make it someplace special tonight. This is a celebration."

June 1969

LaDarla turned 16 in April. I turned 16 on May 3, and Karen Carr turned 16 34 days later on June 6.

Dena and Belinda Roach had started their own two-member clique, so just the three of us celebrated her birthday with a "just us lunch." Karen's mom dropped us off at the mall with $45 where we ate at the Magic Pan restaurant and had fancy chicken crepes and then strawberry crepes for dessert. Our bill totaled $28.60 and we felt very grown up leaving four ones and three quarters on the table for our server with the dreamy blue eyes and mustache. Then we went to the movie theater in the mall and saw a Saturday matinée starring Andy Griffith.

After the movie we bought matching denim hats and strutted through as many shops as we could until it was time to meet Karen's mom at the mall entrance turnaround.

Mrs. Carr was wearing a pink dress, pink pumps, pearls and white gloves when she picked us up.

"Wow, Mom. Why so fancy?" Karen asked as the three of us slid across the back seat of their mint green station wagon.

"You're father and I have been invited to dinner with one of his clients tonight," she said as she checked her lipstick in the rear view mirror. "How was your 'just us lunch' and movie, ladies? You look cute in your hats."

"Super," I offered as LaDarla and Karen confirmed with affirmations of their own.

"Can Josie and LaDarla spend the night tonight, Mom? Please? You look very pretty, by the way."

Mrs. Carr pulled the car to the side of the turnaround and turned to face us all. She had ringlets in front of her ears, probably set with Dippity Do. She looked prettier than I'd ever seen her and it was the first time I ever remembered her wearing lipstick.

"I'm afraid not tonight, Karen," she said. "We have a Salisbury steak TV dinner I thought you could have for your supper, but no friends to spend the night when your father and I aren't home."

LaDarla snarled her lip, probably at the thought of Salisbury steak, but quickly snapped back to neutral and studied Mrs. Carr in the rear view mirror to see if she'd noticed.

"Mrs. Carr, could I ask my mother to see if Karen and LaDarla could spend the night at our house?" I asked.

"Haven't you girls had enough of one another today…"

"Please, Momma! It's the start of summer and it's my birthday!"

Mrs. Carr smiled. "It's actually the day after your birthday, Karen, but okay, if Mrs. Flint is okay with it, you may spend the night."

"Yippee," we cheered in unison.

We'd already set our agenda of records and games we'd play and subjects we'd discuss, so when the station wagon pulled in front of our house and Mrs. Carr suggested that LaDarla and Karen stay in the car while I spoke with my mother alone, the thought of Mother saying no to our plan had long since left our minds.

"I don't want Mrs. Flint feeling pressured into saying 'yes,' if it's not a good night for her," she reiterated. "You girls just sit tight and let Josie find out her family's plans on her own."

"Yes, ma'am," I said and got out of the car giving a quick thumbs up to my friends in the back seat. I knew the back door would be unlocked so I walked to the back of the house.

I saw Mother and Shalene through the kitchen window sitting at the kitchen table. Mother looked like she'd been crying. I grabbed my new hat and wadded it up in my hand. She straightened her back as she saw me come through the door and offered an exaggerated smile to deflect the sadness I'd seen so many times in the past year.

"Hi sweetheart," she said brightly, giving me a subtle nod toward Shalene.

I knew that meant to acknowledge the adult in the room, and I opted to ignore the annoyance of knowing she felt she had to remind me of that lesson.

"Hi Shalene," I said. "Nice to see you. How are Luke and Vivian? And Dexter?"

"They are all wonderful, Josie. Luke and Vivian both had birthday parties to go to today, too. Your mother and I have just been enjoying some girl time. I hear you've had some nice girl time with your friends today too."

I thought of Karen and LaDarla waiting in the car, but I wanted to hold my spend-the-night request until I was certain to receive the answer we were seeking.

"Is everything all right, Mother?"

"Oh, of course, Josie. Shalene and I have had a wonderful time chatting over some sweet tea. Would you like a glass of tea?"

"No, thank you," I said looking toward Shalene.

She dropped her eyes and I knew she was worried about my mother. She'd mentioned many times how she appreciated the fact that I was so mature and how I could be an important shoulder for my mother, though Mother never seemed to expect or wish for that herself.

I saw Shalene make a slight nod to Mother and then look back at me.

I studied the side of Mother's face as she pretended to be looking at something in the back yard. Then she turned to me.

"Does Daisy seem to be doing all right to you, Josie?"

Her question surprised me.

"Daisy? I think so. Why do you ask?"

"Shalene was telling me that Daisy's been making up stories about your father. Denying that he is dead and telling her friends that he's been on a secret astronaut mission and that's why they haven't seen him."

I almost chuckled but stopped myself in time.

"Oh."

I thought about the many times I had wished there was an alternative story to tell about my father and how many times I'd been tempted to lie.

"She seems okay to me."

"Me too, Josie," she said wrapping up her fear as she always did with two claps. "Just let me know if you notice anything. Meanwhile, who would like a slice of pound cake?"

She stood and walked with perfect posture toward the refrigerator where Annie Jo had shared a pound cake her friend Anabelle had made.

"Actually," I began. "I wanted to ask you if it would be okay if I had Karen and LaDarla spend the night tonight."

Shalene shook her head as Mother presented the pound cake so she put it back on the shelf in the refrigerator.

"I suppose tonight would be okay," she said. "Ansley and Daisy should be home soon. They took a walk with Annie Jo."

"Great Mom. Thanks," I said pushing open the screen door, rounding the door frame, jumping the three back steps to the ground and flying around to the waiting car.

"It's a yes!" I said as LaDarla opened the car door and she and Karen jumped out cheering. I saw Mrs. Carr glance at her watch.

"Oh, Mrs. Carr, I'm sorry that took so long. I hope it didn't make you late for your dinner. Karen can wear some of my pajamas and we have some extra toothbrushes in the linen closet."

"Well if you're sure..." she began.

"We're sure," we all screamed in unison.

"Bye, Mom," Karen yelled from the front steps of our house. "Have fun at your dinner!"

Mrs. Carr waved out the window as she pulled away and we raced to the back of the house and into the kitchen.

Mother was on the telephone so I introduced Karen to Shalene and we all chatted a few minutes as we'd been taught, though anxious to run to my room, shut the door and get on with our spend-the-night agenda.

"That was Annie Jo," Mother said hanging up the phone. "Ansley and Daisy are going to spend the night with her tonight. She has a decoupage purse kit they want to work on together."

Our excessive elation at the news was no secret as we thanked Mother, offered our goodbyes to Shalene and ran to my room.

I took it as a sign for the beginning of a great summer when I turned on the transistor radio that Ansley and I shared and Quicksie was just starting to play, "Sugar, Sugar," by the Archies.

We sang along, danced to a few more songs, then decided to play a few games of Rummy before we moved on to records and makeup.

I knew where Ansley kept scratch paper in her drawer of our desk, so I opened it up for a score sheet. She had a pink spiral notebook on the top of the stack and I knew I could tear out a page without her knowing.

I shuffled through her pages of pictures and notes and landed on one of her many pages of penmanship practice.

"I miss my Daddy," she'd written in perfect penmanship for at least 15 lines. Then she'd switched it up for a handful of "I love my Daddy" lines. Below those were two "I hate my Daddy" lines. Both with less care to the penmanship.

I closed her notebook, tucked it back in the drawer and suggested we play another game instead.

March 2004

"Carly says Aunt Ansley has a carousel of slides she wants us to look at," Grace said as I helped her unload the dishwasher in her apartment.

"Slides?"

"Photos of you and Aunt Ansley, Aunt Daisy, Grandmother and your dad when you were little."

"Where did she get those?"

"Ansley says Grandmother gave them to her years ago but they got mixed up with Uncle Trey's things during the divorce. He recently found them and gave them back to her. There is a slide projector and even a white screen on some kind of stand that we can set up to look at the slides."

I smiled as I remembered the tripod stand and white canvas screen that collapsed into a long, black tube that we kept in the hall closet in our house on Duberry Street.

"Well that would be fun. You and Carly would enjoy that. And you'll get a kick out of seeing our old-fashioned version of home movies."

"No we want it to be a family thing," Grace said. "And we want you and Aunt Daisy and Grandmother to be there too. We want to learn about our grandfather."

"Oh, Grace. You know I..."

"I know you don't like to talk about it, but that's not fair any longer. We are old enough to hear the whole story and we want to know more about him."

She took the dishtowel from my hand and folded it in half and then into thirds, just the way I like them and taught her to do when she was growing up at home.

"And Mom, I think it would be good for you too," she said as she handed me a cold bottle of water from the refrigerator and nodded toward the futon she and her roommates used as a sofa. "Why don't you let this final chapter about Izzy's murder serve as the final chapter for all that you've bottled up all these years?"

My impulse to resist had me trying to stand, when Grace pulled me back onto the futon.

"It's been almost 36 years, Mom. It's time to let go. Besides, I know he was a wonderful father to you. He made that toaster clock and that birdhouse. It doesn't get a lot sweeter than that."

I felt my chest burning red and weights growing larger at the back of my eyes as she talked.

"He was a really great father, Grace," I managed.

The clicking sound my childhood Viewmaster made echoed through my head as an image of my father turning to face me as he stood in front of the barbecue grill came into focus. He was smiling and had a red mitt on one hand and a pair of skewers in the other. The smell of pork chops filled my head.

Click.

My daddy and I at our dining room table as he helped me understand Greatest Common Factors. He was wearing his turquoise plaid shirt. And his eyes were steady and sincere as he spoke about divisors and rolled my favorite mechanical pencil between his fingers.

Click.

He and mother standing proudly as Laura Liz's name was called at Honor's Day.

Click.

Licking ice cream cones with my sisters and Donnie and Dena Baker in the bed of his red truck as the UGA fight song played at full blast.

I centered my eyes to my knees and looked up slowly and nodded. Tears were running down my face.

"He was a really great father, Grace. I loved him so much."

"Well, Joey and Carly and Chip and Charlie and I would really love to love him, too," Grace said as she rubbed my arm.

"And we've already set it up."

I noted a hesitation in her voice with the last words.

"What?..."

"We're all getting together tomorrow night at our house," she said with sudden confidence and affirmation. "Carly and I've already arranged it with Dad. Aunt Daisy and Uncle Allen are coming in town in the morning and they're bringing Charlie and the dogs. We are going to watch the slides and we want to hear stories from the generation above us. We want details — good and bad — about growing up Flint."

"Everyone knows about this? What about Mother and Doc?"

"Grandmother says she'll be there too. Doc says he thinks it's a good idea and fully supports our plan. He says he'll pay for pizza delivery."

"And Ansley agreed?"

"Ansley will be there. She's invited Kenneth."

"Kenneth will be there?"

"Mom, we're all family and this is all okay. We can include LaDarla too, if you'd like."

Suddenly I wanted to tell Grace more about my father. I wanted to share the stories I loved with Joe and Joey. And hear how Ansley and Daisy remembered our shared experiences. I wanted my niece and nephews to know our stories of Duberry Street and Annie Jo and my father.

"You know what, you're right," I said. "This is a good thing."

I thought of the photo of me wearing the flowered pantsuit I made when Annie Jo taught me to sew and wondered if it would be among those in the carousel.

July 1969

*E*veryone was excited about the U.S. astronauts being first to land on the moon.

Mother had been saving the *Atlanta Constitution* newspapers for months and took Ansley, Daisy and me to Treasure Island to find the largest scrapbook we could find. We bought a large red scrapbook and three bottles of LePages glue with the rubber top.

We cut out each article from the paper and pressed the edges with the rubber cement glue. The rubber tip had a slit on the top, so we were careful to press just hard enough to glue on the edges of the newspaper articles. We placed them carefully in the scrapbook in order. Then each morning as the moon landing got closer, we would run out to the street to get the newspaper. One of us would read the latest update of the astronauts and their mission aloud. Then we'd take turns clipping the article and adding it to our scrapbook.

Buzz Aldrin, Neil Armstrong and Michael Collins were as familiar to each of us as Elvis Presley and Joe Namath. We understood the framework for how Apollo 11's command module Columbia and its service module would later separate from the lunar module Eagle and launch the three astronauts back to Earth.

Harmon's Pharmacy printed the mission's emblem — an eagle landing on the moon holding an olive branch in its talons designed by astronaut Michael Collins — on the front of its coupon book, so we cut it out and pasted it to the front of our scrapbook.

Daisy, especially, had memorized every fact about the astronauts and the mission.

A dream of the late President Kennedy, the moon landing was a dream that everyone I knew shared. We'd made plans to go to church, bring home a bucket of chicken and eat our lunch while watching the Sunday afternoon news coverage and scheduled moon landing. Until I announced I'd been invited to go to Lake Allatoona with Karen Carr and her family, that is.

"That sounds lovely, Josie, but you don't want to miss the astronauts' landing," said Mother. "Maybe you could go with the Carrs later in the summer."

"No, she's invited LaDarla too. And the Dalrymples leave for the beach for the rest of the summer next week. Please, Momma, I really want to go. This is our only chance! Plus, we can watch it from their lake house."

"Momma, no!" screamed Ansley as she rounded the doorway to the kitchen. "That's not fair! We've been planning this day. You can't let her go!"

Mother promised to think about it, but I nagged relentlessly until she gave in.

Daisy wouldn't speak to me. Ansley locked our bedroom door and wouldn't let me in when I left the room while packing my duffel bag for the overnight trip.

I poked a toothpick into the hole on the doorknob to jimmy the lock just as Ansley opened the door. The toothpick broke off inside the knob.

"Now you've done it," she screamed. "You ruin everything, Josie."

"Quit being such a baby," I said condescendingly. "I'm 16. You don't even know what that's like."

"You're an ugly, constipated ape, Josie Grace Flint. And I hate you," she added as she ran to tattle to mother about the toothpick.

I finished packing my bag and then called LaDarla to see what bathing suit she'd packed. I felt guilty about telling Mother that the Carrs had a television at their lake house since Karen had already told me they didn't.

March 31, 2004

I looked again at the business card as I waited for her to arrive for our 12:30 lunch date. "Laura Echols. Attorney at Law. Fortner, Matthews, Wellstone, P.C., Nashville, Tennessee."

The judge's preliminary ruling was 60 years behind bars for Zachary Beauregard "Butch" Roberts. In a separate hearing, Ronald Eugene Hazelip was sentenced to just five years in prison for tampering with evidence.

We were all present for the final hearing. Cece and Kenneth drove four hours to Valdosta to pick up Isaac Jackson so that he could be there too. Isaac wore a houndstooth jacket and a cobalt blue tie and black and tan saddle oxfords. He was smaller and greyer, but every bit as stylish as I remembered him from the Wilson's New Year's Eve party so many years before.

The evidence against Hazelip was mostly circumstantial, but records did show that he was present at the station when the evidence came in, and they were able to lift a thumbprint from the yellowed tape that matched his. The fact that he was the next-door neighbor to Annie Jo didn't implicate him, but once evidence from Butch Roberts came to light, a plausible theory became more clear. Whether or not it was supposed to come into play for Hazelip's case, it seemed it did.

But breakthroughs in DNA testing tied the bathrobe belt to Izzy. Blood, skin and saliva samples matched those they had collected at Grady Hospital. And the library card's membership number matched one registered to Bailey Jackson, Izzy's brother.

Nothing in the envelope could be tied to Butch Roberts other than my statement that I had left the bathrobe belt at his house. He might have gone free if it weren't for the testimony brought in by Butch's own attorney.

Even though she hadn't seen or talked with her brother in the 16 years since their mother died of pancreatic cancer, Laura Liz came to Atlanta when her brother was first questioned in December. According to what the investigator had shared with CeCe, she thought it might be an opportunity to mend fences with her brother since neither of them had heard from Hank in almost a decade and it seemed clear that the evidence against him was poor at best. Butch said he'd been harassed by the police for no reason at all and needed his sister's help. Her firm had insisted that all attorneys apply for license reciprocity with the neighboring states that would allow it, and she had completed that application just three months before his call. Butch called and Laura Liz came running.

On the surface, Butch seemed correct. Despite several interrogations by police, there was nothing that could tie him to the photos or pen or gum or paper or piece of terrycloth fabric, but once Laura Liz learned that the found evidence had been located among the belongings of Annie Jo Flint, she questioned Butch's story.

But it was the envelope itself that confirmed her thoughts. She recused herself from Butch's case and testified against him.

CeCe filled us in on the limited details she'd learned from the investigator in the weeks before the hearing, but the hearing itself offered little more clarity. Laura Liz and I chatted after the morning's hearing and made plans to meet for lunch. I'd arrived at The Atlanta Fish Market restaurant about ten minutes early, but Laura Liz was ten minutes late.

The waiter was refilling my water glass as I saw her turn the corner. The hostess pointed her in my direction, and she hurried in apologizing for being late even before she sat down.

I stood up to hug her. She lingered long enough to finish her apology and hold the hug almost to the point I was concerned she might be crying.

"I've always wished we were still friends, Josie," she said when she let go and we each took our seats.

Laura Liz — just Laura now — looked amazing. Her highlighted blonde bob was both professional and sassy at the same time. Her seafoam green eyes were set off perfectly by her lilac-colored slim jacket and pencil skirt and white collared blouse. She wore nude colored pumps and no hose. I felt dowdy in my brown cardigan sweater and tweed pants.

"Well, let's be friends again. I'm so happy to see you and happy to see how this day has turned out, but I don't know how to say that to you since it's your brother…"

"You know what, Josie? Right is right," she said. "Your family raised me every bit as much as my family did. Maybe more."

She took a sip of water before she continued. "When I realized that the evidence the police had was with Annie Jo, I knew she couldn't have been knowingly involved."

The waiter came for our order, and we asked for a few more minutes.

"Did you realize that the terrycloth in that bag was the belt from my bathrobe?"

"The investigator told me that you suspected that, but I don't really remember you leaving that at my house."

"Really?" I said. "I asked you about it about a hundred times!"

"Vaguely," she said. "I remember the bathrobe, of course."

"So, how were you so certain Butch was guilty?"

Her eyes steadied on mine, and I got the impression she wasn't going to answer the question.

"CeCe Dalrymple said…" I began.

"I'd seen the envelope before."

"What do you mean?"

When the police showed me that envelope, I remembered one day that Daddy asked Butch to pick me up at the bowling alley. I got in his truck with a full Coke in my hand, and when I jumped in his truck, I spilled Coke all over an envelope just like that. I started to wipe off the spill and Butch grabbed it out of my hand and said, 'don't touch that,' and threw it back into the bed of his truck."

"Did you know what was in it?" I asked.

"I didn't have any idea. But I know it had a label on the front. When the police showed it to me it had been pulled off, but I recognized the Coke stain and the tape that sealed it shut. I honestly had never thought about it since that day in the truck until the police showed it to me," she said.

"When did you see it?"

"When we were teenagers. I tried to pinpoint the day with police, but I just remember it was a hot summer day. Probably not long after your Daddy died."

I was saying a little prayer and smiling at Laura Liz when the waiter came back to our table and I asked for a Caesar salad.

"Same for me," said Laura Liz.

"So, Laura..."

"Yeah, I dropped the Liz part before I got married."

"And your husband..."

"Eddie Echols. I met him in law school. He's a closing attorney from Memphis, but was teaching a real estate class I took. We were both 40 when we met, so no kids. We've been married nine years. Two dogs," she added.

"I'd love to meet him," I said.

"I really want you to meet him," she said. "And I really want to hear about you."

We talked for three hours. And cried about my Daddy and Annie Jo and her momma. We laughed about Ansley's paper maché beaver and Bombardment and the Faulkner twins. I filled her in on my job, my family, my mother, the Dalrymples and Kenneth and Ansley's budding romance.

"You know the Faulkners still live in the same house, right?" I said.

"Really? I'd love to know where Mason and Dixon are."

"It was Mr. Faulkner that saw Annie Jo fall. He said both boys are in Florida. Pensacola and Tampa, I think."

"Can you believe we're 51, Josie? Doesn't it seem like just years ago we were at Seaton Ferry and Northbridge High? Not decades?"

"You're 51. I still have a month to go," I said smartly. "And, yes, it does."

We made plans to introduce Joe and Eddie and get together in Nashville for my birthday in May. I pulled my calendar out of my bag to look at the date options.

"Tomorrow is April Fools Day," I noted.

"Oh, good, let's think of a good trick you can play on Ansley," she said. "Remember that time she put your bra in your lunch bag?"

We came up with three good ideas before the valet brought our cars to the drive.

I smiled all the way home.

I couldn't wait to play a trick on Ansley the next day.

Acknowledgments

Jaybird's Song began with a paragraph about southern women.

I must have been channeling Beverly, Josie's mother, with the first few lines and thought the story was going to be about her. But Jaybird took over and this is the story that unfolded. I credit growing up Danbury, Grandma McClish and Aunt Maxine for some of the fine details, but short of the dirt hill and Bloody Tiger and lots of crafting, marzipan making and tomato picking, *Jaybird's Song* is a story of fiction, and any similarity to any individual or incident* is purely coincidental.

I want to thank my very first reader Monica McGurk. We shared our very first tiny ideas for our stories and she's catapulted into three great novel releases with her Archangel Prophecies trilogy before *Jaybird's Song* saw the light of day. More, I thank my uber-supportive early beta readers: Pam Pomar, Wayne South Smith, Sharon Moore, Jill Florence, Jackie Florence, Linda Gilson, Carol Niemi, LaCreta Wilson, Liz Hackney and Karen Elliott for their encouragement, confirmation, direction and great edits. And of course, I thank my Dream Team weekend focus group ladies: Erin Nydam, Melanie Williams, Paige Graddy, Eleanor Pippin, Shelbe Zimmerman and Wendy Aitchison who redirected me toward a much better ending, pointed out the inconsistencies and confirmed what I was hoping to be true with this story. After incorporating advice from many, it was my book club's affirmation that gave me the final push to send her into the universe. Thank you, Chris Martinek and Debby Dolinski, and to Eleanor, Shelbe and Wendy who read it twice.

I thank my dear friend Sharon Moore for our collaboration on cover design and my blog readers who voted this design into permanent ink.

My sincere advice: If you've got a story burning in your gut, spill it.

This has been so much fun. Many a night, Josie would wake me up with an idea for story line or a nudge toward another chapter. I'm proud and humbled to present her story.

And best of all? That first paragraph is on the cutting room floor. Maybe I'll pick it back up and see where it leads. *KWF*

---

* *Okay, my sister Linda's paper maché beaver project was real.*

Made in the USA
Columbia, SC
13 August 2017